THE STRANGLING OF SATAN

BY

ANTHONY DICKENSON

Strategic Book Publishing
New York, NewYork

Strategic Book Publishing
An imprint of Writers Literary & Publishing Services, Inc.
845 Third Avenue, 6th Floor – 6016
New York, NY 10022
http://www.strategicbookpublishing.com

ISBN: 978-1-60860-106-6
SKU: 1-60860-106-4

Printed in the United States of America

Book Design: Bonita S. Watson

FOR GAIL

ACKNOWLEDGEMENTS

My thanks to Gail, my wife, for her continual support and for painting the front cover.

To ABABIL

Friend & Inspiration.

Best Wishes

Tony

CONTENTS

PROLOGUE

Steve Dalton froze; he couldn't take in what was happening to him. The first brick that shattered in front of his eyes left him momentarily bemused and then, almost in slow motion, he realized that someone was shooting at him! This only happened to hoodlums or army personnel, yet here he was late morning in a sleepy Cheshire village, being shot at in broad daylight; he was a respectable businessman who paid his taxes and who definitely hadn't joined the British Army.

Although he had no Forces training, instinct cut in; he dropped to the floor and rolled under a parked van as even more brickwork exploded above him. The initial shock had ebbed a little, but now he was acutely aware of his heart thumping in his chest and, to his surprise, that his senses were almost cat-like. Survival mode was now fully engaged, thanks to adrenaline, and he was not ready to die!

Where were the shots coming from? The marksman, whoever he was, had to be on the roof of one of the shops on the opposite side of the main street. Thirty feet away there was an entrance to a pub car park that had once been the coach access to the old inn. There was no cover, but if he could just survive the short distance, he knew that there was a rear exit through the grounds of the derelict castle behind.

Thank heavens for local knowledge.

A lull in the shots coupled with fear concentrated his thoughts.

He must be reloading; I must create a diversion! The only thing to hand was his rucksack that somehow still clung to his back. "Shit!" He hit his head on the van chassis as he started to wriggle out of the harness in the confined space. At last his shoulder came free and in one quick move he threw the bag into the road, simultaneously rolling from under the vehicle, crouching, and running for cover. His escape was punctuated with deafening shots that caused the tarmac road to erupt as his rucksack took the brunt. Reaching the cover of the archway, his throat burning with the strain of breathing, but with no time to recover, he pushed himself to keep running up the old castle hill and finally through a narrow alleyway into a side lane.

Steve had not the slightest idea who wanted him dead but since leaving the airport he'd had a vague suspicion that he'd been followed, almost a sixth sense. Nothing concrete, just that feeling that we've all experienced, dismissed, and then found to be right. Whoever was after him would be searching the village, and as there was only one main street, that wouldn't take long.

A sigh of relief escaped when he realized that he was drawing near to Robert's cottage. Robert eked out a living by poaching, doing odd jobs, and gardening and had cut Steve's hedges in the autumn. He was regarded as a loveable rogue and everyone said that he was fine as long as you didn't accept a cheque from him. A bang on the door-knocker resulted in a welcome from Robert's long suffering wife, Sue, and Steve fell into the living room gasping for breath.

"My God! Whatever's the matter?" Steve couldn't answer at first but finally caught his breath and spilled out what had just happened.

"That's unbelievable! You'd better call the police."

"What! With one Bobby to eighty square miles in this area, I don't think we'll achieve much. No, I want to get home and make some phone calls, but I don't want to be recognized; can you lend me one of Robert's coats?"

Wrapped up in an ancient waxed Barbour jacket and a waterproof cap, Steve thanked Sue and asked her to keep things to herself. Sue had had a lifetime of practice in this skill with her husband's escapades, and he felt certain that he could rely on her silence. He decided to walk home along the public footpaths across the fields and leave the car in the village. Obviously the sniper already knew his car and would assume that whilst the car was still in the village, so was Steve. This ruse should give him a good approach view of his cottage from all directions, and he should be able to see if anyone was watching his home.

Suddenly he felt very tired, very frightened, and totally out of his depth; he'd been bored in his previous job but never terrified. What was happening?

The village had still been in sleep mode when all of the action had taken place, and nobody had actually witnessed the attack on Steve. The usual rash of busybodies and a few concerned people had reported that they were sure that they'd heard gunfire in the street; being in a rural area, they could tell the difference between a car backfiring and the sound of a gun. The one overstretched PC eventually arrived in the early afternoon and made a number of futile enquiries, then dutifully reported back to HQ.

The appearance the following day of a mobile incident centre on the public car park caused a ripple of excitement amongst the locals but turned out to be equally non-productive and subsequently departed almost empty-handed at the end of the week. The one fact that had been ascertained was that the gunman had easily gained access to the shop roof from the metal fire escape at the rear. The only evidence left at the scene was a pile of empty cartridges and some size eight footprints in a patch of mud.

The whole business was manna from heaven for the local weekly newspaper, which ran a spread: "GUN WARFARE SPREADS TO CHESHIRE VILLAGE"—jumping to conclusions and linking the event to recent shootings in Liverpool and Manchester. Sales of the paper shot up, the story was sold to a couple of the national dailies, and the editor and his reporter were in a city-centre pub building the foundations of a couple of good hangovers.

Two weeks later it was old news, nobody was any the wiser, a file was gathering dust at the County Police HQ, and village life had returned to snooze mode apart from the occasional discussion in the pub. Life moved on albeit slowly.

1

The alarm clock danced around crazily on the polished bedside table, and Steve Dalton stabbed at it to shut it up before it woke the slumbering Jane. Sometime previously he had bought one of the modern quiet electronic alarms, but it didn't rouse a deep sleeper like him, so he'd gone back to the old-fashioned wind-up bell alarm that would wake the dead.

Jane worked in HR (he still thought of it as "Personnel") for a French pharmaceutical company's UK branch. She'd moved in with him six months previously, and it was proving to be what he could best describe as a comfortable relationship. There was a faun-like vulnerability about her that drew out his protective feelings, and this compensated to some degree for her obsession with safety in the home and the slight lack of passion in the bed department. Sex was satisfactory but somehow never red hot. At first he'd felt deprived by the lack of passion but had gradually accepted that not everyone has the same sexual appetite.

Yawning, he stretched languorously, rolled out of bed, staggered across the room, and looked out of the cottage bedroom window at what he could see of the Cheshire Plain, which wasn't much. The weather was foul: horizontal driving rain, windy, and miserable as yet another occluded front made its way in from the Atlantic, the third in as many weeks. No wonder this was prime dairy country; with rain like this grass shot up like magic.

Now that he was earning respectable money Steve had promised himself to gain his private pilot's license by the time he was thirty-five; in fact he'd qualified the week before his birthday some three months ago. Since then he'd become a daily amateur meteorologist wistfully checking out the weather each morning. Hopefully it would improve and he'd be able to get some hours in when he returned from his business trip to Kuala Lumpur. The UK weather was so changeable that he made a firm decision to study for his instrument rating as soon as he could spare the time. Once that's in the bag, flying hours won't be so restricted.

Having been brought up in a faceless three bedroom semi-in-suburbia, Steve had made a vow to himself that, when he could eventually afford a home of his own, it would be one with character and in the countryside. The chocolate box black and white cottage certainly fitted the bill, but the mortgage was somewhat crippling, and he now realized that character, like most desirable things in life, came at a price. Steve wondered if he'd over-reached himself but quickly banished the thought because the prospect of losing his dream home was just too painful. He consoled himself by reasoning that, if he built the business up quickly, the place would cease to be a millstone around his neck, and the repayments would become effortless. He just wasn't sure if he believed himself.

A degree in electronics had led him into a career in medical control systems, and up until three years ago his job had been technical sales manager for an American medical equipment manufacturer that specialized in intensive care and high dependency products. He'd worked hard, so hard that the job had caused several relationships to wither on the vine—"The trouble with you is that you're married to your job and there's no time left for me" being the recurring comment. Painfully he knew that the criticism was justified, and this, coupled with his awareness that he'd never make real money whilst working for someone else, had propelled him into starting his own business, Foston Medical, the name "Foston" being the merging of his surname Dalton and his partner's Foster.

The Japanese, Koreans, and Malaysians had started to produce cutting edge highly competitive electronic control equipment, and Steve's knowledge, coupled with his partner Ian Foster's money, had been a formula that had created an increasingly profitable business in a shorter time than either could ever have imagined. Rapid growth of turnover had already enabled Steve, with Ian's agreement, to draw a salary that was a significant improvement upon the one he'd enjoyed with his previous firm. However, even with his recent pay raise, the house was still a major drain on his income, and this was his spur to build on what he had already achieved.

Ian was a friend from university days; they'd always got on, in spite of the difference in their backgrounds, and had kept in touch ever since; perhaps it was the attraction of opposites. Ian had read Economics and Politics not out of any great calling, but just because he couldn't think what else to do. The Fosters were well off, due to Ian's great grandfather having originally owned a coalmine in Yorkshire, pre National Coal Board days. Since the mine closure, good investments of the proceeds had produced a sizeable fortune. In fact the family was now vastly better off than it had ever been during its mining era.

Tim, Ian's brother, had entered Sandhurst and was now an army officer whose role was not very clear, but he appeared to spend a fair amount of time in Hereford. A natural linguist, he spoke fluent Arabic, Russian, Mandarin, reasonable Cantonese, and was quite proficient in several other languages. Unmarried he appeared to enjoy army life, the traveling, and the camaraderie that it involved, which was just as well as he'd never really got on with his older brother whom he considered to be totally irresponsible. The tall wide shouldered physique was topped off by a shock of unruly sandy hair, which was only controllable thanks to a regulation Army haircut.

By contrast Ian "worked" for a firm of stockbrokers in Manchester, and life always seemed easy for him. The brokerage company was owned by the family; the job wasn't taxing, and women seemed to fall at his feet whenever he approached them, which he frequently did. He had married Fiona, a handsome rather than pretty woman with a figure that turned heads when she entered a room. Being the daughter of a retired Brigadier seemed to have endowed her with both confidence and capability, but so far the marriage had not produced an heir. She was frighteningly efficient, a great hostess, and didn't seem to mind Ian's constant attention to other women. In short, this seemed like the ideal marriage of convenience.

When Steve had been looking at ways to raise capital to start his own business, he had immediately turned to Ian as he was one of the few people whom he knew with enough wealth to be able to invest. Fortunately for Steve, Ian had immediately seen the potential of the proposed business and considered it a good investment. (People were living longer, but that meant more heart attacks, strokes, surgery, and with an increasing population, more accidents; this had to be a growth industry. What's more it couldn't be long before the Chinese started manufacturing, and this would increase profitability.) He'd decided to look at it as a three-year project, but growth had already way exceeded his expectations.

Ian was sharp and had secured his investment in Foston by a joint insurance policy. If either party died, the policy would pay out the sum of the investment, and that would be paid to the deceased's next of kin and then no further claims could be made upon the business. Steve liked him but couldn't help resenting the ease with which prosperity fell on the Foster family. Mind you, he was grateful for the Foster money that had helped get the Company up and running and just hoped that some of their Midas touch might now rub off on him by association.

In fairness the Daltons had achieved a modicum of success but always by struggling; nothing ever came easily to them. Perhaps they valued people and possessions more as a result, but Steve had an un-admitted ambition to be the first of his family to break the mould, and he felt that affluence would be the sort of problem that he'd enjoy dealing with. Both his parents were dead, and his father had definitely disproved the theory that hard work never killed anyone.

Wandering into the en suite bathroom, Steve left Jane snuggled up in the fetal position. After a long satisfying pee, he showered and shaved. It was funny but he always did his best thinking when shaving, and he was already rehearsing the Malaysian meeting in his mind. Looking in the mirror, he was quietly pleased with what he saw. Strong features with a little mileage now showing in the form of character lines and a mop of dark wavy hair inherited from his father. He remembered, as a little boy, watching his father shave and hoping that one day he too would be tall; in fact he'd made six-two and was taller than his dad. Mind you, daily shaving hadn't come up to his expectations.

Feeling fresher and more awake, he dressed, carried his already packed suitcase downstairs, and made the mandatory pot of fresh coffee. Breakfast could wait until he reached the airport, but coffee definitely couldn't. With his caffeine-level restored Steve penned a short note to Jane and put it under the cup of coffee that he had just placed on her bedside table. Her blonde head was on the pillow and the bed-clothes had fallen away from her. He kissed her gently on the cheek, whispered, "goodbye" and she responded sleepily rolling towards him. Noting the inviting pertness of her breasts under the satin of her nightdress, his body responded, but his watch told him there was no time for such pleasures, and he headed back downstairs.

The cold, damp car quickly extinguished his ardor, and it seemed an age before the heater made life comfortable again; he made a mental note that his next car would have heated seats. Although it was still early in the morning, the motorway was its usual busy stream of traffic with the occasional lunatic driver determined to be ahead of everyone. Steve wondered where all these people came from or where they were heading to—it reminded him of an ant colony which seemed to have a mass purpose.

As he drove into the airport long-stay car park, he cruised along the rows of empty cars finally finding a space next to a new BMW. He'd long since developed a habit of parking next to quality cars: that way you were less likely to get your doors dented. His mind was now fully functional and he quickly estimated a thousand cars in that section; say an average value of only ten thousand pounds and the figures were staggering.

Having finally warmed up nicely in the car, air travel now dictated that he had to wait in a cold, windy bus shelter for ten minutes until an airport bus picked him up and eventually deposited him at the departures terminal. He had to agree with the comedian, Billy Connolly, that the word "terminal" really wasn't a confidence-inspiring choice of name for an airport.

The check-in desk was crowded, as usual, but fortunately the queue moved quite quickly. Steve always booked economy class seats to keep his business expenditure as low as possible, but habitually asked if an upgrade to business class was available. As a lone traveler he was sometimes lucky but today, in spite of trying to charm the dark-eyed young beauty at the desk, his luck was out.

Oh well—you can't win them all and anyway breakfast called.

The inner man duly satisfied, it now made sense to use the waiting time in the departures lounge by checking out the competitors' websites on his laptop. At least modern technology enabled him to legally spy on his rivals, but of course this was a double-edged advantage, and everyone was being careful not to reveal too much detail on their website.

The boarding announcement disturbed his surfing, so he shut down his laptop and headed for the plane. The shuttle to Heathrow, London took less than an hour, and fortunately he didn't have long to wait for his main flight to Kuala Lumpur. After all the preliminaries were out of the way he funneled his way into the crammed-full aircraft. Flying long haul on a Boeing 747 was no longer a novelty, but somehow the size of the monster never failed to amaze him as he turned right and looked down the length of the cabin. Getting the little flying club Cessna 172 into the air didn't stretch the imagination too much, but the thought of getting this beast into the air beggared belief.

Once settled into his well-sat window seat and after the usual delay whilst everyone joined the aircraft and found their seat, Steve was relieved to find that there was nobody sitting next to him. The luxury of elbow-room, the ability to stretch his long legs diagonally, and blessing of blessings, no need to make small talk would be much appreciated. He spread out himself and his belongings, checked out the in-flight films that were on offer, and ordered his ritual gin and tonic, which arrived accompanied by a menu for the food that would be served.

Between some remarkably good airline meals (one of the reasons he chose the Malaysian airline, after a tip-off from a friend) he whiled away the time with reading and watching the movies. Steve also had the enviable ability to sleep anywhere, so the flight didn't prevent him from getting his usual ration of shuteye. By the time the cabin crew roused people in preparation for arrival, he was feeling rested and a quick electric shave and splash of after-shave completed the job.

As the lumbering plane finally shuddered to a halt at the airport satellite, Steve recovered his laptop and jacket from the overhead locker and joined the sheep-like queue of passengers, who always got out of their seats too early, to wait for the aircraft doors to open. Making his way into the airport building, he was surprised to find that there were large numbers of people milling around, yet the place was as silent as a cathedral. Obviously modern architecture had embraced new technology, and it was working. It entered his mind that cathedrals were the biggest buildings constructed in the Middle Ages, and that airports were those of modern times, so the comparison was not that inappropriate. The marble floors gleamed but weren't slippery and there was an air of calmness about the whole place—very different from UK airports.

Having been reunited with his luggage (there was always that sneaking worry that it mightn't be there) and passed through Customs uneventfully, he finally emerged in the huge arrivals hall to be confronted by a sea of drivers waving name signs. After a few moments of scanning he spotted a smartly dressed chauffeur holding aloft a sign headed "Tsang Corporation" and the all-important name "Mr. Steven Dalton" underneath. The system worked. Steve made himself known, the driver took his bags from the trolley, and they headed for a large stretched limo at the curbside. His chauffeur opened the rear door and suggested that Steve make himself comfortable as the journey to Kuala Lumpur was over fifty kilometers. Comfort certainly wasn't going to be a problem as the limousine was cavernous with sheepskin rugs, acres of leather upholstery, and a drinks cabinet complete with crystal glasses and decanter. This is the life, he thought.

The car glided out of the airport and headed close to the Malaysian Grand Prix circuit; he'd seen this on TV earlier in the year. Once clear of the airport complex they picked up speed and headed north. The road was good, the scenery unexceptional, but Steve absorbed everything blotting paper–like as one does when confronted by the novelty of new surroundings. By now he was looking forward to reaching his hotel (he'd booked in at a mid-range, city centre international chain hotel), so that he could linger in an invigorating warm shower as he now realized that he didn't smell at his most fragrant after the long flight.

Thirty-five minutes later, to Steve's surprise, the car turned off the main road and headed through a golf course, pulling up outside a huge and very impressive hotel. The driver parked, opened the passenger door and announced that they had arrived. Steve's protests that he was staying at a city centre hotel were brushed aside, and it was explained that Tsang Corporation had cancelled his booking and were transferring him to this six-star hotel as their guest. He briefly thought, How did they know where I was staying? But he was quickly distracted as the driver ushered him towards the hotel entrance.

The entrance atrium was awe-inspiring and so was the slender Malaysian manageress who met him and escorted him to the lift. As they smoothly glided upwards, she gave him a credit card–type key that granted him access to the fourth floor. Apparently the fourth floor was reserved for VIPs and was out of bounds to the unprivileged. The lift delivered them to a sumptuously carpeted floor; he was shown to his own suite and introduced to his personal butler, Kim, a smart and very fit looking Asian. This level of luxury was beyond Steve's experience, and he was having trouble taking it all in but reckoned that, with a bit of effort, he could get used to it.

Once alone, reality returned and he quickly stripped and headed for the joys of the power shower. Shower controls tend to be different in every hotel, but having finally mastered this latest challenge, he relished the powerful jet stinging his body; it was that close borderline that encompassed both pain and pleasure. A good wet shave and the application of thoughtfully provided expensive cologne completed the invigorating revival. Wrapped in the unbelievably thick toweling robe, he relieved the mini-bar of a miniature malt whisky, threw himself on the enormous bed, and telephoned Jane to tell her that he'd arrived safely but more importantly to describe his unexpectedly luxurious surroundings.

The phone rang and rang, but there was no answer. Ten minutes later the calm of the room was suddenly shattered by the sound of the phone ringing. Steve physically jumped then quickly recovered and picked up the receiver. The receptionist asked for his permission to put through a call from the Tsang Corporation, and he was immediately connected to Mr. Liu whom he remembered from correspondence was the marketing director of this huge company. The Oriental voice with a hint of American accent at the other end of the line enquired, "Was the hotel satisfactory? Had his journey been good? Etc." Steve affirmed everything and thanked Mr. Liu for his kindness in arranging the change of hotel, and they finally agreed that a driver would pick him up and take him to the company headquarters for a meeting at 3:00 p.m. the following afternoon to enable him to get some rest in the meantime. Steve pondered that Tsang Corporation was obviously very influential, and he had that sneaking butterfly feeling in his stomach that he might just be batting out of his league.

With the meeting arranged, he managed to put such negative thoughts out of his mind, exhaustion started to take over, and he decided to sample the comfortable looking bed and try to overcome his jet lag. Initially he quickly fell into a deep sleep that soon became fitful until finally he got up, switched on the TV, and flicked through the channels. Nothing really caught his interest, so he drew back the curtains and found that he was looking out over a huge lake with several motor launches gliding swan-like across its mirror surface and a golf course on its far side.

Is the lake man-made or natural? I'll ring Jane again; with a bit of luck I'll catch her before she leaves for work.

The phone yet again rang and rang but no answer.

She must have already left and forgotten to put the answer-phone on.

He called her mobile, was transferred to her voicemail, and left a brief message; her phone must be switched off too—Jane and technology had never been very compatible, perhaps that was why she'd chosen an occupation that dealt with people rather than machines. Feeling somewhat deflated at not being able to share his experience with anyone, he decided to explore the hotel blurb and immediately found the answer to his lake question: apparently the lake had been a huge tin mine many years ago and had flooded after falling into disuse but had since been landscaped and turned into a feature after the building of the hotel.

Thoughts of tomorrow's meeting crowded into his mind, and he felt the adrenaline start to pump. Tsang Corporation was huge in Asia, Australia, and America, but to date, they had no representation in Europe, although they did sell some products directly into the E.U. If Steve could swing this deal and become the European agent for Tsang Corporation, he and Ian would be in clover. (Come to think of it, Ian already was in clover!) One thing puzzled him though; there were other similar organizations to his in Europe that were much bigger than Foston, so why had Tsang invited him to discuss being their agent? Come to that, how had they even heard of him?

Researching Tsang had shown him that the company was massive with interests ranging from shipping, pharmaceuticals, electronics, aerospace, and even to property development. Public awareness of the company was limited, because they owned a large number of individually well known companies due to takeovers and a high degree of asset stripping, which had been a specialty of the Chinese founder M. L. Tsang who had died some years previously. The company was now a truly international conglomerate, and their annual budget would have been the envy of a number of small countries. Steve felt that at last he was playing with the big boys. The range of possibilities raced through his mind.

He would advertise Tsang products, they would supply directly to the customer, and he would pick up a percentage on each sale. Advertising would be costly but could be sustained if the commission was high enough.

Tsang would consign goods and paperwork to him in the UK, and he would advertise the products and be paid commission on each sale made. He would have the advantage of not paying for stock but because of having to rent storage would need a higher commission than in the first scenario.

Tsang would do all their own advertising, feed him leads, and he would be paid commission on any resultant sales. This would be ideal as he would have no initial outlay and would only have to employ additional staff once the leads were coming in thick and fast. However, this was cloud cuckoo land, because the only advantage to Tsang was that they weren't actually funding a full-time sales force and most of the benefit would be to Foston. He should be so lucky.

Having mulled over the main possibilities, he realized that he would have to do battle over the first two options, and he had no doubt that Mr. Liu would be a hard adversary, not least because the big fish was dealing with a minnow. On the other hand, he had nothing to lose so he might as well put up a fight. Feeling listless, he e-mailed Ian to keep him in the picture and then tried to work out when he would be able to catch Jane on her return from work. The eight hours difference made things complicated, but he finally worked out that if he set his alarm for 6:00 a.m. the following morning, he should catch her before she went to sleep. There was little else that could be done today, so he decided to blow the cobwebs away with a walk around the golf course. What was left of the day disappeared in a haze of disorientation; the journey had taken its toll.

The travel alarm clock bleeped, but in truth he was already awake as sleep had been elusive. He eagerly dialed Jane and this time heard her voice at the other end of the line. She was apologetic, she had left for work, and, yes, he'd been right; she'd forgotten to switch on the answerphone or her mobile. "How was he? Had the journey been very tiring? Etc."

Strangely, pleasurable experiences are never really totally enjoyable unless they are shared. At last he had someone to share his news with, and Steve lost no time in describing what had happened to him since leaving the airport. Jane was totally disinterested in the stretched limo but wanted to know everything about his hotel room including curtains, décor, and the bathroom.

The possibilities of the afternoon meeting fell on the same stony ground as the limo; the gulf between the interests of men and women was alive and well. They talked for a while, and Jane said that she was missing him, and that he was to behave himself with all those beautiful Asian women whom he would doubtless meet. He reassured her that he was going to be fully occupied with meetings and that he was only interested in business. Finally they said their goodbyes.

Showered and reinvigorated, Steve started to feel human again and ready for the fray. The lightweight "non-crease" suit had partially lived up to its name although "less-crease" might have been a more honest description. A glance in the mirror reassured him that he looked sufficiently respectable for the battle to come and he headed for the dining room, although in all honesty he didn't feel that hungry—still it was something to while away the time. Kim, the butler, greeted him and handed him a menu covering a wide range of food that he really couldn't face, so he settled for his favorite strong, black coffee and a Danish pastry.

Returning to his room, he noticed that his laptop had been moved; it must have been the chambermaid, yet his room hadn't been cleaned yet. His immediate thought was that someone had been snooping. God, he was becoming paranoid. More likely she'd been in to clean and then left for some more supplies. It would be nice to leave the four walls of his room and head for one of the numerous hotel lounges to rehearse his forthcoming PowerPoint presentation. It made sense to be as well prepared as possible.

Rewriting some of his notes absorbed him and a quick glance at the clock shocked him as he realized that there was just enough time for a quick snack before his lift arrived. This time his stomach told him that he was hungry. Returning to the comfort of his now refurbished room, he called room service and was soon demolishing the best club sandwich he'd ever had. The effects of the food and yet more strong coffee quickly revived him, and he started to feel normal once more and ready to do battle. The laptop was fully charged; his briefcase had all the papers that he needed; and, although it was still a little early, he couldn't settle, so decided to make his way to reception.

The teak lift doors glided open on arrival at the ground floor, and he gazed upwards taking in the incredible height of the atrium. The volume of the entrance was vast, and Steve's mind fell into its usual habit of calculating how many rooms could have been accommodated in this space and how much revenue the hotel was forfeiting as a result. It dawned on him that he was a victim of small-scale thinking and that if he were going to be really successful in business, he would have to bury this habit once and for all and start thinking big. The manageress appeared as though on wheels from nowhere, almost unnervingly, and wanted to know if he had everything that he needed and could she get a taxi for him? Steve thanked her and explained that a car would be arriving for him within the next five minutes, and as though by magic a driver walked into reception and asked them to page Mr. Dalton. This place is spooky. Steve made himself known to the driver, and they headed out into the bright sunlight and the gleaming car.

Cecil Liu was on edge, not that anyone outside his office would know; they hadn't seen him pacing up and down for the last twenty minutes. Cecil had been born in Taiwan with parents who originated from Beijing and, like most Chinese, had been given a Western name at school by one of his American teachers.

Today his thoughts were a jumble; one moment he was thinking of his frail father in Taipei, the next of the Chinese businessmen whom he had become involved with in London, and finally of the impending meeting with Steve Dalton who could be the answer to all of his problems. So much hung on this afternoon's meeting.

Several months ago Cecil had read a trade magazine that had published a small piece on Foston Medical and its driving force, Steve Dalton. The company was obviously small but progressive, the sort that would be grateful for business from Tsang, so Cecil was confident he'd made the right choice for his purposes. His contact at Steve's hotel had also e-mailed him all of Steve's projections and his presentation, so he felt that he'd done everything that he could to ensure the right outcome from today's meeting. It had certainly been worth relocating Dalton to a hotel that was prepared to be helpful and was indebted to Tsang, who represented a large percentage of the hotel's corporate income.

Steve too was anxious but for different reasons. After a short journey of twenty minutes or so, the car swung into the entrance gates of Tsang Corporation's headquarters and pulled up in front of the main entrance. As he got out of the car, he craned his neck, feeling like a tourist in Manhattan, trying to see the top of the building, which could only be described as a skyscraper. Inside the reception area was equally imposing, and almost before he could take in his surroundings, an Armani-clad figure appeared at his side and introduced himself as Cecil Liu. The man was taller than any Chinese whom Steve had previously met and cut an impressive, immaculately tailored figure. He had a long but not gaunt face, and his jet- black straight hair had been superbly cut.

Formalities over, they quickly made their way to the high-speed lift and were zoomed almost silently to the tenth floor where they waded through an obscenely deeply carpeted corridor and finally entered a boardroom. The central table was the biggest that Steve had ever seen, and he admired the craftsmanship that had gone into it. Cecil beckoned to a seat at the table and picked up the phone—"We're ready to start"—after a short pause the door opened, and Sheila McAllister entered. Cecil introduced Steve to his personal assistant and explained that she would be handling all the details of their negotiations.

Steve's eyes pilot-like ran a quick appreciative scan: tall, elegant, immaculate makeup, expensive fitted suit, no jewellery (except for a ladies Rado watch), great legs enhanced by classic high heels. Sheila's face had gained the best features of her Malaysian mother and Scottish father, neither of whom were still alive, and could only be described as beautiful.

She placed a folder in front of Steve—"This is the complete product range that will be available for Europe." The voice matched the appearance: self-assured yet soft. "I'll organize some coffee, and then we can have a look at a presentation that we've prepared outlining our strategy for your area of the world."

Steve flicked through the folder, and his mind started to race—included in the range was a new ground-breaking compact home-dialysis unit. There had been rumors that Tsang had been working in this area, but here it was and it appeared that they were making it available to him in addition to the hospital range. The revenue potential was mind-blowing if he could only persuade them that Foston was the right company to handle their products. Steve could feel his heart rate increasing.

Sheila set up her laptop with the projector and commenced a slick presentation that explained the very ambitious plans that Tsang had for European penetration. The slideshow completed, she shut down the laptop, leaned back in her chair, and courteously gestured to Cecil to continue. He, however, demurred and said that he was happy just to listen for the moment. Sheila smiled and turned to Steve—"Do you have any questions at this point or would you like to outline your proposals first?"

"I'm more than happy to leave questions to the end," said Steve and started to set up his laptop.

"Here, use our mains lead it's already plugged in," Sheila offered, and as she bent over Steve's shoulder with the power lead, he caught a hint of her perfume and a glimpse of lace bra as her blouse gaped open. Steve couldn't believe that he was registering such things when he was under so much pressure; it just showed the power of hormones.

The computer sprang into life, and whilst his PowerPoint was workmanlike, he was painfully aware that it was nothing like as sophisticated as the one he'd just watched. However, it was the best that he could manage, and it would have to do, but he made a mental note: If you're working with professionals you need to be professional! Oh well—here goes.

Steve filled in the gaps that weren't covered in the presentation and had to admit to himself that the implication was that Foston Medical was larger than it was in reality, but a bit of poetic license was allowed wasn't it?

"Interesting," said Cecil. "You appear to have the same organizational aims as ourselves, so I don't see any snags in that area. Basically, it would seem that the only likely points of controversy will be the terms of commission."

Steve's heart sank a little: But this is where I expected the battle to be, so don't be negative, start to fight your corner.

He decided to test the waters and asked Cecil where he saw Foston's positioning. Cecil replied that he and Sheila had been in discussion on and off over the last few days and had finally come up with their proposals; would Sheila fill him in? The ever-efficient PA produced a leatherbound folder and placed it upon her exquisite crossed legs.

"Well, Mr. Dalton—"

"Steve," he insisted.

"Steve, we have given the matter a great deal of thought, and we feel that the most mutually beneficial arrangement would be for Tsang Corp. to handle all the advertising as we have excellent in house advertising and marketing staff. We also think that we should feed firm leads from our promotional campaigns to Foston Medical and pay commission on any resultant sales. This will leave Foston free to concentrate on closing the deals."

Steve felt as though someone had just winded him, this deal was way beyond his expectations, and he hadn't even had to negotiate, it had been handed to him on a plate. Even the commission rate was generous.

I mustn't let my feelings show!

"Well, that seems very reasonable and I don't see that Foston will have a problem with that," he heard himself say.

I'll bet they won't—Cecil thought but recovered quickly to say, "Good, let's shake hands on it." All three shook hands to seal the deal. "I'll have our lawyers draw up a contract. Are you free for dinner tonight? If you are, we could bring the contract with us for you to sign, and we could then celebrate the Tsang/Foston link at the same time." Steve thought his heart would thump right through his chest, and his temples would burst as he said that he certainly was free that evening and he would look forward to it.

With Dalton heading back to his hotel with a spring in his step, a grin on his face, and feeling as though he'd just won the lotto, Cecil Liu sighed deeply; it looked like he'd pulled it off. It was ironic that Steve was thinking exactly the same thoughts. Sheila, on the other hand, was not so happy; she was confused, very confused. She had always respected Cecil as a hard but fair negotiator, and whilst she'd taken an instant liking to the tall, good-looking Englishman herself, at her boss's insistence, she had just given Foston Medical the dream deal of a lifetime, one that wasn't in Tsang's best interest!—It just didn't make sense. Cecil was normally razor-sharp.

Sheila had never had any cause to doubt Liu's loyalty to the company, but she was now concerned that she had been made to handle the deal and could be held responsible if the "powers that be" decided to investigate. Her innate caution came to the fore, and she decided to check if there were any unethical links between Dalton and Liu. She hadn't risen to her present position in the company without being very aware of office politics and the need to cover one's back. Fortunately, as PA to the marketing director, there was no problem in accessing most company records, and she now ran searches on expenses, stock options, travel records, etc.

In spite of all her efforts the only thing that she could unearth was a visit to London the previous July, but there was nothing to show that Liu had met with Steve Dalton on this visit.

How can I check if there was a link between the two? Suddenly, it dawned. The hotel would be holding Steve's passport, and she would be able to rule him out if he was not in the UK when Cecil had visited.

On the other hand, just because he was in the UK at the time doesn't necessarily rule him in.

A quick call to the hotel (they were used to her making reservations) connected her with reception, and she explained that they were trying to work out when Mr. Dalton's least busy traveling times were, so that they could send him an invite to one of their conferences that he'd be able to attend. Could they check his passport to see if July was a possibility? The more she thought about it the more flimsy the excuse seemed to be, but the receptionist appeared unconcerned and returned to say that July didn't look good as Mr. Dalton had been in America, France, and Germany. The whole of September, however, had been spent in the UK.

Well, that looks like a blind alley!

There was very little else that she could do other than to keep her eyes and ears open and possibly quiz Steve when she got the opportunity. She was somewhat surprised to feel relieved that, if Liu was up to no good, Steve at least didn't appear to be involved. In the meantime, as a precaution, she set up a file on her computer to record her worries and what action she'd taken.

Back at his hotel Steve flopped on top of the bed and gave free rein to his thoughts. He was feeling elated, yet he too was unnerved at how easily Tsang had acceded to what appeared to be the deal made in heaven—somehow it didn't quite add up. The newly decisive him quickly put such negative thoughts out of his mind.

Don't look a gift-horse in the mouth. Time to call Ian with the good news and then to have a chat with Jane at work. Wow. What a day!

Cecil felt as though a massive weight had lifted from his shoulders. The world seemed to revert to color instead of grey. He rang his father and was surprised at how clear the line was to Taiwan and then chided himself; he of all people should know of the efficacy of fiber optics. The old man sounded thrilled to hear from him, but the phone betrayed his frailness, and Cecil recalled the semi-transparent parchment of the old man's skin when last they had met. He knew that his father's days were numbered but couldn't contemplate the thought that his actions might result in his father being harmed or his end being hastened.

2

After a short call from Steve, who had seemed very excited, Jane put down the phone. Unlike Cecil's call, the line had been poor with every word echoing and Steve said he would ring again in the hope of a better connection. Jane was experiencing a mixture of emotions; she didn't enjoy her own company, the place seemed empty without Steve, yet she valued being able to please herself. There was also a tinge of guilt, because deep down she knew that she was using Steve, which was difficult for her to justify because he was a decent guy (the most considerate she'd ever met), and she had to admit that the sex was good too.

Jane's father, Geoffrey Kemp, had been a Major in the army but had mysteriously resigned his commission. He was a somewhat remote figure who found it difficult to show emotion. Strict and very reserved. She craved her father's approval, rarely got it, and was, therefore, always jealous if he showed interest in others. There had been rumors in the family that he'd been involved in Mess fund irregularities, but neither he nor her mother had ever discussed the matter with Jane. Her mother was a somewhat neurotic but well-meaning woman who lived on her nerves, enjoyed bad health, and was renowned for having "one of her headaches." For years she had relied on medication to enable her to cope and sleep, and the doctor had long since given up on the idea of trying to wean her off her drugs, knowing that he'd only make a rod for his own back.

Childhood, like that of most Forces kids, had inevitably involved moving a lot, and she had been brought up in such diverse places as Salisbury, Hong Kong, and Germany. Moving house and changing school had been a constant pain, because as fast as she had made friends and put down roots, they were on the move again. She was always left with the feeling that both school and newly acquired friends were rejecting her. Secondary schooling had been mainly in Germany and this had given her the advantage of being fluent in the language.

Fortunately her father's alleged indiscretion had occurred after her equivalent to "A" levels, and she had returned to the UK to take up a place at Manchester University. Shortly after their arrival back in the UK her father had driven his car to a remote spot and taken a fatal overdose. Everyone was in a state of shock with the exception of her mother who, for once in her life, coped admirably. Jane was a bit concerned that she too was coping far better than she would have imagined. The general consensus was that the recent problems had been too much of an ego dint for her father and that he'd taken the only way out that he could see. Jane felt guilty for hating her father for leaving her before she'd ever gained his approval, but there was no denying the fact that that was how she felt. She also resented the fact that she'd had to leave her latest boyfriend back in Germany thanks to him causing their return to the UK.

By the end of the summer her mother was still on an even keel and actually seemed happier than she'd been for years (the merry widow). So, Jane had no qualms at leaving her for Manchester to start her degree course, and to her great surprise she had found Manchester to be a vibrant city with plenty to do and yet within easy reach of lovely countryside, not the least like the stereotype image that she had held. The university sociology course was good, although, like all courses, it had its moments: some poor lecturers and lots of padding. However, her fellow students made up for the shortcomings, and being away from the restrictive army family-life and living in her own flat, Jane, like most students, went a little wild. Her naturally blonde hair, petite but shapely figure, and endearing smile made her one of those rare people who were popular with both the male and female students and for once she was not short of attention. The pleasures of alcohol, weed, and sex were all new experiences and she didn't stint on any of them!

It was during her third year that two realizations dawned:

1. If she didn't get down to some serious work soon, she was going to fail.

2. She was worried about Bruce Foster.

Jane had been seeing Bruce, a talented electronics student, for the last six months. He was a good-looking lad in a sullen sort of way: tall, slim, and with almost black hair. They'd met at a disco in the student union and exchanged mobile numbers before heading their separate ways. He had phoned her the following week, and the relationship had developed. Initially he'd been great fun to be with; she knew that he smoked a bit too much weed and had been a little shocked to see him use Ecstasy at an all-night party they'd been to but had chided herself for being naïve and unsophisticated. However, Bruce had recently become withdrawn, irritable, and unable to sleep, a totally different Bruce from the one that she'd thought that she knew.

At boringly regular intervals she'd asked if there was anything wrong and had been told sullenly, "No!" In fact she'd recently given up enquiring after being accused of nagging. Insomnia had become an even worse problem, and in the hope that a different approach might meet with more success, the previous night in bed she'd snuggled up to him and suggested that she give him their favorite "sleeping pill." This seemed to meet with approval, yet despite all her efforts, Bruce couldn't sustain an erection; in fact he had trouble achieving what might even be called an excuse for one. He became upset and turned over, refusing to talk, and she found that worry evaporated her frustration. The one thing that had been consistent in their relationship had been sex and now that was gone too.

After tossing and turning most of the night, Jane finally resolved that she would make one more attempt at getting Bruce to discuss his problems, and if that failed, she would have to end the relationship and concentrate on her studies. She woke feeling as if she'd never slept; he was snoring or pretending to snore and showing no obvious signs of consciousness. A glance at the clock threw her into a spin; she'd forgotten to set the alarm clock and would be late for lectures. A hurried shower, fling on some clothes, no time for breakfast, and head the car for Uni. Jane hated days like this; somehow nothing ever went right once you started late.

In fact, contrary to expectation, the day went very quickly and surprisingly well, and it really didn't seem very long before she found herself driving back home. For the first time in the day she had time to think about the Bruce situation—Will he be in when I get home? Will he talk?

To her amazement she found herself turning into her street without being able to recall driving from the university. Must have been on automatic pilot.

The flat was empty, no signs that he'd eaten, the bed a crumpled mess, and no note. He could at least have made the bed the lazy bastard! Anger welled up. This was a give and take relationship; she gave and he took!

Eventually her anger subsided, and late that evening she gave in and rang the communal phone in the house that Bruce shared with four other students when he wasn't at Jane's. It took the usual age before anyone answered, but eventually Wendy, an art student, answered, and said that Bruce wasn't in and that she hadn't seen him since she'd gotten home. The next three days produced the same result, and by now Jane was becoming very worried; should she ring the police? That seemed a bit of an over-reaction, and he certainly wouldn't be overly pleased if they traced him and found him stoned. Bruce could be moody and even in the early days of their relationship would go off in a sulk, but never for three days! In spite of her anger and worry, Jane still experienced that warmth welling up inside her whenever she thought of Bruce.

This guy had definitely got to her she thought. Damn him!

Saturday morning, thank God for a lie-in. By now it was Jane who was suffering from insomnia. The sunlight was streaming through the bedroom window and showed just how dirty it was; she snuggled under the covers—just another half hour. Her mobile rang:

Shit!! – Where the hell is it?

Stumbling out of bed, she stubbed her foot on the chest of drawers and eventually located the ring tone coming from her jeans that were on the floor where she'd peeled them off last night.

"Is that Jane Kemp?"

"Yes, who's asking?"

"This is Police Sergeant Dave Peters; do you know a Bruce Foster?" Her stomach did several somersaults.

"Yes, have you found him? Is he alright?"

"Well, he's in Manchester Royal Infirmary in intensive care. He was found in Salford. I'm afraid he's been badly beaten up. He's unconscious, but the doctors say he should make a full recovery, but he's going to have one hell of a headache when he wakes up. Your name and phone number was the only contact that we found in his wallet."

Jane tried to glean more information over the phone, but all the officer would release was the ward number. Having flung on some clothes and, on one of the rare occasions, no make-up, she headed the car back towards Manchester and, instead of to university, towards the hospital not that they were far apart. What has the silly bugger been doing getting into a fight, but is he okay? Bruce is definitely high maintenance!

After a tour of the very full hospital car park she eventually found a parking space and followed the signs to intensive care. The directions reminded her of the London Tube, color coded and seemingly winding endlessly before delivering you where you wanted to be. A few minutes later she located the security door of the I.C.U., rang the bell, and a nurse immediately opened the door. Jane explained that she was the girlfriend of Bruce Foster (somehow she didn't feel that she was anymore), and the nurse showed her into a small office. "The doctor will be with you in a few minutes."

The Crash Team instructions on the wall brought home the gravity of the situation, but before she could reflect any further, the door opened and a short, very tired-looking Indian doctor entered.

"I'm Dr. Sharma, you must be Miss Kemp. The police told me you would be coming, and firstly, to put your mind at rest, we are reasonably confident that he will make a full recovery, but can't be certain until we can get him down for a brain scan. Mr. Foster has received some very nasty injuries including a fractured jaw. I feel I must warn you that he's not a pretty sight; in fact you may not recognize him due to all the swelling and bruising but be assured it will all subside."

"May I see him?"

"Of course, he's on your left as you go through the door."

She gingerly opened the door; in spite of Dr. Sharma's warning, she still wasn't prepared for what met her; she actually didn't recognize Bruce's face, which was swollen beyond belief, and all those tubes and wires! The nurse encouraged Jane to talk to Bruce as it often helped the patient to recover consciousness. Jane felt guilty for feeling self-conscious; there was something bizarre about talking to someone who was unconscious. However, she dutifully chatted, as suggested, for about fifteen minutes until the nurse returned to say that Sergeant Peters was in the office and would like to talk to her.

As she walked into the office, she could see that Peters was also absorbed by the Crash Team notice. He turned to her, smiled and beckoned her to take a seat. Peters reminded her of everyone's idea of a grandfather; portly, with graying hair and ruddy cheeks, he was a comforting presence.

"I need to ask you a few questions."

"Okay."

"Did you know that Mr. Foster was into drugs?"

"Well, he smoked a bit of weed, but that doesn't really count does it?"

"Well, that's a matter of opinion, but his blood tests show that he was on heroin."

Jane felt herself gasp and was aware of a physical pain in her gut. Heroin! This was serious stuff, and she felt completely out of her depth. She was shocked yet it all made sense now. She was confused because she was almost surprised that she felt shocked; deep down she'd known something was radically wrong.

"I had no idea he was on hard drugs." As she uttered the words, she felt as though she was entering an alien world.

"Did you know any of his friends? Did they use drugs? Do you know who supplied him?"

For the first time she realized how little she really knew about the man who had been her friend and lover. Scraping the walls of her mind, she could only name five of his friends, and to the best of her knowledge only Gaz did a bit of weed. As for the supplier, she had no idea whatsoever. She spilled out everything that had happened recently and Peters listened intently.

"Well, this lad is in real trouble; we have a witness statement, and it looks like he was done over professionally. I'm afraid he's made some pretty nasty enemies, and we need to find who his dealer was, preferably yesterday."

There was a gentle tap on the door, and the nurse popped her head around to advise that a Mr. Foster had arrived. Peters gestured to show him in, and an impressive six feet four inches, bronzed, very fit guy announced in a deep brown voice, "Hi, I'm Tim Foster, Bruce's cousin."

Peters explained that they had contacted the university pastoral officer and had been given Tim as the family contact. Apparently Bruce's parents had been killed in a rail crash, and he had always felt closest to Tim ever since. Both Peters and Jane could understand why—cousin Tim exuded confidence yet appeared very approachable. The position was quickly explained to Tim whose immediate reaction was "Stupid bastard!" However, he wasn't judgmental but wanted to know what was being done to nail the sod that'd done this to Bruce. Was the drug squad involved? What about the Special Branch? Jane sensed a military background from his bearing, seeming lack of shock, and a manner that appeared to outrank the police sergeant. Peters also seemed to realize that this was a man of influence and quickly brought things to a close by suggesting that Mr. Foster might like to see Bruce, and that she might as well go home and, no doubt, the hospital would advise her of any change.

As Jane made her way to the door, the nurse smiled reas-
suringly and said that she could visit at any time. She made
her way back to the car park and realized that she felt confused and very weary but at least reassured that cousin Tim
was not the type to rest until he had a result. However, her
confidence was not rewarded as within the week Bruce had
improved dramatically, and when she visited on the Friday,
she was stunned to find that he'd discharged himself from
hospital without a word to her.

Two years passed since his disappearance, and nobody had
seen sight or sign of Bruce. Initially she had received the occasional call from cousin Tim confirming that Bruce was still
alive; phone and credit card records had placed him in various
places around London, but London was a big place to get lost
in. She was grateful that Tim had been decent enough to keep
her in the picture, but gradually the phone and Visa usage had
dried up. Jane had been devastated and felt totally rejected, yet
strangely she didn't feel that it was all Bruce's fault; something
must have happened to him. He wouldn't just leave her. Or was
she just telling herself this to ease the pain? At least she knew he
had survived. However, Tim's calls had ceased, and she had no
contact number for him.

Her girlfriends all said that Bruce must be out of his mind to reject
her; most were mildly jealous of her naturally blonde hair, size eight
figure, and striking looks but couldn't help liking her. They'd all tried to
be supportive, but, although they were well meaning, she'd found their
match-making attempts to be a pain in the arse. Men were definitely a
no-go area for her, and her social life revolved around a group of her
girlfriends and their friends.

A few too many drinks one night had caused concerns
amongst her friends, and one of the girls, Helen, who lived near to
the bar where they'd been drinking, had volunteered to take Jane
back to her flat to sleep it off. Jane had woken during the night
to find Helen's warm body pressed up against her, and a gentle
hand exploring her. Her first reaction was shock, but almost immediately pleasure and curiosity overtook her. This turned out to

be the beginning of an exciting and passionate interlude, the first to brighten her life for a long time, and in fact she had to admit that she was happier than she could ever remember.

The affair fizzled out after a couple of months primarily because Helen had gotten a new job that necessitated her being away a lot. Both had agreed that they weren't committed gays but had just been satisfying their curiosity and enjoying the different gentleness of female sex and, joy of joys, their knowledge of how to turn a woman on. They'd both been hurt by men, had never envisaged landing up in a same sex relationship, but had to admit, to their surprise, that they'd loved every minute of it. There was no embarrassment, and they knew that they would always be close friends. Jane felt a temporary void but not rejection.

Since then there had been a few short unsuccessful relationships; the most recent was one with a guy she'd met in a Manchester bar who'd been a great lover but turned out to be married and just using her. Some eighteen months on and she'd met Steve at a flying club party that she'd been invited to by Pam, one of the girls at work. Pam was having flying lessons, but her interest seemed to be more focused on the instructor rather than on flying. Jane was a bit fed up and had nothing better to do on that Friday night, so the invite was well timed and there was a good atmosphere in the bar. Pam had headed off to snare her quarry, and left Jane alone with her drink and a bowl of olives. Steve was the guy sitting next to her, he'd struck up a conversation, and she'd found him comfortable to talk to. She noted that he was quite good looking in a distinctive sort of way, but it was his gentle manner and his ability to make her feel important that attracted her. They had initially chatted about his flying ambitions, and his enthusiasm was almost schoolboyish, but he quickly curbed his technical talk and turned the subject around to her and her ambitions. He seemed genuinely interested in everything that she had to say, and she found it refreshingly novel to discover a man who for once wasn't totally obsessed with himself.

At the end of what, to her surprise, had turned out to be a very enjoyable evening and that had passed very quickly, they headed home their separate ways, and she was half surprised and half disappointed that he hadn't asked for her phone number or suggested that they should meet again. However, her disappointment melted away on the Monday morning when he rang her at work.

"How did you get my number?" she heard herself saying only to feel foolish when he explained that every club member had to register their home and work number with the club. He'd simply rung Pam, and she'd been happy to hand over the number—let's face it they'd all been hoping to match-make Jane.

A few weeks and several dinners later they'd slid into a relationship. Neither had delved much into the other's past. She knew that work had ruined several previous relationships for him, and he knew that she'd had one long-term relationship that hadn't worked out.

The sex was good for her, he was a considerate lover, not as exciting as it had been with Bruce in the early days, but good nevertheless, and whilst she couldn't forget Bruce, Steve's easy company helped to dull the pain. Inevitably they had drifted into living together, and apart from that slight lack of a spark, she was surprised to admit to herself that she felt quite happy. She'd been flabbergasted when she learnt of the indirect link between Steve and Bruce via Ian. The only thing that marred the situation was a slight pang of guilt at being aware that she was using Steve as a comfort when deep down her thoughts centered on trying to contact Bruce. She also knew that if she managed to trace Bruce, and he got his act together, she would be off like a shot to wherever he was.

However, even those feelings faded away when she snuggled close to Steve's warm, firm body in their king-size bed; she felt safe with him. They'd both agreed that the bed was a must-buy even though it dominated the cottage bedroom. In fact there was only just enough room to walk around it, and friends always made ribald comments about how important it must be.

3

Cecil Liu had been born in Taipei, Taiwan some forty years previously, and being an only child was a Chinese rarity for that time. His mother had nearly died in childbirth and had undergone a hysterectomy the following year for health reasons. He'd been an exceptionally well-paid executive for a number of years now but had, like many of his kinfolk, been an inveterate gambler. Two years ago he'd hit a bad run and had resorted to the lethal recipe of trying to bet his way out of trouble. His bank was not an option for obtaining a loan, as they would want references from his employer, so he had turned to loan sharks, and recently they'd been putting the squeeze on him big time. These parasites had done their homework well, and they'd made it crystal clear that they knew his father's address and that the old man's health would take a severe turn for the worse if Cecil didn't make a substantial payment to reduce his debt.

Once again he'd returned to Macau (for a gambler, the equivalent to an alcoholic joining a brewery social club) for one last attempt to solve his gambling problem at the gaming tables. Between sessions Cecil was drowning his sorrows in the bar; his body language spoke volumes to anyone perceptive, and he had got into conversation with a fellow punter. His new-found companion, who called himself Tony Pang, became very interested when he discovered that Cecil lived in Kuala Lumpur. Did he have any links with the chemical or transport industry he enquired?

No, Cecil wished that he did work in the transport game; to him it was money for old rope. Transport costs were his highest overhead because his products were bulky and unevenly shaped. He didn't like the fact that he was paying to ship cartons around the world that were half full of air.

Tony Pang had been watching Cecil for some time after a friend had pointed him out, and he quickly recognized a man who was in financial difficulty and who was struggling just to tread water. Pang played him like an expert angler plays a trout and, after listening to Cecil's comment regarding transport, asked which export agents Tsang used. He sounded perfectly convincing when he exclaimed that his London-based water analysis and wood treatment chemical company used the same firm, but because his company was much smaller, they were unable to command a decent discount and were paying extortionate rates. They bought a lot of their chemicals in Malaysia, and if Cecil were prepared to dispatch some of their low volume chemical packages along with the Tsang Electronics products, he would be happy to split the profit with Cecil and there was no need for Tsang Corporation to be involved.

Understandably Cecil's immediate reaction was "What sort of chemicals?"

"Mainly arsenic, aluminum, and copper-based compounds; just wood treatment and water analysis chemicals" was the reply.

Cecil decided not to probe further except to ask how frequent the consignments would be, and Tony said they could discuss details when Cecil was next in London.

July had been sticky, unusually hot and humid, and Cecil would have given a lot to head for somewhere cooler and more comfortable than the Turkish bath conditions of Kuala Lumpur. The Monday after his return from Macau was to be taken up by a meeting with a supplier, but the representative's secretary had phoned to cancel the meeting because her boss was ill, so Cecil was now left with a whole afternoon to marshal his thoughts. The idea of not involving the company worried him, yet they were already paying the shipping costs, and he could do with the additional income to help fill the huge hole that his stupid gambling had produced. He was sure that he would be able to square the arrangement with dispatch department; "samples and spare parts" should suffice as an explanation. There really didn't seem any risk in the arrangement, and it would certainly solve his immediate problems. In fact, the more he thought about it the more he managed to convince himself that this was the right thing to do, so he squared the circle.

A quick call to Corporate Travel Dept. had a flight arranged to London, and two days later he landed at Heathrow Airport, London. Cecil had a real distaste for Heathrow; he just couldn't understand how any so-called civilized country could run such an important, busy airport in such a noisy, chaotic manner—or, he wondered, was he just spoilt by the serenity and cleanliness of Kuala Lumpur airport?

The usual taxi drive through grinding traffic into London and the leaden sky did little to lift his sour mood, but, surprisingly, the arrival at his hotel did. From the outside the building was a classic Victorian monolith in the middle of Marylebone, but as he entered reception, it opened into a towering atrium that was vast with a glass roof and contained tall, real palm trees. Apparently this area had originally been an interior cobbled courtyard but now was a marble floored space that was full of light, the amazing centerpiece of this five-star hotel. It would seem that the UK was catching up at last. After an efficient booking-in, he was shown to his room, which was very tastefully furnished and accompanied by a beautiful white marble bathroom.

Feeling fresher after a shower, Cecil rang the phone number that Tony Pang had given him and the switchboard operator announced the company as "Anglo Oriental Trading." Cecil's instant thought was that this was a handle that would cover just about anything. However, on request, he was promptly put through to Tony, who invited him to be his guest for dinner that evening. Tony would pick him up at the hotel at 7:30 p.m., and they would dine at one of his favorite restaurants. Cecil was almost as compulsive a shopper as he was a gambler and thought he'd kill some time by wandering around the shops, but jet lag suddenly caught up with him, and he had no option but to climb into the massive bed and was soon crashed out.

A couple of hours later he woke feeling revived and much more alert. Thumbing through the hotel list of services, he saw a picture of their swimming pool and decided that a swim would loosen up his stiff muscles. The pool and surrounding layout was palatial, and after an hour's leisurely swim and wallow in the warm Jacuzzi, he opted for a relaxing massage from a very sinuous Turkish masseur. In fact he rated it as one of the best massages that he had ever experienced; he now felt revitalized and totally un-knotted after his long flight and realized just what a toll recent events had taken. Returning to his room, he dressed and then made his way to the hotel main entrance, where Tony was already waiting for him. They exchanged pleasantries and walked to a top of the range Mercedes parked on the forecourt. This guy Pang must be doing all right if he's running cars like this!

Tony gave the driver some hurried instructions, and the huge car nosed its way into the Marylebone traffic and headed for Soho.

Cecil was aware of the male delights that Soho offered and was, therefore, surprised to find that Tony's favorite restaurant was located in this controversial area. However, on entering through the somewhat anonymous doors, he was impressed by the superb décor of the bar/lounge and even more impressed by the menu that the maitre d' handed to him. The wine list was equally classy, yet for London the prices were not extortionate. Tony seemed to read his thoughts as he explained that he particularly liked this restaurant because it was as good as any of the West End's best yet more reasonably priced due to its location. This meant that he could indulge himself more frequently without feeling too guilty or breaking the bank.

Pang proved to be a charming, interesting, and considerate host, and when Cecil tried to bring the subject around to business, he was quickly told that tonight was for enjoyment and tomorrow would be for business. Cecil felt a little frustrated but decided that he had no option but to comply, and he had to admit that at least he wasn't being high pressured; that, of course, was exactly Pang's strategy. The food exceeded the descriptions in the menu, and that was a rarity in Cecil's book, and the excellent wines quickly mellowed his frustration; What the hell—go with the flow.

Feeling totally sated but suddenly very tired, Cecil was delivered back to his hotel. He strolled over to reception for his key and was a little taken aback to be handed a sealed document folder that had been delivered for him and that bore the logo of Anglo Oriental Trading. Curiosity suddenly cancelled out his weariness, and the lift seemed to take an eternity to get to his floor. His frustration gathered as he struggled to open his room door. The credit card–type key refused to turn the light to green for about five times before he struck lucky, and the door finally gave under his pressure. So much for progress.

Throwing his jacket on the bed, he quickly tore open the package. The letter inside the company envelope was signed but typed on un-headed paper and gave details of the chemicals, weight, volume, and quantity of packages that Anglo Oriental were shipping along with dispatch dates. The existing freight charges were indeed considerably more expensive than those that Cecil's company was paying, and he could see why Pang would want to improve on his present deal. Fortunately, it looked like this could be a win win situation. Jet lag again caught up so Cecil surrendered to bed, and, with the help of the copious amounts of the superb wine and rich food that he'd consumed coupled with the feeling that his problems were about to be solved, he slept deeply for over eight hours.

Waking with a start, his first thoughts were Where am I? What time is it?—the usual confusion of being away from home and in a strange place. He quickly became orientated and the bedside alarm clock told him that it was 7:30 a.m. Time to get up and after breakfast arrange a meeting later in the day with Pang to go over the fine detail of their proposed hopefully mutually beneficial deal. He dressed in a leisurely manner, checked himself over in the full-length mirror and was pleased with what he saw. Yes, he looked sharp but not too affluent in the Hugo Boss suit that he'd chosen for today. His usual Armani suits made an obvious statement, and he didn't want to put himself at a disadvantage in any negotiating that would inevitably take place. Big business was just as much about haggling as the local market stalls were. He was also pleased to see that his recent worries had not left their mark; he still looked a good ten years younger than he actually was.

The hotel restaurant was light, and whilst it couldn't be described as sumptuous, it reeked of class. The breakfast was excellent, the service understated, and having re-charged his batteries, he returned to his room and rang Tony. The morning and early afternoon were clear for Tony (the guy didn't seem to be overworked), so Cecil suggested that they meet in the hotel lounge mid-morning and that Tony should join him as his guest for lunch. The meeting was very informal, and as an added tidbit he dropped the fact that European deliveries would be increasing due to a new link with Foston Medical. As a result the meeting really didn't involve any haggling, so both parties felt satisfied and were able to enjoy an excellent lunch.

In marketing terms Cecil would be described as a "Red"— he didn't queue, never procrastinated, and couldn't abide people who did. Having shaken on the deal and bade farewell to Tony, his savior, he immediately rang the concierge to try to get him on the earliest flight to Kuala Lumpur. Fortunately there was an early evening flight and seats available in business class. As he retraced his steps by taxi to Heathrow, Cecil had to grudgingly concede that this was one UK hotel that matched the best that he'd stayed at anywhere in the world.

Several hours later he was at thirty-six thousand feet and heading back home with a warm sense of achievement and a feeling that his troubles were over for the time being. In fact these thoughts turned out to be the case as the mutually beneficial arrangement progressed profitably for both parties for several months after his return, and his worries about his father evaporated.

4

Steve's phone conversation with Jane had left him feeling uneasy. She'd seemed either withdrawn or preoccupied, nothing he could clearly identify. He was sure that there was something wrong, but when he'd asked her what was wrong, she'd offered the usual female reply: "Nothing." Oh well. There was no way that he could pursue the matter from this distance if she wouldn't communicate, and he was right out of crystal balls. No other man understood the workings of a woman's mind so why would he?

His thoughts returned to business, and he was still having difficulty in believing that things had worked out so well for him; it's Ian who has things fall in his lap, not me! Gradually the details of the deal percolated into his consciousness, and he decided that he should celebrate by returning Tsang Corporation's hospitality. Letting the Jane matter drop, he rang Cecil's secretary and asked if her boss was free for dinner that evening and was a bit surprised to hear himself add that if she was available, he would also like Sheila to join them. Perhaps she would confirm? Oh, and as his hotel had a selection of excellent restaurants, they might like to join him there unless they had a particular preference elsewhere.

Later that morning Steve had wandered down to the hotel lounge in search of a bit of company; no matter how good they are, hotels can be lonely places. He had got into conversation with an Australian engineer who ran a chemical contracting company that specialized in desalination plants. The time passed pleasantly over a couple of coffees, and his companion proved to be good company and a vast source of hilarious experiences from around the world. In fact he was quite disappointed when the hotel paged him and asked him to go to the nearest phone.

Cecil's secretary confirmed that both he and Miss McAllister would be delighted to be his guests for dinner, what time would suit? Having agreed on 7:30 in the bar, Steve hung up and was a little embarrassed to find that he was pleased that Sheila went under the title of Miss and not Mrs. He had noticed what he'd thought was a wedding ring but didn't know what the custom was in this part of the world.

Steve headed for the bar for a pre-dinner drink. A gin dry martini should hit the spot, he thought, and the barman certainly knew how to make a good one! He slowly savored his drink and was lost in thought, twirling the olive in his glass when he saw Cecil and Sheila walk in. Cecil was his usual sharp-suited self and looked very relaxed whilst Sheila looked absolutely stunning in a peacock colored satin dress that even from a distance showed off her figure and seemed to complement her jet-black hair. Steve noticed that several guys at the bar had turned to appreciate the scenery.

Cecil opted for a Campari and soda and Sheila for a whisky sour, and once the drinks and nibbles arrived, they settled down to the serious business of deciding which restaurant to opt for. The general consent was for the Italian, and then the even more serious tasks were to go through the menu and wine list. Cecil opted for veal, Sheila wouldn't eat veal on principle and settled for venison, and Steve joined her. The maitre d' found them a good table in an alcove, and Cecil banned any talk of business for the evening. The food was outstanding and the excellent Barolo mellowed them quickly, so that the conversation flowed as easily as the wine.

Steve was amazed at what similar tastes he and Sheila had in music, art, and food, and they both enjoyed discovering things about each other. He told her about the cottage that he loved so much, although to his own surprise, he omitted Jane from the picture and he heard that Sheila had recently bought a new apartment in the centre of Kuala Lumpur and had been in shopping heaven furnishing and decorating. Meanwhile Cecil seemed somewhat distracted and asked if they would excuse him if he left early because he had a meeting the following day and needed to be on the ball. The meal and company had been a delight and a great way of celebrating their association, which he knew was going to be very successful.

For Steve the evening was drawing to a close all too soon, and he found it hard to believe that Sheila had awakened such profound feelings in him in such a short time. He had to confess that he was quite pleased at the early departure of Cecil, and he desperately wanted to suggest that he and Sheila finish the evening with a nightcap in his room, yet somehow he was frightened that this would break the spell and spoil things. This was a new experience for Steve; he'd never been backwards in coming forward with women previously. Sheila was definitely something different, like no woman he'd ever met before. He compromised by suggesting that they have their coffee and liqueurs in the lounge; it would feel more intimate, and they could talk more easily without being overheard.

The waiter ushered them to a secluded, large comfy-looking settee, and they both sank into the soft down cushions. The coffee was good, and he noticed that like him she drank it black without sugar; yet another coincidence. Armed with a large Armagnac, he relished the warmth and closeness of her body next to his and also noticed, with satisfaction, that she made no attempt to draw away. Sheila turned to him, hesitated and then said, "When are you intending to return to the UK?"

"Probably Monday. I thought I'd give myself the weekend to explore Kuala Lumpur."

"Well, I can be free tomorrow, and it would be my pleasure to show you around my city, unless you want to be on your own?"

Want to be on my own? You must be joking!

Steve accepted her offer and made it very clear that he could think of no nicer way to see the capital city than in her company.

She smiled the smile that lit up her face and in turn said that she would enjoy showing him around her home patch and would pick him up at 10:00 a.m. tomorrow. They made their way to the hotel lobby, and the thought of the following day eased his disappointment that she wouldn't be staying longer with him to-night. A taxi was called and as usual appeared in lightning time. She slipped her coat over her shoulders and thanked him for a wonderful evening. Awkwardly, he didn't quite know how to respond, but the moment was rescued when she confidently leaned over and kissed him on the cheek.

"Until tomorrow."

"Roll on 10 o'clock!"

A whisky night-cap is what's needed.

Steve settled into a deep, comfortable bar armchair and asked the barman to bring him a Glenlivet and the phone. With malt in one hand and the phone in the other it was time to update Ian.

5

Ian had long since found that leaving home early enabled him to miss the worst of the traffic and likewise leaving work early offered a better journey home. It made for a distorted work day, but he got through more work and was actually less tired by the end of the day than if he'd battled with traffic.

With his routine glance at the Financial Times headlines over, he was now sipping his first cup of strong coffee and re-savoring last night's "business dinner" and subsequent bedroom antics with his latest diversion; she'd certainly been athletic, bloody near killed him, and great though it was, he could have done with a little more sleep. His direct-line phone rang disturbing his thoughts.

Steve's voice sounded excited as he briefly outlined his successful negotiations with Tsang Corporation. He was sinking celebratory malt for both of them until they could catch up on his return. What was the UK weather like, etc.?

Ian put the phone down slowly. He had to hand it to Steve; it looked as though he'd pulled off the deal of the century that was going to push Foston into the big league. God only knows how he's done it; I never really saw him as a big player.

Mind you, he wasn't complaining. He could do with accumulating yet more money to keep up with his extramarital flings, which were becoming ever more costly. Unbeknownst to Ian he had started to be seen as a meal ticket by a number of available and somewhat vacuous women with whom he associated. He was in danger of becoming an easy touch and like a moth with a candle flame was keeping ever more dangerous company.

During the last couple of years Ian had set up a couple of off-shore companies as covers for his own investments and had become more attracted by the predicted profit of various deals and less choosy about the ethics of some of the ventures. The purported activities of several companies that he backed were dubious with fairly transparent covers, but he chose to believe the blurb rather than delve deeper. Also, on several occasions he had sailed very close to the wind with regard to the possible accusations of insider dealing, but so far he had led a charmed existence and all had gone well for him. He'd rationalized his personal financial dealing as being a need to create an overseas hedge fund in case Fiona ever decided to cease tolerating his philandering and press for divorce. It was almost as though he couldn't help himself from getting involved with other women yet sensed that it was going to wreck his marriage. If it all goes belly up, there is no way that I'll let her take me to the cleaners!

However, in reality, he had become addicted to the adrenaline of dealing (and screwing) and like so many gamblers was chasing the crock of gold, but that would be too uncomfortable for him to admit to himself. As usual though fate smiled on him and he was amassing significant funds abroad; his expenditure was increasing proportionally with many "business trips" to attractive places with equally attractive but "on the make" companions.

When Steve had first approached Ian about the business, he had seen a potentially good return on his capital investment but had never thought of the business as becoming a major source of income. Now, however, having listened to Steve's phone call, he could feel his pulse racing and for once it wasn't a woman who brought the glint to his eye. He genuinely thought that this could now be a big money spinner. He sank another black coffee and then started his company work, but throughout the day his mind kept drifting back to the earlier phone conversation, and if Ian had one overriding talent, it was his ability to assess potential and he was sure that this was going to be a big one!

Meanwhile, in Malaysia, Steve was feeling quietly self-satisfied; Ian had been very complimentary about his achievement, and he was rarely generous with his praise, and as he strolled back to his room, he felt an inane desire to skip. He'd never felt so excited, but he realized to his surprise that it wasn't the business that had him so elated; it was Sheila, and he'd never experienced this level of feeling about anyone before. With a slight pang of guilt, he had to admit that Jane was not in the same league when it came to stirring up his emotions or his hormones. Sleep was elusive as he kept putting the evening on "replay" but eventually he drifted off into a fitful somewhat exhausted sleep.

Back in the UK Jane had been due some time off from work and had enjoyed a luxurious lie-in with a pile of magazines. She had just relished a sinfully late brunch when the phone rang—Probably Steve, 'cause he's left several messages.

She picked up the phone, but the voice wasn't Steve's but a rather clipped male voice asking if she could take a call from Major Foster. It took a moment for her to register that Major Foster was, in fact, Cousin Tim.

"Yes, of course, please put him through."

"Hi Jane, I've come up with a few developments but need to meet up with you for a talk. What are you doing this evening?"

"Nothing in particular, do you want to come here, and I'll make us dinner?"

"That'll be great—see you about eight o'clock."

Jane couldn't settle for the rest of the afternoon. Where the hell had Tim been? What had he come up with, and why couldn't he discuss it on the phone? How could he just call as though their last contact had been only yesterday? Preparing dinner took her mind off the subject, and she settled into the routine of cooking. She was a confident, good cook and enjoyed experimenting on guests. However, she guessed that with Tim's public school and military background, his tastes would be fairly simple.

The gravel on the drive crunched, and then shortly afterwards the doorbell rang. Quickly checking the oven and running her fingers through her hair, she glanced in the mirror, straightened her dress, and then answered the door. Tim's bulk filled the doorway, and he looked somewhat embarrassed as he quickly handed over a bunch of flowers.

"Something smells wonderful!"

"I hope it tastes as good as it smells! Would you like a drink?"

"A gin and tonic would hit the spot perfectly."

They moved into the cozy sitting room and armed with their drinks sank into the winged armchairs. There was a moment of stilted silence, but then Tim said that he'd been wary of talking on the phone because you never know who might be listening. Jane thought that this all sounded a bit sinister but decided not to comment, just listen.

"I'm also sorry that it's been so long since I've been in touch."

"Where have you been?"

"Let's just say The Middle East."

Jane felt that it was pointless pursuing the matter further; his tone made it quite clear that he was not going to elaborate; there was something mysterious about Tim. She reckoned that his work must be secret but also that he quite enjoyed the cloak and dagger impression that he gave. Men's egos!

As they continued talking, it became obvious that Tim certainly had been busy since his return to the UK, but he still hadn't been able to trace Bruce. However, through one of his contacts he'd been able to examine CCTV recordings in the area where Bruce had been found after the assault and, as a result, identify his attackers who were known to the police as small-time drug dealers. Jane didn't like to ask how it was that Tim had managed to achieve what the police hadn't, but her respect for his contacts was increasing dramatically.

The dealers had been arrested, questioned, and charged, but the police had been unable to make any further progress and the alleged attackers had been released on bail until their court appearance.

"Well that's that then," said Jane.

"Well, not exactly—I had a talk with one of them, and we've managed to trace his supplier."

"How on earth did you manage that?"

"Don't ask! But one thing has led to another, and we're now getting somewhere. Anyway, the rest can wait till we've had dinner."

Jane suddenly realized that she'd been so engrossed that she'd forgotten all about dinner and dashed into the kitchen to make sure that the food wasn't cremated— it wasn't! Tim followed her into the kitchen, and she asked him to open the bottle of red that was sitting on the counter. She was about to fill serving dishes, but he suggested that they serve directly onto their plates as this would save washing up. Cousin Tim the ever practical. They ate in the farmhouse-style kitchen. The steak, kidney, mushroom, and claret pie was a hit; she'd given him what she considered to be a generous portion, but he managed an equal-sized second helping.

"That's the best food I've eaten in twelve months," he declared, patting his stomach in appreciation.

"Well, I hope you've left room for apple crumble?"

"How did you know, that's my favorite?"

"Oh! Just guesswork . . ."

"We could do with you in Intelligence! Come to think of it, we could do with you in the Mess kitchen as well!"

Having dined amply, they made their way back to the sitting room and settled down with a brandy each in front of the log burner.

"Come on, put me out of my agony; tell me all that you know."

"Okay."

It turned out that the dealer had been legitimately working as a sales rep for a company called Anglo Oriental Trading and was regularly traveling between Europe and the Far East. Tim had approached the company about his activities, and they'd feigned horror and ignorance of his dealing, sacking him on the spot. In spite of pressure from Tim (and she could only surmise what that might mean), the dealer was not forthcoming with any further information so was handed over to the police.

Tim, however, was not convinced that Anglo Oriental had been as ignorant or innocent as they had made out. Subsequent investigation by some of his "friends" had proved him to be spot on. For starters, several employees in Holland and Germany had been caught dealing, and this was pushing coincidence beyond belief. It turned out that Tim was not alone in his suspicions about this organization. Both Customs and Interpol had been keeping a watch on the company after several spot checks had found discrepancies between the manifest and the actual container contents. Admittedly, they had not found any contraband, but their suspicions had been aroused. With Tim's additional facts, and doubtless his background, they'd decided to spontaneously search cargo in Kuala Lumpur, Taiwan, Manchester, and Rotterdam.

Taiwan proved fruitless as did Rotterdam, but they'd hit the jackpot in Kuala Lumpur and Manchester. Initially the examination of Anglo Oriental containers had only revealed legitimate cargo as per the manifest. It was a sharp-eyed Customs officer in Manchester who had made the breakthrough by spotting a reference to a joint consignment with an electronics company on an invoice. Thanks to the wonders of modern communications, all four centers were e-mailed the new information, and in no time at all officers were crawling all over the electronics company's containers. The search quickly revealed Anglo Oriental cartons which, when opened, revealed various packages of chemicals used in water analysis along with a number of packages which weren't—in short, heroin! The next step had been to raid Tony Pang's offices and impound computers and files. Pang had been arrested and was in custody helping police with their enquiries. Meantime, Anglo Oriental was under a microscope.

Jane sat back bemused.

"This is fascinating but it doesn't help us find Bruce though does it?"

"No, not directly, but the more links we find to him, the more likely we are to eventually find him, and I feel more optimistic now than at any time since he went missing."

They drained their glasses, and Tim said that he'd have to leave because he had an early start the following morning, but he would keep in touch and update her as news came in.

Thanking her for a wonderful meal, he made his way to the front door, hovered, and then somewhat awkwardly kissed her on the cheek and evaporated into the darkness.

She heard the car start and the throb of its engine as he drove off and was finally left to her thoughts: I do like Tim. Wonder what he really does? Will any of this bring Bruce back to me? If it does, how will I cope with the Steve situation? Questions, questions, questions!

As a rule Jane would never leave dirty dishes in the kitchen (it was one of her obsessions), but tonight her head was in a whirl, and she felt weary—what the hell! She'd do them in the morning. She headed upstairs, undressed, and climbed into bed.

Ten minutes later it dawned on her that she hadn't even cleaned her teeth; maturity was bringing decadence. Thinking of Bruce and how things had been originally, she finally drifted off but woke with a start because the phone was ringing. She must have been asleep for a long time because it was now broad daylight.

"Hello?"

"Hi, it's me."

Jane felt a pang of guilt as she heard Steve's voice. She hadn't really given him a thought for the last twenty-four hours. He told her that he was staying on in Kuala Lumpur over the weekend to do a bit of sightseeing as he had seen nothing of the city since his arrival. All was going well, and he'd booked a flight for Monday and should arrive at Manchester on Tuesday morning.

How was she? Was everything okay? Etc.

It was only after he'd rung off and she'd thoroughly woken that she sensed something was not right. His phone calls, when away, were normally quite erotic; in fact they often enjoyed phone sex, yet today there hadn't been a flicker of interest. Not that she felt sexually inclined towards him herself at the moment, but it just wasn't like him.

Come to think of it, he hadn't even asked if she'd missed him. Perhaps he was just tired what with jet-lag, etc. Anyway, at least she needn't feel guilty for pleasuring herself, whilst thinking about Bruce, before drifting off to sleep last night.

6

Usually when Steve's alarm clock roused him, he turned it off with a curse, but today when it heralded the new day, it was a joyful experience, and he sprang out of bed and bounded into the shower. Feeling totally alive, he slid back the wardrobe doors to decide what to wear. Like most men he loathed having to decide what to wear when he needed to be smart casual. Formal wear was easy; with suits you really couldn't go wrong. Having dressed and undressed three times, he finally settled on stone colored chinos, a navy polo shirt, linen jacket, and a comfortable pair of loafers. However, he still wasn't confident that he was in the right things.

Still in a quandary he wandered into the private dining room and breakfasted on fresh mango and pineapple washed down with the inevitable coffee. Kim, the butler, asked him what his plans were for the day, and he explained that he was being taken sight-seeing in Kuala Lumpur—did Kim think he was suitably dressed? Steve was mortified at his own lack of confidence, but that's the way it had always been. Kim suggested that he just sling the jacket over his shoulder as he wouldn't need it during the day, but that the temperature could drop quickly in the evening.

So, feeling a little reassured by Kim's comments, he made his way to the lobby and couldn't believe that his heart was bounding like a teenager's. After what seemed an age, but in reality was only ten minutes, an electric blue Mazda MX-5 with roof down swung into the entrance, and Sheila beckoned him into the passenger seat as she apologized for being late. She'd forgotten that she needed gas and the local gas station had been closed because of a fuel delivery. As he maneuvered his long legs in alongside her, she offered her cheek and he needed no second bidding to kiss her; once again he registered her unusual perfume. She was wearing a white and navy summer dress with shoe-string straps that really showed off her shapely shoulders. In fact once again she looked stunning.

Sheila gunned the engine and the little sports car leapt past the gleaming statues and out onto the main road towards Kuala Lumpur. She proved to be a fast but competent driver so he relaxed and settled back to enjoy the ride. He absorbed the scenery feeling elated that he was going to spend the whole day with this beautiful fascinating woman. It was Saturday morning, and as the little sports car wove through the traffic heading into Kuala Lumpur, Steve was totally unprepared for the site of the Petronas Towers. These two linked buildings had been the tallest in the world until a couple of years previously, and no petrochemical company could have had more impressive headquarters. They dominated the skyline, and once in the city centre they dominated everything.

Having parked the car in a friend's office car park, they headed to a smart coffee shop where they enjoyed an Americano and people watching. Steve was amazed at how sophisticated everything was; the women were stylishly dressed, the men equally smart, and the shops were full of Gucci, Versace, Armani, Hugo Boss, etc. As he expected, the traffic contained its fair share of Protons, but what he hadn't expected were the BMWs, Jaguars, Porsches, and the smattering of Ferraris and other exotica. This truly was an affluent, vibrant city.

They lingered over coffee and enjoyed the sun and people watching. The coffee worked its magic, and Sheila took Steve by the hand and led him into the twin towers. The lift was super smooth and transported them at an ear-popping rate to the bridge level. As he looked down from the glass bridge, he felt giddy. What must it have been like to work on the construction of the building?

This was a completely different sensation to that experienced in an aircraft; here there was something joining you to the ground, and you could see the towers disappearing to a point beneath you. It actually took a level of courage to walk out onto the bridge, and he noticed that a number of people opted not to. The view was stunning looking way out over the city, which was a blend of old colonial buildings and ultra-modern additions.

Sheila reveled in showing him around her city, and they eventually arrived for a late lunch at The Colony Club, which hadn't changed perceptibly for donkey's years. She suggested that he should try the specialty that the club was famed for; its sattay. He was more than happy to go along with whatever she recommended. They started with chicken and beef skewer sattay, which didn't disappoint, and then proceeded to a Malaysian vegetable curry, which was both hot and fragrant. It reminded Steve of a Thai curry that he'd enjoyed in London but was better than anything he'd ever tasted before. Sheila's smile was radiant as she watched him devouring his food like a young schoolboy at a party. Finally, feeling extremely full, they both declined dessert and settled for a Java coffee.

Steve was looking around the large dining room with its swinging fans, wicker and leather furniture, and sumptuous drapes, but as he turned back, he realized that Sheila was looking intently at him.

"Would you like to carry on exploring this afternoon or would you like to come back to my apartment for a rest and then do the town tonight?"

"I think a rest and then the nightlife sounds great."

"Okay let's get the car; it's less than fifteen minutes to my place."

They rescued the Mazda from its office car park and sped through heavy traffic to Sheila's home. The car turned into a side street with mature palms and pulled up in a parking space in front of a modern apartment block. Sheila let them in, and they took the lift to the third floor. He followed her along the corridor enjoying the sway of her hips until they reached her front door.

Letting herself in with a credit card–type key, she beckoned him inside. The small entrance hall opened into a large sitting room that expertly blended large traditional furniture with modern pictures and lighting.

Pointing to the settee, she said, "Take a seat and I'll get us a beer." Steve wasn't sure what came over him; perhaps it was because Monday was so close, but he just pulled her close to him, held her tight, and kissed her. She didn't resist, thank God, in fact she seemed to respond. Guilt forced him to pull away slightly and apologize. "Don't apologize; I was hoping that you would make the move before I had to."

Steve pulled her back to him and drank from her lips. He could feel her thighs against his and that tantalizing pressure against his ever-increasing hardness. They half sank, half fell back onto the settee with him fumbling at the buttons of her dress and her tearing at his polo shirt to get to bare skin. She giggled and suggested that they should make life easy and head for the bedroom, and so, in a state of disarray, they did just that. She slipped her dress over her head, and he felt himself gasp as she stood there in matching cream lace bra and panties that contrasted with the gorgeous coffee color of her skin. God she was beautiful.

She sauntered over to the bed and draped herself tantalizingly on the duvet. He stripped easily, unselfconsciously, and followed his manhood to the bed. Lying alongside her and feeling her body touching his was the nearest thing that he'd experienced to ecstasy. Gently stroking her shoulders, he played at the straps of her bra, holding back before eventually undoing it to reveal those beautiful pert breasts that he'd always known were there. The nipples were already hard, and he quickly realized, whilst toying with them, just how sensitive they were as she started to purr and mew catlike.

Having held back as long as he could bear, Steve traced with his fingers the line to her navel and after dwelling a short time traced the faint line of dark down that led tantalizingly to her welcoming mound. As he touched her moistness, she let out a little childlike cry but then pulled him onto her and guided him in.

It was dark when they woke up wrapped around one another, and they talked and talked and talked. Everything had seemed so natural and uncontrived, and they both felt it was the best lovemaking that either had ever experienced. Steve realized that for the first time in his life he was in love—deeply in love. He stretched lazily and yawned as he shifted his position to feel her firm breasts against his chest.

"That tickles!" she said as she played with the hairs on his chest.

"Are you complaining?"

"Definitely not!"

"Then do we explore the city or keep exploring one another?"

Steve didn't get an answer, well not a spoken one.

7

The clock was ticking like a sledgehammer, and the sun streamed viciously through the grimy window as Bruce woke. His hangover could best be described as "a pain in the brain," a very apt phrase often used by an Irish friend of his. The last two years had been the worst in his life. He'd lost the one person whom he now recognized was the most important person in the world to him, been beaten up, suffered hepatitis, gone through cold turkey detox, and lived in constant fear of being found by the drug suppliers whom he still owed.

Having signed himself out of hospital he'd headed for London. God only knows why!

The only good thing to come out of that experience so far was that he'd seen a drug rehabilitation course advertised in Camden. They'd sent him for a medical before accepting him and fortunately he'd been negative HIV but positive for hepatitis, a legacy of sharing needles. They'd enrolled him in a treatment course at a teaching hospital, and he'd responded well. Three months later he'd been clean, was feeling healthy again, and was proud to say that he hadn't touched anything since.

London, on the other hand, was the loneliest place that he'd ever lived. He'd started off at a hostel that couldn't have altered much since the days of Oliver Twist, but now he had a base-ment bed-sit opposite to Clissold Park in Stoke Newington, north London. This had been made possible once he'd landed a job as a hotel porter. The pay wasn't good and the hours were appalling, but they'd taken him on without references, and he was paid cash in hand. How they managed to square that with their books he would never know, but that wasn't his problem.

Like many in the catering business, he was anonymous and didn't exist officially. There was a certain common bond with his fellow Thai, Filipino, and Eastern European workers, most of whom he suspected were illegal immigrants. He'd stopped using his credit card, partly because he'd been broke and partly because he didn't want to be traced. The mobile phone had gone for the same reason. He now lived entirely by cash, and what he couldn't afford he did without. Actually, he felt quite moral as for the first time in years he didn't owe a soul with the exception of his persecutors.

It had often passed through his mind to try to contact Jane, but he didn't want to hurt her anymore, and being realistic, he was terrified that she might be watched in the hope that they could trap him through her. Ironically, the pushers were no longer interested in him; they'd given him a damned good beating, frightened him so that he'd never cross them again, and moved on to new addicts. The effort and cost of further shadowing just didn't add up to the amount owed. So, like most of us, he was running away from something that was never going to happen.

Stoke Newington was handily placed on a direct line to the hotel and was close to Highbury for Arsenal home games, now that his finances were more healthy. The place partly owed its fame to being the birthplace of the famous author Daniel Defoe and partly for the Kray Brothers, a family of murderous crooks who had once been very active in the area. In fact Bruce's local pub was The Robinson Crusoe where he often enjoyed a quick pint when coming off duty.

Having dropped into his local at the end of a shift, he became introspective over a pint. He could tolerate his own company, but there were times when he felt as though he was existing rather than living. He'd made a few drinking friends amongst the porters, but it was very much a man's world, and he now started to realize just how good life had been with Jane; he hadn't valued it, just thrown it away. If only he hadn't been such a dickhead; actually, thinking back to those times, this wasn't a very apt description. He shuddered to think of how low he had sunk with drugs and made a vow never to tread that path again. Slowly he finished his drink with one eye on the big screen TV then, as there was nobody that he knew in the pub, decided to head home to the flat. Once home, he fixed himself a cold meal from fridge leftovers, turned on the TV to see the end of the Arsenal away game that he'd been watching in the pub, and eventually woke with a stiff neck and a mouth like the bottom of a birdcage. He dragged himself off to bed and then typically couldn't sleep as his mind kept wandering back to Cheshire, Jane, Cousin Tim, the bastards who'd nearly killed him, etc. After what seemed an age, he drifted into a disturbed sleep whose relative peace was shattered when the alarm clock went off.

After the night's kaleidoscope of thoughts he made a firm decision to get out of the rut he was in and start to live life. Moving abroad would be essential, and, as languages were not his forte, it made sense to pick an English speaking country. He had a late shift, so after demolishing egg and bacon he headed to the travel agent around the corner for inspiration. It was virtually impossible to browse nowadays; he'd only just picked up the first brochure when a young girl teetered over asking, "Can I help you?" His reply of "I doubt if anyone can!" sent her scuttling off with a pout but left him in peace. Twenty minutes later he'd narrowed things down to Australia, New Zealand, Canada, America, Hong Kong, and India.

The States really appealed, and whilst at university he'd prepared a portfolio of his ideas that he thought might be taken up by the US market. However, he knew that because he hadn't completed his degree he wouldn't have any hope of securing a job in electronics in the US. In fact the more he thought about it the only likely place was India. This was a country with a burgeoning electronics industry, huge population, and cheap labor. In short it was likely to become the next major economy alongside China, and everyone spoke English.

On his way back to the flat he dropped into the corner newsagent and picked up this month's copy of his favorite electronics magazine. Sitting at the kitchen table and armed with a mug of steaming, strong black coffee, he scoured the overseas jobs section. There were only two positions advertised for Indian companies, one in Mumbai and the other in New Delhi. He made a note of the agency phone numbers and went in search of a public callbox. The first one had been vandalized, but the one further down the road was in working order, and he quickly got through to the first agency only to be told that the job had already been filled from within the company. His luck was better with the second, and he was asked to attend an interview the day after next. As he headed back home, for the first time in ages, Bruce felt a spring in his step. Somehow he was sure that things were looking up.

During the next couple of days the thought of the interview worried him as he'd been out of the swim for so long, but the reality proved far less daunting. The central London hotel was impersonal, but the panel, which included a senior project manager from the company A. I. Electronics, soon put him at his ease. Firstly they outlined the company's product range, which primarily covered security in all of its forms. They produced everything from laser sights to electronic camouflage for the armed forces and a host of other products (both hardware and software) to overcome industrial espionage.

When they turned their attention to him, he was able to answer all of the technical questions satisfactorily, but then came the dreaded one: "Why didn't you finish your degree when you were so close to doing so, and why are you working in the hospitality business?"

Bruce had rehearsed the reply—he'd had a health challenge just before his finals but was now recovered. Since then without his degree he'd been unable to secure a job in the industry. He'd taken the job in the hotel, as he didn't wish to be a burden on the State and to earn enough to enable him to save money to support himself when going back to university to finish his degree. However, he'd seen the job advertised and considered that he was perfectly suited to the position.

To his amazement and delight they accepted his explanation and outlined what the job would involve. They felt that, due to the initial heavy workload liaising between three sites, the job would be best suited to a single man and that they would like to have a discussion amongst themselves if he would care to step outside for a few minutes.

Sitting in the outer office alongside the receptionist reminded him of having to wait outside the headmaster's office during his schooldays. After what seemed an age, but was probably only a few minutes, he was called back into the inner sanctum. Yes, they would like to have him in their organization. He was to be on a three-month trial on a modest salary, which would be reviewed at the end of the probation period. How soon could he start?

Bruce recovered his composure and said that he could start at the beginning of the following month. They would post all the fine details to him that evening and looked forward to a future together. Bruce thanked them and left in a daze. He had expected to have to attend a lot of interviews before getting a job or maybe not be able to find employment at all. Yet here he was, successful at his first interview with a starting "modest salary" that doubled the hotel pay. It just went to show that you can be successful if you just grab life by the scruff of the neck. This was the start of a new chapter, and boy did it feel good. The rest of the day passed quickly, and for once Bruce entered the hotel without feeling depressed. Only another four weeks.

As promised, the details all arrived in the following day's post complete with full job description, contract for signing, and returning, and confirmation of electronic booking for the British Airways flight to Mumbai. His frugal existence proved to have one distinct advantage in that he had very few loose ends to tidy up before leaving. Four weeks later the BA captain announced that they were now making their approach to Mumbai, and Bruce was incredulous that he could actually smell the city in the aircraft. That strange mix of spices and sewage managed to penetrate the air conditioning system even at several thousand feet above ground.

Shortly after arrival Bruce was settled in an apartment in the suburbs of teeming Mumbai. The factory was some distance away, but in view of the odd shifts that he'd be required to work, a car arrived to pick him up each day making him feel like a latter day member of the Raj. Initially he wondered if he would ever become accustomed to the heat, the crowds, the poverty, and the smell, but amazingly everything slid into place very quickly. At the moment his senses were on total overload but fortunately the factory was an oasis of tranquility and air-conditioned cool. He also felt slightly foolish at being surprised when he found himself amongst a very small minority of people with pale skin; somehow it hadn't entered his head that he would be different from everyone else. The other pleasant surprise was that the company was as high tech as any he'd seen, and he just knew that he was going to have a great future with them. It felt wonderful to be valued (the drugs counsellor had been right), and for the first time ever he felt a warm glow of security.

If only Jane were here!

8

As usual, Cecil was the first person to arrive in the building; the time was 7:00 a.m. He'd long since realized that he only needed four hours sleep a night and that lying in bed awake was just a waste of time; as he only had himself to please, he was invariably early for work. Also, he always took work home with him and worked till late at night, and it was largely because of these extra hours that he was able to devote to work that he'd risen to such a senior position within the company at his relatively young age.

His reverie was broken when his direct line rang; he picked up his phone and was surprised to hear the chairman, Alec Jackson, on the other end. Jackson was an abrasive American who had built an awesome career as CEO of a variety of blue chip companies before taking over at Tsang. His typically American brashness didn't always go down well with his Oriental colleagues but, in spite of this, they all respected his ability and judgment.

"I'm calling from our Tokyo office to let you know that I will be flying back this afternoon. I want a meeting with you tomorrow at 8:00 a.m. prompt in my office. Meantime, I want you to take the day off. Don't take your company mobile with you and don't tell anyone where you are."

"Yes but—"

"No buts! All will be clear tomorrow."

With that the line went dead. Cecil felt a deep sense of foreboding. The chairman had never spoken to him like this before; could he know about Cecil's extra-curricular activities? Surely not. Perplexed, he headed back to the car park where he had so recently left his company Mercedes. Having been totally absorbed in thought, he retraced his journey back home but realized on arrival that he had no recollection of the drive from his office. The next twenty-four hours were to drag interminably.

Driving to work early the following morning conjured up the image of the lamb going to the slaughter, and yet he could see no way that any of his actions could be traced back to him. Perhaps it was about something totally different and he was worrying needlessly, but somehow he couldn't totally convince himself; there was still that nagging dread inside him.

Swiping his security card failed to open the door, and Cecil was forced to return to reception, which was at this early hour manned by a night security officer.

"My card doesn't seem to be working; can you re-program it for me?"

"I'm sorry Sir, but I have strict instructions that I can't let you in and that you are to wait here until Mr. Jackson arrives."

Before Cecil had time to reflect, the automatic doors opened, Jackson barged through, acknowledged the security officer, and as he swiped his security pass, told Cecil to follow him. They headed for the lift and were soon in the "Ivory Tower" as the executive floor was cynically referred to by lesser individuals. Jackson deposited his briefcase on a side table and settled in his chair behind his remarkably modest desk.

"You'd better sit down."

"Thank you."

"Doubtless you are wondering what this is all about. Let me make it quite clear that my concerns are purely to protect the interests of this great company; nothing else matters to me."

Cecil shifted uncomfortably as Jackson stood up. He had an intimidating habit of walking around the room as he addressed meetings, and he paced about searching for the right words before getting to the point.

"I was contacted two days ago by our CEO who advised me that he had been visited by Customs and Excise and an officer from Interpol concerning a large quantity of drugs found in one of our containers in Manchester. Further investigation at Kuala Lumpur revealed more drugs in one of our containers awaiting shipment to Rotterdam."

Cecil breathed a sigh of relief. It wasn't good news for the company, but it couldn't have anything to do with him. Jackson continued: "It turns out that a character named Pang who fronts an organization called Anglo Oriental Trading was sharing our containers and shipping genuine products along with heroin. He's now in custody and, after a little persuasion, mentioned your name as a contact. Our paperwork shows no tie-up with this company, and I would value your comments as to how this could possibly happen and what role you played in this arrangement."

Cecil knew that all was lost. There was nothing to do but to come clean. He started to explain that he had been assured that the chemicals were innocuous when Jackson interrupted him:

"You conniving little shit! You've shafted this company! You can save your excuses for Customs and Interpol; they're downstairs already, and I propose to call them up now." He picked up his phone, barked instructions to security, and several minutes later two very ordinary looking men were ushered in by the uniformed officer. The stupid thought went through Cecil's mind that men like these really ought to look remarkable; they didn't. He walked out of the building flanked by the two anonymous men feeling totally disconsolate but at least secure in the fact that by paying off his debts he had succeeded in protecting his father from coming to any harm—he could never have lived with that.

Monday morning seemed to come around incredibly quickly; weekends just flew by. Sheila made her way through the same doors that, unbeknownst to her, Cecil had departed through so ignominiously on Saturday. She was very early, having seen Steve off on the first flight, and hoped to get ahead with her work before Cecil arrived; it would also take her mind off the aching void that she had felt as Steve's plane had climbed out into the hazy dawn. She showed her pass to the security officer.

"For once it looks as though I've made it before Mr. Liu."

"I don't think you'll have a problem doing that in future," he replied. She didn't really register his comment until she was on the way up in the lift. What did he mean by that? It was a strange thing to say.

Without the constant ringing of the phone Sheila became immersed in her backlog of work and felt a sense of accomplishment that for once it looked as though she was going to clear it all before Cecil's customary morning phone call summoned her to his office to brief her on the week's meetings. As if it was responding to her thoughts, the phone rang, but to her surprise it wasn't Cecil; it was Robert Young the finance director. Young had been head-hunted from Price Waterhouse and had a formidable reputation for his knowledge and expertise, yet he was rarely seen out of his office.

"Can you come up to my office right away please?"

"I'll be right up."

Feeling slightly puzzled, Sheila knocked on Robert's office door, and it dawned on her that she'd never been in his office. In fact she had never actually even had a proper conversation with him. They'd just acknowledged one another in the lift, etc.

"Come in! Do sit down; tea or coffee?"

"Coffee please, black, no sugar."

Robert was well prepared, poured from a silver coffeepot, and handed her a delicate china cup complete with the nowadays mandatory cinnamon biscuit in the saucer. "I want you to treat what I'm about to say as confidential for the time being. Is that understood?"

"Of course."

"Right, well I've been asked by Alex Jackson to confide in you. This may come as a shock to you, but it is doubtful that Cecil Liu will ever return to this company. He has allegedly been running a dubious business of his own under the auspices of this company, and it seems that drugs have been involved. Obviously we have to presume him innocent until proven guilty, but I have to say that it looks very damning. The company will come up with a plausible reason for his absence as we don't want any loss of confidence to occur."

"Phew!"

"Yes, I thought it would be a bolt out of the blue for you. Alex contacted me for some guidance as to who could temporarily take over Cecil's job, and I suggested you. I like to keep a low profile, but not much goes on in this company that gets past me, and I have seen how competently you have handled things when Cecil has been out of the country. Would you be prepared to stand in?"

"Well, yes but this isn't what I was expecting when I came in this morning."

"Quite. I will arrange for a generous salary raise because of the extra responsibility and for a dress allowance as you will need to travel more. I think we should work on a three-month trial basis, and if we are both happy after that period, then we will establish you fully as marketing director with the commensurate salary, pension rights, and options. Would that be okay?"

"That sounds very generous and yes, I would be delighted to stand in. May I ask for some more detail on the Cecil business?"

"I'm sorry but I'm not at liberty to say any more at the moment, but you will be the first to know once we have all of the relevant information."

Sheila hesitated. "There's something I feel that I should bring to your attention; Mr. Liu recently instructed me to handle a deal that, in my opinion, was not in the best interests of the company—in fact I was so concerned that I did some research and opened a folder on my computer."

"Yes, I know about the Foston deal, and I have to confess that I instructed IT to check out your computer. Alex Jackson and I were impressed that you had taken such steps to protect the company's interests, and it was part of our reason for offering you the position. However, we won't renege on the deal as it would put the company in a bad light, but we will watch things with interest."

Sheila let herself into her office and felt as though her brain had been scrambled. What had Cecil been up to? Did this link with her suspicions about the generosity of the Foston Medical deal? God, was Steve involved? Don't let him be involved; don't spoil things.

Thoughts milled around frantically in her mind, and she physically jumped as there was a knock on her door. It was the maintenance crew to move her things into Cecil's office. Robert certainly didn't let the grass grow under his feet. What shook her even more was that as she approached his old office, she saw that her name was already on the door.

She longed to put a call through to Steve's plane to tell him of her meteoric promotion but knew that she couldn't because of the confidentiality agreement. The sudden realization that her desperate need to share things with him meant that this man had gotten to her more than any of her previous boyfriends took her by surprise.

9

The relentless ringing of the phone gradually bored into her consciousness, and Jane stirred from her deep sleep. Glancing blearily at the alarm clock, she registered that it was 6:00 a.m. Who the hell was ringing at this time? She picked up the cordless phone and was surprised to hear Tim's voice.

"Hi! Is that you Jane?"

"Sure is! Couldn't you sleep?"

"Why what time is it there?"

"6:00 a.m.!"

"Oh shit! I'm ever so sorry; I thought I'd got the time difference right. Anyway, don't be too angry I've found Bruce."

Jane's stomach leapt inside her. "Where? How? Is he alright? Have you spoken to him?"

"Whoa! One thing at a time please."

Tim explained that he was in India, that Bruce was fine and holding down a good job with a computer company, and that he was highly thought of. He didn't want to discuss much more on the phone but was leaving for the UK today and would fill her in once there.

"Where are you flying in to?

"Manchester."

"Give me your flight number, and I'll meet you and drive you back to the cottage."

Jane's mind was spinning, but she was up with the lark the following morning to meet the early flight from Mumbai. She'd gunned her car and arrived early. Stupid idiot! My arriving early isn't going to make the plane arrive any quicker.

For once the luggage must have been delivered to the carousel promptly after the landing announcement, and the arrivals hall started to fill with a colorful array of Indian men, women, and children of all shapes and sizes, dressed in gorgeous vivid colors and carrying "hand baggage" of enormous proportions. Occasionally an out of place pallid European emerged, and eventually the solid figure of Tim loomed into view.

Tim's face lit up with a smile as he spotted her at the barrier, and after a perfunctory kiss on the cheek, they made their way to the payment machine so that they could retrieve her car from the short stay car park.

He looked tired and admitted that he hadn't slept well on the plane and was longing for a hot shower. So, although she was bursting to bombard him with questions, she settled with difficulty for small talk until they got home and he could freshen up. The journey back to the cottage seemed twice as long as the outward one.

"Right, that feels better, and I'm sure I smell more fragrant than before. So, let me fill you in about Bruce, but first let me try to marshal my thoughts." Tim let his mind drift back to the recent happenings in India.

Police investigators often say that their major breakthroughs frequently come about as a result of happy accidents, and tracing Bruce had been just such an occurrence. The British Army was interested in a very sophisticated computer encryption programme that was being marketed by an India-based company, and Tim had gone over to see if it was capable of handling their needs. Imagine his amazement when the M. D. had called in the technician responsible for the project, and the door opened to reveal Bruce.

After their initial mutual shock they had spent the day covering the business in hand but had met up in the evening for dinner and a long and very much overdue revealing discussion.

Bruce had explained somewhat sheepishly to Tim all that had happened to him prior to and after his leaving Jane, and, to his surprise, he'd found Tim to be a good listener, non-judgmental, and actually complimentary with regard to his efforts to turn his life around.

Bruce's first question had been: "How's Jane?"

Tim had initially told him that she was fine, without mentioning the Steve situation, on the principle that it was better to drip-feed information rather than deluge it. He'd also been able to reassure Bruce that the drug dealers were unlikely to be any further problem to him as they now had bigger fish to fry. Later in the evening and halfway through a bottle of whisky Tim dropped the bombshell of Steve and Jane. Bruce had looked crestfallen but admitted that it was only what he deserved. Were they happy? Did he think it was for real?

Tim had to admit that he really didn't know, as he hadn't seen them together but that Jane had certainly still been very worried about him. Bruce surprised himself by saying that he was determined to win her back. This really is the new resolute me!

Having got the personal side of things out of the way, Tim had steered the subject around to the encryption program and told Bruce how impressed he was with its performance and that it would actually exceed their requirements. The designer must have been a whiz- kid to come up with something so revolutionary. Bruce smiled, "I wrote that program when I was in my last year at university along with several other programmes and gizmos."

"Really! What a pity you didn't copyright it."

"I did."

Tim was flabbergasted. "Does your company know that you own the rights?"

"I don't suppose they do. I just gave the technical department the original programme, and we tweaked it a bit to make it attractive to the military fraternity."

Tim had pointed out that Bruce was in a position to make a great deal of money if the product took off as he thought it would and that he should clarify the situation with his employer immediately. Bruce kicked himself that it hadn't entered his head to exploit the product, but he had to admit that it did make sense, although he suspected he wasn't going to be too popular with his bosses.

Obviously, Tim couldn't commit the army, but he felt confident that, with his recommendation, they would be placing a considerable sized order, and it would be wise to have the details signed and sealed before then. The evening passed all too quickly as they covered a lot of Bruce's recent past in more detail, and Tim was left feeling that the young chap had indeed turned his life around and was going to be okay after all, no matter what happened with Jane. The two said their goodbyes, and Tim had headed back to his hotel in one of the Ambassador taxis that roam throughout India. He had to admit that the 1950s design whilst simple and easy to maintain was both spacious and comfortable. So much for progress!

Tim returned to the here and now and Jane listened eagerly as the edited highlights of the story unfolded. The one place she would never have thought that Bruce would be was India.

"Does he look well? Is he off the drugs? Did he ask about me? Did you tell him about Steve?" These and a host of other questions spilled out as Tim came to the end of his saga. Tim answered her questions, and she particularly latched onto Bruce's reaction to the Steve situation. She asked the name of the company that he was working for, his address and then went back to questions about his health again.

By the time that her cross-examination was over it was lunchtime and they sank a chilled bottle of Pinot Grigio as an accompaniment to the seafood salad, which Tim thought that she produced as if by magic. Chairs pushed back they both relaxed, and he said that he mustn't get too comfortable as he needed to get back to London to report to the M.O.D.

Jane gave him a lift to the mainline station at Crewe and saw him off on the train to Euston a quarter of an hour later. Driving back home with her mind racing, she felt that she was on emotional overload: Bruce was alive, off drugs, probably back to his old self, concerned about her . . . .

10

In true Hammer horror film fashion the lock on the remand cell door rattled, and the door opened with a rusty screech to reveal a prison warder accompanied by two men: an insignificant man who was introduced as being a senior Customs official and a military-looking type from Special Branch. Tony Pang was relieved that the boredom had been broken but somewhat disturbed at what the interruption might involve. He revelled in the soothing blast of cool, fresh air that the door let in. Since arriving here, he had become acutely aware of simple things that he had previously taken for granted.

Pang and his family had long-standing links with organized crime in London's China Town with tentacles spreading to Liverpool, Manchester, Hong Kong, and Macau. He had made a conscious effort to divorce himself from the past and thought that he had managed to escape into respectability by setting up Anglo Oriental Trading. He'd seen boxers and footballers occasionally spring the crime and poverty trap, and he wanted to follow in their footsteps. In spite of his worldliness, his arrest had had a devastating effect upon him, and he was not coping well with remand. Loss of face and loss of freedom had both taken their toll, and he felt very alone. The food hardly deserved the name. Who else was in the frame except him?

After a long and searching conference, his expensive lawyer (more than he could really afford but what price was your freedom?) had offered some hope of pleading mitigation if he co-operated with Customs and police and was meantime working on his brief. Let's hope he knows what he's doing.

The two investigating officers knew far more than he ever imagined possible, but then he was unaware that his business had been under scrutiny for more than two years. Both had been more pleasant than he had expected, and against all of his instincts he found that he rather liked the grey Customs officer who had a wry sense of humor.

The one area that they seemed to be most interested in was the funding of Anglo Oriental. The company was Virgin Isles–based, and as a result Companies House had been of no help to them; what could he tell them?

Tony was loath to offer any assistance but felt as though he was on a film set when the Special Branch officer uttered the classic line: "Look, you help us and we'll see what we can do to help you." His mind went back to his interview with his solicitor, and he weighed up his options. He was unlikely to avoid prison so in essence it was a question of trading names for years; a no-brainer when you boiled it down. What's more, there seemed no point in employing an expert and not taking his advice, so he might as well try to reduce his sentence by cooperating. Fortunately, none of the present backers were Chinese so at least he wouldn't be in trouble with the Triads, and he knew only too well what their retribution would have been like; they didn't take prisoners. He vividly remembered a great uncle in Liverpool who had fallen behind with protection payments on his restaurant and had been run down and killed by his own Mercedes.

Half an hour later the two satisfied visitors left Pang's cell with a list of the three shareholders in Anglo Oriental: two small and one large, the latter also having links with Cecil's company. The last pieces of their jigsaw were now slotting into place, and this was the breakthrough that they'd been looking and hoping for. The heroin trade that pedals short-term ecstasy and long term misery and death is incredibly profitable but requires major investment to function. This financial backing is the lifeblood of the business, and if it can be cut off, the trade will wither. The backers had to be their main target, but they were so difficult to locate as they invariably hid behind legitimate businesses and overseas registrations. Recently, the law had changed to enable the confiscation of assets accrued from drug-related business along with both financial and custodial punishment. At last the measures that Customs had been pressing for were being implemented if only the perpetrators could be identified.

The door clanged shut, the walls closed in again, and Tony became aware of the sweat running from his armpits. This had not been one of his better days. His mind wandered back to the early days of the company when it had genuinely only dealt in innocuous chemicals. Unfortunately, cash flow had been poor, and he had been facing closure when, whilst talking to one of his relatives at a family wedding, a solution to the problem had been suggested. If he were to sign over his shares in the company, take on several employees of their choosing, and act as manager, his salary would be the same plus a profit sharing bonus. The last thing that Tony had wanted was to sign over his company but at least this offered a solution, and he retained the face-saving but meaningless title of managing director. The only other requirement was that he turned a blind eye to the contents of consignments.

Once the business was back on track, his distant uncle had moved on to pastures new and had sold the company to other backers with the proviso that Tony retained his position. This was due less to altruism than to reaping a profit and sticking with a successful formula. Pang had worked hard to improve profitability, which benefited the investors and boosted his bonus. Everyone had been happy until now, and the only person in the firing line was him.

Meanwhile in a cell thousands of miles away Cecil Liu was in conference with his barrister. In the Far East, unlike the West, court proceedings like funerals happen very quickly after the event. He was advised that his best approach was to stick to the fact that he had been assured that the chemicals were harmless, and fortunately he actually had the exact details of the chemicals in writing. With a favorable judge and a following wind there was every reason to expect that the maximum charge would be "Fraudulent use of Tsang Corporation transport." A vastly lesser charge than one related to drugs. The old gambler came to the fore:

"What are the odds?"

"About fifty fifty."

"Well it could be worse I suppose."

The lawyer headed back to his chambers and once again Cecil had time to contemplate his future. He felt that there wouldn't have been any future if he had let anything happen to his father, so anything else was a bonus as long as his father didn't find out what had happened; the loss of face would be more than he could bear. Having no idea how he would cope with long-term imprisonment, he prayed that he wouldn't have to find out. If his lawyer could sway the court not to impose custody, he would be free to find employment, which would be essential as he still had debts to pay off. Obviously, a reference would not be forthcoming from Tsang Corp., but he still had good contacts from the past, and with a bit of luck he would be able to call in a favor or two. The salary drop would be difficult to cope with, but he was capable and with a lot of hard work, and a little luck, he should be able to re-build his career.

Two days later Cecil was escorted to the courtroom where the prosecutor, armed with information provided by Tsang Corp. and the Customs authorities, pressed for a custodial sentence based upon fraud and drug trafficking. By the end of his submission Cecil felt a cloud of depression descend; the case seemed compelling and sounded extremely discouraging.

Undaunted, Cecil's lawyer was very persuasive as he highlighted his client's impeccable career, to date, the lack of any previous convictions, and he made great play of the signed but un-headed letter detailing the safe chemicals that Cecil had expected to be handling. Handwriting experts' testimonies confirmed the authenticity of Pang's signature on the letter, but it was admitted that there was no excuse for his fraudulent behavior although the motivation had been the protection of his father and not personal gain. It was an established fact that compulsive gambling like alcoholism was due to an obsessive personality trait and might even be genetic in some cases, etc. At the end of the proceedings the judge adjourned to his chambers to consider the submission and read all the testimonies in detail. Half an hour later the clerk ordered those present to stand; the judge returned and gave Cecil a severe dressing down but finally issued a six months suspended sentence.

This was better than Cecil could ever have hoped for, his spirits soared, and he thanked his lucky stars that he had chosen such a competent advocate. Somehow in the crevices of his mind he felt that justice had been done as he knew that he wasn't evil, just weak and desperate, and he was now content to pay the price of losing his job. Life wasn't that bad after all, and he reckoned that he could live with this.

Leaving the courtroom, Cecil was struck by the incongruity of his lawyer congratulating him on the outcome of the case. "It's not you who should be congratulating me but vice versa: I should be congratulating you on your brilliant handling of my case. I can't thank you enough!"

"Yes you can. Don't ever let me have to represent you again; that will be thanks enough!"

Cecil left the court chastened, a free man but with the caveat that any further law infringement would invoke the six months sentence immediately and the unpalatable fact that he now had a criminal record. However, there was no shortage of successful people who had not found that to be a hindrance to rebuilding their careers. The glossies were full of authors, industrialists, and media moguls not to mention politicians who had dubious pasts, including prison sentences, but very large bank accounts. Here's to my next career!

11

Steve was thankful for the thickness of the blackthorn hedges that surrounded the fields around his home and which gave him excellent cover as he circled his cottage. The black and white cattle were nosey and eyed him suspiciously, but otherwise the place seemed deserted. From the cover of a nearby bush he lobbed a pebble at a downstairs window, but there was no response. He dialed his home number on his mobile and could faintly hear the phone ringing but nobody responded. What should he do?—the place seemed deserted but he couldn't be certain. Approach the back door cautiously and be prepared to get the hell out of the place if you're not happy.

The back door was locked; he slid the key in, turned it, and quietly entered creeping from room to room with his heart pounding but the place was empty. Returning to the kitchen, he spotted an envelope on the table with "Steve" in Jane's writing. Inside was a briefly scribbled note:

"Gone away for a few days will ring a.s.a.p. someone rang, just as I was leaving, asking for Ian; told them he didn't live here but they rang off before I could give his phone number.

Love Jane."

That's odd she rarely goes away with work and no mention of where she's gone. She did seem odd on the phone—oh well, no doubt she'll explain when she rings. At least I haven't got to deal with cross-examination and the Sheila situation.

The next moment the kitchen door crashed open, and in an instant a small athletic man had rolled across the floor, taken an upright stance that enabled him to watch Steve, but still see through the kitchen door window, and was pointing a gun at him. The whole thing had happened so quickly that Steve hadn't even had time to be surprised, but now he felt terrified. Guns weren't his specialty, but he recognized that this was a serious no nonsense weapon with automatic action and telescopic sight; this must be the guy that was using me for target practice in the village. Hell I'm in serious shit!

To Steve's relief the sound of crunching gravel signaled the arrival of someone. The gunman didn't react other than to glance out of the door and give a "thumbs up" signal; Steve's relief evaporated. It must be his accomplice, not the bloody cavalry!

Steve was ordered to sit on the nearest chair, and as he did so, he was trying to puzzle out where his assailant was from. Definitely Oriental-looking but not Chinese or Japanese, yet the features were familiar and reminded him of someone. Suddenly it clicked: Kim the ex-Ghurkha personal butler at the hotel. These guys had a fearsome reputation, and you didn't pick an argument with them. What the fuck was he going to do?

"So, Mr. Ian Foster, you thought you were being a smart arse and could outrun us?"

Perfect English and obviously not on his own.

"The name is Steve Dalton not Foster."

A crashing blow to the side of Steve's head that left him gasping and seeing double was the reply. Breathing heavily, Steve fought not to lose consciousness and with a mammoth effort managed to explain that his passport was in his jacket pocket and that it would prove that he was not Ian Foster.

Without his eyes even once disengaging from Steve's, he moved to the other chair and felt in the jacket pocket, but all he pulled out were airline boarding pass stubs. "Try the other pocket," Steve yelled before he got another reminder of who was in charge. This pocket bore fruit, and flicking the passport open, his eyes quickly digested the photograph and the identity.

"Let's get things straight, you own Foston Medical, right?"

"Well yes and no—my partner and financial backer is Ian Foster."

It dawned on Steve that someone must have checked out Foston Medical at Companies House and seen that Ian was the shareholder with greatest liability, but how had they latched onto him? Then he remembered the feeling of being followed since he left the airport and realized that he had probably been followed all the way from Kuala Lumpur and possibly even whilst he'd been there.

"You're saying that Foster is the financier for the business."

"Yes."

"Have you had any contact with a company by the name of Anglo Oriental Trading?"

"Who are they?"

"Yes or no?"

"No!"

The reply seemed to satisfy and the gun beckoned him to stand and turn around. With the weapon prodded uncomfortably between his shoulder blades, he was forced to make a tour of the cottage. Each time they reached a phone extension, it was wrenched from the wall, and then Steve was forced to empty all of his pockets to reveal his mobile phone, but it had been left in his car at the village.

Once it became obvious that they were alone and that there was no means of communicating from the house, he was warned not to try anything clever and shoved unceremoniously onto the floor. With the barrel pressed against Steve's temple the gunman barked: "Give us Foster's phone number and address." Feeling a traitor but realizing that he had no option, he gave the Manchester address and number rather than put Fiona at risk. He was kicked roughly onto his side, the door slammed, a powerful car throbbed into action, and with gravel scattering they left as quickly as they'd arrived. Steve's mind was in a whirl: what had Ian done to cross them? How could he warn him?

Rummaging around in the garage, he found enough plywood to board up the damaged kitchen door. Next he bundled some clean clothes into a bag and walked briskly along the lane to the village. His head was still pounding monstrously after the pistol whipping, but he gritted his teeth and pressed on. A cautious approach to his car revealed nothing suspicious, and he concluded that his assailants would be well on their way to Manchester by now to nail Ian. Sliding into the safe familiar surroundings of his car, he rummaged in the glove box and retrieved his mobile. Ian's apartment number rang and rang, but nobody answered so he tried the office number and was instantly put through to Ian.

"Don't ask loads of questions just take it from me that you are in great danger. Drop whatever you're doing and get a taxi to Barton Aerodrome, and I'll fly there in one of our club's planes to meet you. You'd better believe me; I've just been looking down the business end of a gun barrel!"

Before Ian could get a word in, Steve had clicked the phone closed and headed his car to his local flying club. Mondays were never busy and he quickly booked out a Cessna 172. Thank heaven the weather's okay.

Pre-flight checks complete he radioed for permission to back track the active runway, and once vital checks were over, his headset crackled giving him clearance for takeoff with altimeter setting, wind speed, and direction. The engine roared sweetly, and the little aircraft climbed out to the south. After changing frequency and adjusting the altimeter setting Steve headed north and thirty minutes later was radioing for permission to land at Barton. The landing was not one of his best, but it was the first time that he'd landed on a grass runway—well that was his excuse anyway.

Booking in at the clubhouse, he was relieved to see Ian walking over; obviously he had taken the warning seriously.

"What the fuck is going on?" was Ian's greeting. Steve briefly explained what had happened and the color drained from Ian's face.

"What in God's name have you been up to Ian?"

Ian's mind scrolled through all the deals he'd been involved with and also all the women (it could be an enraged husband or partner who wanted him dead), but he couldn't bring anything specific into focus. He felt fear bubbling up deep inside him.

"I don't bloody know!" he yelled.

"Okay, but look Ian, I think you need to get away for a while to let things cool down; where can you go?" Ian thought for a minute and then replied, with a wink, that he could go to a friend in Antibes, but he'd have to pick up some clothes and toiletries from home first. They clambered into the aircraft, and Steve set heading for Shobdon, an airfield close to Ian's home.

Ian used his mobile to contact Fiona and asked her to pack a bag and meet them at the airfield. Half an hour later the little plane cleared a patch of woodland and immediately the airfield appeared beneath them. They landed (a better effort this time) and taxied to the apron; silence returned as the engine stuttered to a halt. The ever-efficient Fiona was waiting with an overnight bag as requested; she didn't even quiz Ian about where he was traveling to but did seem surprised to see Steve. She gave him a hug and a peck on the cheek before walking back to her Audi TT, and in no time she was disappearing into the distance before they'd even lined up for takeoff.

Once again the Cessna clawed its way into the air and this time headed north for Liverpool. Landing on the jumbo-sized runway left him with what seemed like miles to taxi before he could deposit his passenger at the terminal. In fairness Ian was profuse in his thanks and said that he would pick up a budget airline flight to Nice. He'd got his laptop with him and would e-mail once he was there. Steve slapped him on the shoulder and in no time at all he was retracing his steps to the flying club wondering what on earth Ian had got himself into and also wondering if he would get back to base before darkness. He did, just, but made a mental note to train for a night rating as soon as possible in addition to his instrument rating.

With the plane refueled and returned to its hangar Steve signed the flight sheet. His stomach reminded him that he hadn't eaten all day, so he made a stop to pick up fish and chips on his

drive back home. The food hit the spot, and he washed it down with a cold beer before checking his answerphone to see if Jane had rung. There were no calls recorded, so he switched on his mobile and picked up a text message from Sheila which read:
MISSING YOU DARLING!
AMAZING DEVELOPMENTS AT WORK.
SWORN TO SECRECY.
WILL TELL ALL AS SOON AS CAN.
DON'T WORRY, IT'S ALL GOOD NEWS.
RING ME WHEN YOU CAN.
LOVE S. XXX

12

Jane's plane commenced its descent, bucking and bouncing its way through sullen rain clouds, and her heart started leaping as the old anxiety reared its head. Somehow she'd never liked the landing bit of flying even though Steve had tried to explain it to her and stressed all of the safety factors. She still felt frightened, and the fear only lifted when the plane finally came to a halt. In fact she had to admit that she didn't really like any of the aspects of flying and if it weren't for the time factor would opt to sail everywhere. Anyway, liners have a romance about them that aircraft have never managed to achieve.

Bruce had sounded delighted when she'd rung him at work and told him that she'd booked the first available flight. She lugged her suitcase off the carousel and made her way through the Customs hall. Bruce had said he'd be waiting for her in what was jokingly referred to as the arrivals lounge. Looking around her, Jane came to the conclusion that you'd go a long way to find anywhere less comfortable or lounge-like and now understood what he meant. As she pushed her luggage trolley towards the exit, she scanned the sea of faces and quickly spotted a bronzed, healthy looking Bruce almost unrecognizable from the gaunt, pale-faced version that she had last seen.

They flung themselves at one another, and as he felt her body clamped to his, he couldn't believe his luck. All of the horrors of the last couple of years melted away, and he wanted to shout and tell everyone that he was the luckiest man alive to get a second chance with this lovely woman.

Christ! Am I jumping to conclusions? What about the guy she's supposed to be with now?

They hadn't talked about the future yet, but somehow he felt an underlying confidence. Yes, this is me feeling confident!

When they eventually parted, it was to pick a taxi from the tangle of clamoring drivers. The heat hit her like a hair dryer, and she was overwhelmed by the teeming mass of people, many of whom seemed to be transporting all their worldly belongings with them. So this is India.

They settled into the taxi and the manic driver attacked the traffic; Jane clung to Bruce, and he suggested that she should try doing what he'd learnt to do: look out of the rear window as it was less frightening than looking out of the front. Jane was convinced that they weren't going to survive on at least three occasions during their journey to the suburbs, but they finally did arrive in one piece at Bruce's apartment. Luxurious it wasn't, but clean it was, comfortable and better than she'd imagined.

The air conditioning unit clattered into life, vibrated, and noisily blasted out its cold air. The room soon became more bearable, and Bruce returned from the fridge with a couple of ice-cold beers. As they settled into the sagging, ancient sofa that was surprisingly comfortable, the cold bitterness of the beer hit the spot, and Jane asked him to fill her in with all that had happened since he had absconded from hospital. It was a long story, and she listened intently but found that her eyes were becoming heavy towards the end. The journey was catching up with her. He suggested that she should catch up with some sleep. He'd taken the day off but had to go into work for a short time to clear up a few outstanding preparations for an important meeting the following day. Tim rang with a query, and Bruce proudly told him of his new arrival. Tim wasn't surprised, wished him luck, and said he didn't envy him dealing with the Steve situation but Good Luck!

Sleep found her at long last, and she woke after a couple of hours feeling vastly better. A bath would be nice.

It didn't take her long to explore the flat, and with a woman's perception she noted that there was no sign of a feminine touch in the furnishings and, more to the point, no female items in the bathroom or bedroom. After a long soak in a hot bath the old Jane returned and having toweled herself down with a hand towel because she couldn't find a bath towel, she cleansed her face, re-applied her makeup, and put on her Agent Provocateur lingerie and clean, cool clothes. The full-length bathroom mirror, the only one that she could find in the flat, reflected what she wanted to see, and having smiled her approval, she was startled to hear her mobile ringing in her handbag. Tim's distinctive voice told her that he'd spoken to Bruce, but more to the point he'd had a call from Ian, who was gallivanting somewhere in the South of France (she knew where that would be), and it appeared that Steve was back at the cottage. He thought she ought to know. Good old Tim, he was looking out for her.

Bruce returned late afternoon, and his eyes feasted on how lovely she looked. Her high heels showed off her long legs, and her dress clung to her figure in all the right places. "We can eat out, or I can knock something together here which would you like." After a moment's thought it was decided to eat out so that she could see a little of the city and taste authentic non-anglicized Indian food. Anyway, she felt that having dressed up she would like the foreplay of being wined and dined.

Remembering Jane's fondness for Indian food, he chose a restaurant that specialized in food from the north: creamy and taste bud explodingly spicy but not too hot. They lingered over their meal, and Bruce asked her about the new man in her life; was it serious? She'd been trying to convince herself that it was until she'd heard that Bruce was alive and well. She was shaken to hear herself say that she'd leave Steve, give up her job and come to India if Bruce wanted her to, with the proviso that he promised to stay off drugs; otherwise it was a no, no.

"Believe me drugs and me are over! I'm never going down that road again."

He tentatively rubbed his leg against hers under the table and was encouraged that she responded. The conversation drifted to his work, and he proudly told her about securing the rights for the encryption software and that his company had agreed, somewhat reluctantly, to continue production and to pay him royalty dues. In short, thanks to Tim's advice he was going to be comfortably off, particularly now that they'd just secured the first large order from the M.O.D. for their huge networks. Bruce paying his own way! Now that's a new experience.

The food was the best that Jane had ever tasted, and her mouth tingled as a reminder of the panoply of flavors that she'd just experienced. The newly chivalrous Bruce called for a taxi and ordered the driver to take a trip around the city centre for a bit of sightseeing the easy way before returning to the apartment.

Jane was amazed at the hodgepodge of impressive buildings interspersed with shabby crumbling ones and then areas of squalid heart-breaking shanty-towns. There were people everywhere and even folks sleeping and living on the street pavements. Beggars plied their trade in whatever area they drove through, and she had never seen so many people pile onto one motorbike. There was a brisk trade in second hand bicycle and car tires many of which had been cobbled together with neatly sewed twine. Life was cheap here! So much for health and safety!

By contrast on their way back they passed a wedding ceremony with the groom sitting on a white horse and attired in magnificent clothes with all of the relatives in their finest throwing rose petals and accompanied by blaring but exciting rhythmic music. Jane had never seen anything so beautiful and sumptuous in Europe. It was like having their own private Bollywood performance.

The cool of the flat was delicious as they abandoned the stifling taxi and the rancid smell of the driver's sweat. They both agreed that it had been a lovely evening, and a couple of ice cold beers later they wandered out onto the balcony and surveyed the twinkling jewel-like lights of the city. She savored the sights and the aromatic smells that wafted on the wind and for the first time in ages actually felt contentment. Eventually bed called. Bruce didn't want to rush things and said that she was welcome to the bed, and he'd sleep on the sofa. She replied by grabbing his hand and pulling him toward the bedroom, and minutes later they were re-exploring one another. She realized with relief that passion had re-entered her life. The lovemaking was frantic and hungry; it had been a long time, and they both needed it. The third time left them both sated, and she lifted herself onto one elbow and looking earnestly into his eyes, she asked, "Why didn't you contact me when you went to London?"

"I don't know, I suppose I was frightened that you would lead them to me if they were watching you."

Bruce's reply hit her like a fist in the stomach; it was actually physically painful. "Charming! You bastard! So, you were only thinking of yourself and not a thought for how I would be feeling. What's more, you didn't trust me." The old feelings of rejection welled up powerfully inside her and once again she felt alone, uncared for, and rejected.

"I'm sorry, no, it wasn't really like that but you're right, I should have been more considerate. I promise it won't happen again."

You bet it won't!

It had been a long day and there seemed little point in pursuing things any further, so she dropped back onto her side, let him cuddle her, and they both slid into the arms of sleep.

A beam of bright sunlight suspending a myriad of dust particles was stabbing the room through a gap in the heavy curtains when Jane eventually woke. She turned towards Bruce who was breathing heavily and obviously still deeply asleep. Well everything worked properly this time and the old sleeping pill obviously still worked. Same thing all over again; I can't believe he could have left me like that!

Scouting around the kitchen and the fridge, she managed to produce scrambled egg on toast, coffee, and orange juice. Having put everything on an ancient wooden tray, she went to her handbag, took out a small pill case, and dropped the tablets into one of the glasses of orange juice.

Bruce was woken by the viciously bright sunlight as Jane pulled the curtains back.

"God, you're an early riser!"

"Well, I thought you'd like breakfast in bed."

It was only then that he saw that breakfast had been delivered
to both of their bedside tables. He muttered his thanks, heaved
himself up on his elbow, and started demolishing the eggs. She
thought, Nothing's changed; he was always hungry after sex.
Rubbing his lips clean with the back of his hand, he washed the
eggs down with orange juice and then sipped his coffee. Jane
ate a little of her eggs and pushed the rest around her plate. She
drained her coffee cup and told him to enjoy the rest whilst she
showered. Coffee downed, he heard the shower buzzing away,
beat his pillow into submission, and gave in to the tiredness
that was suddenly enveloping him.

Showered and having washed all traces of Bruce from her,
Jane dressed, re-packed her case, checked on the deeply sleeping Bruce, and quietly pulled the front door behind her as she
walked the hundred yards to the taxi rank that she'd spotted on
their return last night. She caught the eye of the driver at the
front of the queue.

"To the airport please."

13

Life had taken on a special sparkle since meeting Steve Dalton, and Sheila was dressed, organized, and ready for work when her phone rang. He'd got the time difference right, bless him, and it was lovely to hear his voice. He filled her in briefly with the happenings since his return, and she was horrified to hear what had happened to him. "Are you sure you're alright my love? I couldn't bear it if anything happened to you!"

Steve glowed inside and assured her that he was fine, apart from a few bruises, and the conversation reverted to lovers talk. His parting comment was that he was off to bed and just wished that she were coming with him. "Me too" was the reply. He drifted off with thoughts of Sheila floating through his mind.

As she drove to work through the heavy business traffic, her mind was working overtime. Could the attack on Steve be connected in any way with Cecil's activities? But why would the thugs mistake Steve for Ian; it doesn't make any sense.

She'd been that busy at work that she hadn't given the Cecil situation much thought, particularly as her transition into his job had gone so smoothly. In fact she'd only just come to realize that she'd been doing most of Cecil's work for a long time just not getting paid for it. Mind you, she was enjoying every minute and had already received some complimentary comments from the Ivory Tower. She was determined to justify their trust in her and make the position permanently hers.

By the time she'd reached the office, her mind was made up: she'd have to confront Robert Young. Young's secretary made an appointment for her to see him at 10:00 a.m. In the meantime she waded through her in-box and weeded out the urgent from the non-urgent. Trouble was that there didn't seem to be many "non-urgent."

He'd already seen her, through his office window, approaching his door and opened it before she had time to knock.

"Do come in; what's troubling you?"

She explained that she fully understood his need for secrecy with regard to the Cecil saga, but that she found herself in a difficult situation. Robert was very disturbed to hear what had happened to their new associate. He was very receptive and quite understood why Sheila needed to know if there was any link between the company that Liu had been dealing with and Ian or Steve; he also wondered if her concern for Dalton ran deeper than just business. He would check through the records and clear things with Alec Jackson but, he couldn't see that there would be any problem.

Leaving his office, she felt relieved that he'd been so helpful and hoped it wouldn't be long before she had a phone call giving her permission to bring Steve up to speed. Under normal circumstances her previous call from Steve would have left her in high spirits, but she felt that she was under a cloud, a very large leaden one that looked likely to hang around unless she could be certain that Steve wasn't linked to Cecil's murky dealings. No sooner had the thought entered her mind than she felt guilty at her lack of trust. Of course Steve wouldn't be involved.

An hour or so later Robert called her to his office and told her that the only link that they'd found was an admission from Tony Pang that he'd logged the fact that Tsang would be working with Foston Medical and that this venture should increase European trade considerably. Don't know if that's any help said Young, but it's all we've been able to dig up. She thanked him and said that she would tip off Dalton in case it was of assistance to him. A wave of relief flooded through her and her anxiety cloud partially evaporated, but there was still the worrying thought that someone had wanted to harm her Steve.

In the UK Steve's lunch had come from the freezer, as he still hadn't had time to shop, and he was just enjoying a coffee when he took Sheila's phone call. So that was how they'd got Foston's name and probably Ian's and his names as directors; at least things were making a little sense now. They chitchatted for a while, and he promised to ring her tomorrow. Steve was left to his thoughts. Where the hell was Jane—not a word so far!

As so often happens when thinking about someone, his mobile purred and a text message appeared:

ARRIVE MANCHESTER 7:15 a.m. TOMORROW. BA FLIGHT FROM MUMBAI. CAN YOU MEET ME?—J. X

India! What the hell has she been doing there?

There was nothing he could do until tomorrow so he booted up the PC in the spare bedroom, which doubled as an office, and checked his e-mails. Joy of joys amongst everything else—five leads from Tsang! With five appointments made, two relatively local and the others scattered around, the rest of the week and the week after were now fully booked. He leant back to stretch the computer ache from his shoulders and spotted a new e-mail from Ian:

THANKS FOR EVERYTHING. LIFE IN SUN O.K. COMPANY GREAT!

IAN

God, the guy's incorrigible!

Steve e-mailed Ian outlining what Sheila had told him and asked for a landline phone number so that he could keep in contact, and within a few minutes he received a reply.

The rest of the day was taken up with paperwork and a long overdue foray to the supermarket to restock the now depleted larder, fridge, and freezer.

Early the following morning, mid breakfast, he switched on his mobile to read:

SORRY, FORGET MEETING ME TODAY. HAVE ANOTHER BUSINESS MEETING. WILL CALL WHEN ON WAY BACK. LOVE, J. X

This was becoming a joke, not that he relished bringing up the subject of Sheila, which he knew couldn't be avoided and that he would have to do very soon. Deep down he had always known that there was something missing in his relationship with Jane and that it wouldn't last forever. In fact painful though he knew it would be, he'd decided to tell Jane as soon as he'd returned. Some chance with her flitting all over the place! Frankly, he reckoned this was taking the piss!

A phone call to one of his potential local clients resulted in him being able to bring the meeting forward so that the day wouldn't be wasted. In fact it turned out to be highly profitable as he secured a sizeable order. On his return he e-mailed Sheila, to keep her in the picture, but also because he missed her and wanted to feel close to her. It looked as though the Foston/Tsang link was going to pay off, and as long as nobody else tried to eliminate him, all would be well.

14

The average person has no idea how unsecure e-mail is. The criminal fraternity most definitely understands and relies on it for their ill-gotten gains. Steve's recent assailants had reported back to their masters, and whilst not pleased at the outcome, it had taken them no time at all to locate Ian in his Mediterranean love nest turned hideaway.

A short flight to Nice, a hire car picked up at the airport, and now two anonymous hit men were quickly back on the scent. The car wove along the spectacular and ever-busy coast road in the afternoon sun heading for Antibes. Even they could appreciate why this place had remained so popular; both scenery and weather were perfect. Better still, they were being paid to be here.

Ian was staying with Jackie, a wealthy late thirties widow who'd been thrilled when he turned up. She'd been married to Terry, a brash workaholic fifteen years older than her, who'd made a lot of money from property development and then had the decency to die from a heart attack and leave everything to her. She'd met Ian in London and fallen for his charm, but she'd been looking for commitment. He had conveniently forgotten to mention that he was married and as a result had run backwards as fast as his hairy legs could carry him. Now that he was in survival mode, he'd decided that it seemed like a good time to rekindle things and to become less commitment shy. The Fiona business would have to take care of itself.

Ian's sudden arrival had given Jackie fresh hope that she could tame him, and she'd welcomed him enthusiastically plying him with as much food, booze, and sex as he could cope with. No mean achievement where he was concerned. Not wishing to rock the boat, she hadn't questioned his change of heart. Let's face it, last time she'd only applied a little pressure, and he promptly slid off the hook; she wasn't going to make the same mistake this time.

Friday was traditionally Jackie's Pilates morning, and she had always lunched with her girlfriends afterwards. She'd apologized for leaving him on his own, but secretly Ian was quite pleased to have some time to himself as he was feeling more than a little suffocated and was for the first time ever starting to appreciate Fiona's apparent lack of concern at his wanderings.

Thanks to Satnav the apartment had been easy to find, and the two guys entrusted with Ian's demise were both glad to escape from the still hot afternoon sun as they parked in a shaded area of the private car park. Fifteen minutes of surveillance had resulted in no sign of movement on the top floor. The apartment block was very plain although the beautiful surrounding gardens and sea view made up for any aesthetic deficit. Jackie's penthouse was spacious and had wonderful views across the Cap from the spacious balcony, and that was the feature that had sold it to her.

As usual the team split up. One stayed in the car ready for the off, and the marksman took the stairs to the top of the building—much less chance of meeting anyone than in the lift.

The door looked typically feeble and gave easily to his shoulder charge. Gun to the fore, he made his way, Special Forces style, through the entrance hall taking in the kitchen en route until he reached the sitting room. A man was apparently asleep in an armchair with a glass and what was left of a bottle of wine next to him.

Pissed I'll be bound!

Even amongst assassins there appeared to be a code of ethics; it went against the grain to kill someone in their sleep, so he yelled at his target to wake up. No response. Keeping his gun at the ready, he cautiously approached and shook the drunken bastard. Nothing! He felt for a pulse—nothing!

Either he's snuffed it or some bugger's beaten us to it! Shit! We may not get paid the second half!

He retraced his steps down the rear staircase at a leisurely pace, rejoined his sidekick, and they left as quietly as they'd arrived. The hire car was returned to the incredulous Hertz agent, and they walked the short distance across to the airport where they informed their clients by public telephone that their problem no longer existed, but that they couldn't take credit for the removal as his lease had expired before their arrival. They were taken aback by the news but delighted that their problem had been disposed of and that nothing linked any of them to the proceedings. The two should return to Manchester on the next available flight and a courier would meet them with an envelope.

There was no doubt that this was the easiest job they'd ever had, and as long as the envelope contained the necessary, they weren't about to complain. After booking in for their flight, they sauntered into the bar for a cold lager to celebrate. The beer must have been good because neither of them took any notice of an attractive blonde, perched on a bar stool, sipping at a glass of white wine to pass the time before joining the same flight as them.

The flight was short and uneventful, and as they walked through immigration and showed their passports, they noticed a small commotion at another booth where a slender young lady was being escorted away to some hidden security office and to God only knows what fate. The scene was one that regularly featured in their nightmares and was part and parcel of the business that they were in. However, once again it was someone else that had been apprehended and not them. Long may it last!

In the arrivals hall Steve was waiting and pacing with a mixture of anxiety and annoyance. He'd received yet another text asking him to meet Jane from her new flight. I am supposed to just drop everything at her beck and call without any explanation!

Small groups of people started to emerge, and then a flood cascaded through but no Jane—this really was the limit. He waited to see if there were any stragglers, but no, there weren't. Better check with the airline to see when the next flight is, looks like she's missed this one.

He explained to the bored-looking girl behind the desk that he'd been asked to meet a passenger off the recently arrived flight. Could she tell him when the next flight was due and if his friend (he was surprised to hear himself use "friend" and not the usual "girlfriend") was booked on it?

"Her name please?"

"Jane Kemp."

The boredom disappeared in a flash. "Can you just wait here while I get someone to speak to you?"

She clip-clopped off on four-inch stilts and was soon back with a somewhat austere looking man in a charcoal suit. He beckoned Steve into a back room and offered him a chair alongside his desk.

"I believe you were aiming to meet a Miss Jane Kemp? What is your relationship with Miss Kemp?"

Steve felt it more appropriate to revert to "Girlfriend."

"Well I'm afraid that she's been arrested and taken into custody."

You could have knocked Steve over with a feather; he'd had some surprises in the last week, but this ranked way up with the biggest. It was explained that she'd been taken to a police station for questioning and would be allowed to phone once questioning was over. In the meantime the best thing that he could do was to go home and stay by the phone. He asked what she was accused of but was told that they were unable to discuss any detail with him. With that he was politely shown to the door and he walked to the car park in a daze.

What has she been up to? Christ, she won't even exceed the speed limit!

Letting his mind drift back to the early days, he wondered if it had anything to do with someone from her past life. Was

it something to do with his predecessor—she never mentioned
him, although Ian had said it was a relative of his: a chap called
Bruce. Come to think of it he now realized that he knew very
little of her past at all; it just wasn't something that they'd discussed. Frustrated and disconsolate, he made his way home, but
no phone call arrived until mid morning the following day. It
was a solicitor who'd been appointed to act for Jane. She was
still being interviewed but had asked him to call Steve. She was
being questioned about the death, under suspicious circumstances, of a Mr. Bruce Foster.

"Are you suggesting that she was involved in this guy's death?"

"I'm not suggesting anything. When they've finished their
questioning, she'll either be released or charged dependent upon
what evidence they have. I'm afraid that's all that I can tell you
at present. If I hear any more, I'll call you."

"Thanks."

Steve put the phone down. What had she been doing with
Bruce in India?

He needed more information and quickly, so he rang the
landline number that Ian had given him. A woman's voice answered (no surprise there), but when he introduced himself and
asked to speak to Ian, she burst into floods of tears. Oh God!
This is all I need. What's he done now?

"I'm so sorry, there's no other way of saying this, but
Ian's dead."

"What! How?"

She briefly described coming home and finding the door broken in and him dead in the chair. "We don't know anything else
yet, probably a heart attack; they're doing a post mortem." She
sobbed. Steve pulled himself together enough to apologize for
disturbing her and offered Jackie his condolences. She asked for
his number and said she would call as soon as she knew any
more. Gutted was a pretty good description of how he felt right
now. Ian was young for a heart attack. He wasn't overweight,
but he certainly had lived life to the full and beyond. Amazing
he didn't die on the job really.

Hell! I'll have to ring Fiona.

Never mind the time of day he needed a stiff scotch be-fore tackling that phone call. The alcohol surged warmingly through his body, and he felt his shoulders drop; the phone call had to be made. Fiona was in, and he broke the news as gently as possible. There was silence at the other end, and then she started to cry gently but not for too long; public school and army upbringing cut in.

"I suppose he was with some woman?"

Steve stayed silent. She continued, "Wouldn't be surprised if the sod died on the job!"

This broke the tension, and they both laughed rather too heartily. "Look, Fiona I'll call you as soon as I hear any more, but in view of the post mortem don't be too surprised if the po-lice call you. Would you like me to come down and be with you?"

"You're very kind but no. Tim's coming over this evening. I'll be fine."

The next twenty-four hours were to stay engraved on Steve's mind for the rest of his life. Firstly he'd had a phone call tell-ing him that Jane had been charged with the murder of Bruce and was being held in a remand centre. A matter of hours later he'd had another call from Jackie saying that the police thought that Ian, his friend and partner, had died from a heart attack but couldn't be certain until they had the results of a post mortem.

15

Sheila sifted through her e-mails in the hope of seeing one from Steve; she wasn't disappointed and her heart leapt. She'd tried ringing him on several occasions, but he'd obviously been busy and at least the e-mail maintained a link and gave her a feeling of closeness. Her frantic work schedule had been a blessing because it meant that she didn't have much time on her own. On her own she was worried sick about what might be happening to Steve.

Life had been hectic for her as well, although not as crazy as Steve's. Cecil's case had been concluded without any adverse backlash on Tsang Corp, which was a relief. Not wishing to risk confidence-sapping publicity, the company resolved not to take any civil action against Cecil. She'd had a long phone conversation with Alec, and he'd told her everything that had happened with Cecil and Anglo Oriental Trading and had given her permission to release the information, if necessary, at her discretion. He also had added that they had total confidence in her ability and were impressed with what she'd already achieved in such a short time.

Once he'd rung off, she felt good as she digested what he'd said, and she decided to let Steve into her confidence as soon as possible. She e-mailed him an invite to attend the first sales meeting to commemorate one month of their merger. Could he confirm that he'd be able to attend? She clicked the mouse and the invite sped westwards towards Steve. At the receiving end

Steve was in the middle of forty-eight hours that would be in-
delibly marked on his mind for the rest of his life. Previously
he'd had the call to say that Jane had been charged with Bruce's
murder and was now held in the remand centre.

Jane, a murderer; it didn't seem possible, just bizarre.

Now, twenty-four hours later, a distraught call from Jackie
in France had told him that Ian's post mortem had revealed that
he had not died from a heart attack but from a mixture of alcohol
and a sedative overdose.

God! Never thought of Ian as the type to overdose. He must
have been either very frightened or desperate.

Shortly afterwards he'd taken a call from Fiona, just as he'd
been about to call her, saying that the police had interviewed her
after telling her the results of the post mortem. They'd wanted
to know if Ian had been depressed recently or even in the past.
She'd replied definitely not, and that if things had gotten bad
for him, he'd always sought solace in a bottle or with a woman,
more likely with both.

His emotions were being stretched to breaking point because, on the positive side, he'd also then taken a call from one
of his recent contacts and had just received the largest order in
the history of Foston Medical. To top that he'd now just read an
e-mail from the most alluring woman that he'd ever met inviting
him back to Tsang for a sales meeting. His mind was spinning in
free fall, and he was an emotional wreck feeling both elated and
devastated at the same time.

The call that he'd put through to the remand centre had informed him that Jane would not be allowed any visitors until
her psychiatric assessment had been completed, and that would
probably take at least a fortnight. Well, there was no way that
he could beat the system, so he might as well accept the Tsang
invitation. He e-mailed his acceptance, arranged his flight, and
couldn't wait to get away from the disaster area that he'd been
plunged into. What was left of the month was spent on everyday
Foston business and spending time with his solicitor sorting out
the mess that Ian's death had created. A lot would depend upon

the contents of Ian's will; would Fiona be financially secure? He felt awful at not being able to help Jane in any way but couldn't deny the great sense of relief that he felt as he climbed aboard the aircraft and departed for Kuala Lumpur.

Sheila met him from the airport and was shocked to see how drawn he looked.

"Whatever's the matter?"

"Have you got a couple of days to spare?"

She knew better than to pursue it further at that point, and having put his luggage in what passed for a boot in her car, she put her foot down hard to get them home as soon as possible.

He told her everything; nothing was left out: Jane, Bruce, Ian, Jackie, Fiona, the whole damned saga. She listened intently eyes opening wide at times. He felt that he had to apologize for not mentioning Jane previously; he didn't feel good about that. She understood, she was a big girl and it would have been unrealistic to think that there wouldn't have been another woman around. However, if they were going to get through all of this, could they at least make a pact to be totally truthful as of now? Relief took over his emotions, and the tears started to flow; this hadn't happened in years. She held him tight, let him cry his fill, and then took him to bed and loved him to sleep. They both woke early the next morning and he tried to apologize again, but she refused to listen so he asked her what had been happening to her.

"Not much compared to you. But I suggest that you shower; I'll fix breakfast and tell you all about it."

He wandered into the kitchen/diner and realized that he'd never seen her in jeans and t-shirt before. Christ! She looked fantastic even like that. Mind you, he reckoned she'd look great in a sack—funny how some people look good in anything, and yet others look awful even in good clothes.

As the whole of her story unfolded, he found it hard to believe how profoundly their lives had changed in such a short space of time. It was certainly hard to believe that someone as commanding as Cecil Liu could disappear off the scene so quickly. Neither of their lives were going to be the same again, and welling up inside him was that same mixture of fear and excitement that he'd felt when first experiencing aerobatics as a student at the flying club.

By the time breakfast was out of the way, they'd agreed that he should return to the UK after the sales meeting and give Jane whatever support she needed until the court case was over. Sheila was adamant that he should do everything that he could to help Jane or their future would be jeopardized by him feeling guilty. She was happy to offer any help that she could but felt it was probably better if she stayed in the background and gave him support when he needed it. Later they went through the agenda for the afternoon's meeting, and Steve checked his e-mails to update his figures.

The meeting went well and it gave Steve the chance to meet the other worldwide agents. Sheila was impressive as she outlined her plans for the next twelve months and beyond, and he realized that here was a lady who was going places. It was also a relief to have his mind occupied by business rather than worry and grief.

The evening was relaxed; they stayed in, she cooked, and they ate cuddled together whilst watching a film on TV. He wished that he could just run away and stay here with her forever, but he knew that he would have to return to reality and all that it involved. All too soon the alarm clock heralded the new day. She had to be in work early for yet another meeting, and he took the long taxi ride to the airport wondering what would meet him at the other end.

16

Steve arrived back home to find a message on his answer-phone from Jane's solicitor telling him that she'd been moved to a secure criminal psychiatric unit and giving him the phone number to arrange a visit. It still didn't seem possible that the woman that he'd shared his life with could be capable of criminal activities and in this mess. A short phone call later and he'd arranged a visit for the following morning, although it wasn't a trip that he was looking forward to.

As he drove into the hospital grounds, he was taken by surprise; the gardens were immaculately manicured, beautiful and totally ordered giving no hint of the mental turmoil that they surrounded. A psychiatric hospital was a new experience for him, and he found that, although the staff were kind, nothing could alter the oppressive atmosphere that hung over the place. He was ushered into a small, cluttered office, and after a few minutes wait a psychiatrist entered and introduced himself as Dr. Avery.

"How long is it since you last saw Jane?"

"I guess it's just over a month."

"Well I'm afraid you are in for a bit of a shock. She's gone into a withdrawal state and is totally uncommunicative. We're hoping that you, being a familiar figure, may just shake her out of it. I suggest that you spend some time with her and then get a member of staff to page me, and I'll try to answer some of the questions that you are likely to have."

Without further preamble the doctor called a nurse who showed Steve into an adjacent room containing two armchairs, a small table, and a few pictures on the walls that attempted to de-institutionalize the room. Shortly afterwards the door opened and a woman shuffled in accompanied by a nurse and was helped into a chair. Involuntarily Steve gasped at the realization that the crumpled figure in front of him was Jane. The woman in front of him looked at least ten years older than Jane, and there was a disturbing emptiness in the eyes, yet there was no denying that these were Jane's features. No makeup, hair unkempt, and a hospital dress added to the metamorphosis.

"Hello Jane, how are you? What have you been doing?"

No response.

"Jane, this is me, Steve. You know me don't you?"

Steve tried everything that he could think of to produce a response, but nothing worked. She just sat staring ahead and constantly playing with and clicking her fingernails. Once again Steve felt tears welling up as he witnessed the shell of someone whom he'd been so close to. It was so sad, so horribly sad. Nothing could have prepared him for this.

After what seemed like an eternity the nurse returned and asked him if he wanted to stay longer; it was almost as though she'd sensed that he'd had enough. He said that he'd like to speak with Dr. Avery, and she picked up the phone and paged him. Almost immediately Avery returned beckoning him to follow into his office, drew up a chair, and sat down whilst the nurse led Jane back to wherever she was being cared for.

"Fire away, doubtless you have questions."

Steve wanted to know exactly why Jane was in this state, would she recover, etc., and what was all the nonsense about Bruce's alleged murder?

Avery made it clear that he was limited in what he could say because he was preparing the psychiatric report for the court proceedings. However, he could talk in general terms and would do his best to be helpful, as he appreciated the difficult situation that Steve was in.

"Firstly, it is not uncommon to find people who go into withdrawal after either a serious shock or a series of shocks. It is as though the mind is refusing to admit that anything has happened and is shutting out feeling. This fulfills a function by preventing the person from feeling pain but creates a problem as they equally cannot experience pleasure either. In other words they are existing within life rather than living it.

"These sorts of conditions often owe their origins to childhood and the relationship with siblings or parents. People often unwittingly copy the way that members of their family cope with trauma. Many patients recover from their withdrawn state, but, in fairness, some spend the rest of their lives emotionally shut off from the rest of the world; it is as though they have committed emotional suicide. Electro-convulsive therapy has proved useful in some instances but can't be relied upon and the same applies to various forms of psychotherapy and medication. Obviously we will try all approaches to help with her recovery."

He regretted that he could not comment on anything to do with the allegations made against Jane but was prepared to say that, as she was at the moment, he would not consider her to be fit to stand trial.

This was a lot of information for Steve to take in, but he was grateful to the doctor for talking in everyday language and not blinding him with science. It was agreed that it might be helpful if he were to visit regularly, although he must recognize that it might be a thankless task. Having been shown out through a variety of locked doors, he took in great gulps of air in an attempt to purge the place from his body. He sauntered on aimlessly and relished lingering in the peace of the gardens before disconsolately making his way home.

Poor Jane, poor Jane!

It had made sense to arrange the hospital visit in the morning as this gave him time to have a meeting with his solicitor later in the day. The letters regarding the business had been batting to and fro, and it still wasn't clear what Steve's position was likely to be. Lawyers and accountants always left Steve frustrated; they seemed to talk in either financial or legal jargon, and he was never any wiser at the end than he had been at the beginning. Today, however, was an exception because the lawyer explained that he had drawn up a life assurance policy for both partners when they had entered into the partnership. Steve had completely forgotten this but realized that it could be the solution to his problems. They had both signed an agreement that the sum assured would be paid to the surviving next of kin in the event of the death of a partner. The sum paid out would represent the sole claim upon the business of any next of kin.

Thank God he didn't commit suicide or the policy would have been null and void!

It seemed sensible to ask the lawyer's view with regard to Jane's situation, but he was loath to offer an opinion without having all of the facts. However, in basic terms he pointed out that if she was proven innocent, her only problem would be in recovering from her present state. If she were guilty and didn't improve from her present state, then it seemed unlikely that she would be held responsible for her actions.

As Steve walked back to the car park, he felt a deepening sense of loss with regard to Jane; the person he had known seemed to have left him. On the other hand, he sensed that a great weight had lifted from him concerning the effect of Ian's death on the business and that he could now see his way to moving on. There were still a myriad of problems to deal with, but at least one was resolved. Once home he rang Fiona and updated her, but she seemed relatively unconcerned. It emerged that she had an income from a portfolio inherited from her family, and the policy would just be a useful bonus. As he digested this information, it went through Steve's mind that it was amazing that she'd put up with Ian when she was financially independent. She must have loved the guy, warts and all, at least in the early days anyway.

17

Sheila had arrived at her office earlier than usual and had only just sat down when a call was put through to her. She had hoped that it was Steve, but it turned out to be a call from Alex Jackson.

"I've been looking at the sales figures for Foston Medical, and they are quite remarkable. That young man certainly knows what he's doing, and I think we should have a meeting with him in the near future to see if we can offer any more support. If he can achieve what he's done in such a short time without us throwing resources at him, just think what he might achieve with additional help."

Sheila felt a glow of pride mixed with a tinge of guilt. She'd been so busy that she hadn't checked Steve's figures for a while.

"Yes, I've every confidence in him, and I'll let you know when he's available to visit."

The file made interesting reading. Foston had already won orders for a few hundred home dialysis units, and there were respectable orders for most of the rest of the range. More excitingly there were letters of intent for some really large orders for two private hospital groups. It struck her that Steve must have been throwing himself into work to escape all of his other problems.

Well it's an ill wind. Cecil may have introduced Steve for the wrong reasons, but Tsang were certainly gaining from the arrangement.

Late afternoon she placed a call to Steve and felt herself lurch inside as she heard his deep voice. She filled him in on Jackson's comments, and he was delighted and said that he would be happy to meet up with Jackson in a couple of weeks time and even more happy to meet up with her at any time.

"Occidental man speaks with silver tongue!" she replied in a pseudo Chinese accent.

They both laughed and he told her about the good news from the lawyer, and she could sense what a great relief this had been for him.

"Jackson has asked for this meeting, so Tsang will pay your airfare."

"Thanks! Cash flow is a little difficult until the estate is wound up."

"Yes, I thought it might be and anyway it's our call."

The rest of the conversation was very much non-business, and they both agreed that they couldn't wait to hold one another again and that it was going to be a very long fortnight. She put the phone down and once again was left with that feeling that no other man had ever had such a profound effect upon her. In fact she was almost frightened to say it, but this was the man that she wanted to spend the rest of her life with, and if anyone had told her that she'd be thinking like this, she would have laughed out loud at them.

The following day Sheila was going through some of Cecil Liu's old files when her attention was drawn to the transport company that they used for Europe. She wondered if Cecil had been getting a "backhander" and ran a check on costings from several other competitors. Cecil obviously hadn't been underhand in this area, but she was able to achieve some savings where certain countries were concerned, particularly into some of the old Eastern Bloc countries. She wondered what had happened to Cecil. He'd been a fair boss, and they'd had a good working relationship and, although he'd been a little austere, she had liked him.

Dinner had been a solitary affair, tray on knee watching TV, and having washed up, she rang Cecil's mobile number. The call was answered immediately by a very surprised Cecil. He seemed genuinely pleased that she'd made contact and some-what embarrassedly said that there was no fool like an old one and that he'd been an idiot. However, very generously he said that he thought she would be very successful in his place.

He had set up a company to coordinate research in the phar-maceutical field to create a database of information that would be available to the industry. However, very cleverly he had been researching some of the research and come up with several drugs that could prove very successful in other areas of medicine than the ones that the original company had been involved with. Ac-cordingly, at very little cost he was now the proud owner of sev-eral patents and was confident that he was going to make a lot of money. Totally honestly this time he laughed.

The clever old devil, I always knew he'd bounce back.

Sheila went to bed with a sense of satisfaction. It had been a good day, and she couldn't help feeling pleased for Cecil whom she couldn't regard as being anything other than a man who'd weakened whilst under great pressure.

It was only a few days later that she opened the newspaper to see banner headlines: BREAKTHROUGH: DISCARDED TRANQUILIZER PROVES SUCCESSFUL IN TREATING TUMOURS

The article went on to explain that a tranquilizer that had proved to be no more effective than existing ones had been found to de-prive tumors of blood supply. The tumors were shrinking and, in a number of cases, disappearing altogether. Inset in the article was a picture of Cecil, the owner of the patent and manufacturing rights. He's back! she thought. The industry better look out!

The following week passed much more quickly than ex-pected due to work pressure, and once again she felt her heart pounding as she headed south to the airport to pick up Steve from his flight. The plane was on time, and he soon appeared thanks to only having hand luggage. They wrapped themselves around one another, and the world felt right. To those watching it seemed like an age before they peeled off from one another and headed to her car.

The meeting was scheduled for the following day, so they had the rest of the day to catch up, make love, catch up some more, and make love some more. Dinner was great and they both did justice to it having worked up an appetite. They eventually fell into a sated sleep wrapped in each other's arms.

Once pleasantries were out of the way, it was down to facts and figures. Alex was very complimentary and extremely keen to offer support in whatever form Steve thought would be useful. Sheila picked up on the fact that he said on several occasions that Steve had engineered himself a fantastic deal with Tsang. She later checked with Steve to see if he'd logged the comment, but he hadn't and added that he thought that she was overly suspicious although it was understandable after the Cecil saga. However, her woman's intuition was flagging up warning signs, and in spite of Steve's reaction she filed them in the back of her mind.

Steve gave Alex's offer considerable thought and finally settled for help in manning trade stands at several trade fairs that he'd booked for the rest of the year. Tsang would produce background boards and posters for the stands in the various relevant languages. They'd also make staff available, and it was suggested that Sheila should attend the more important events. Once again Steve couldn't believe his luck, and Sheila was taken aback but delighted at the idea.

During the evening they'd synchronized their diaries, he'd pointed out the biggest trade fairs where her presence would be helpful, and she'd made notes concerning the sales aids that he would need. "Quite a team aren't we?"

"Yes," he heard himself reply. "A team for life I hope."

"Are you proposing to me?"

"I'm really in no position to propose anything at the moment, but provisionally yes, I suppose I am."

"Then the answer is also provisionally 'YES,' I can't think of anything that would make me happier!"

The whole turn of events was completely unplanned, but they both felt deliriously happy and both knew that there was nobody else for them. That night they slept better than they had for months and knew that they could now face whatever was thrown at them.

The following morning meant heading their separate ways, he to the airport and she to the office, but this time they didn't feel disconsolate at the separation; somehow it made a huge difference now that there was commitment, and they knew that it was only a matter of time before they would be together permanently.

Sheila's in-basket was brimful, and she quickly became engrossed with work. In fact it was almost lunchtime when her phone rang and brought her back to reality. It was Alex asking her to let him have a copy of the Foston/Tsang contract a.s.a.p.

What the hell is he up to? Looks like my suspicions were right!

She arranged for her PA to fax the contract to him but in the meantime took the trouble to read every detail of the document herself. It certainly was a good deal for the agent but seemed watertight to her, but then she was no lawyer.

I'll ring Cecil tonight and see what he thinks.

It had been a grueling day, but finally she shut the door of the apartment, retrieved a chilled bottle of Pinot Grigio from the fridge, poured herself a large glass, slumped into the sofa, and dialed Cecil's number.

Cecil was adamant that the company lawyer had drawn up the contract and that there was no way that Alex could renege on it without incurring punitive compensation, but he wasn't surprised that he was trying to find a loophole, because that's how he'd gotten to the top, by being wily and ruthless.

"Doesn't sound like a very nice guy!"

"He's okay as long as you are aware of what you are dealing with. There's many much worse than him!"

They chatted on for a while, and she congratulated him on his new cancer therapy that she'd read about in the newspaper.

He admitted that he'd been lucky to have success so early in his new venture and that it should make him very well off if all went to plan. With the phone call out of the way she sat back and breathed a sigh of relief now that it looked as though Steve's contract was bulletproof, and she had to smile to herself that Cecil had come up smelling of roses.

The following morning she took a phone call from Alex concerning a contract that she'd been re-negotiating with an Australian company, and after bringing him up to speed she decided to take the bull by the horns and asked him why he'd wanted the Foston contract. His answer was straightforward and without hesitation: "I wanted to see if we could wriggle out of it because I don't like giving that much away to an agent. No chance though, 'cause that bastard Liu made the damned contract watertight in Dalton's favor."

He was obviously annoyed but accepted that he was powerless to alter the situation. It did, however, give her an insight into how the man worked, and she found it chilling. There was obviously no room for sentiment in business where he was concerned, and she'd do well to remember this when dealing with him in future.

I must warn Steve what he's like, so that Steve's wary in any future dealings.

18

Leave was due to Tim, so he had taken it and stayed with Fiona until Ian's body had finally been released for burial. The funeral was held at the local parish church, which seemed the logical place due to its proximity, yet equally appeared hypocritical because it would be hard to find anyone less religious than Ian had been. To add to the sense of unreality Fiona had, to her credit, invited Jackie as she had been the last person to see Ian alive and must have had a terrible shock. Tim found Fiona's attitude difficult to understand, yet he secretly admired her for being so strong and realistic about the situation. Perhaps it was her way of drawing a line under things, and she'd long since given up on being hurt by Ian.

Steve arrived just in time for the service and recognized some of his old university friends in the congregation. It was intriguing to see how much some of them had changed in such a relatively short time whereas others looked just the same. The vicar rambled on, obviously knowing nothing about Ian, and the whole performance had farce written all over it, but everyone went through the motions. Fortunately the sun had made an appearance when they all poured out of the church porch and the mood lifted. Fiona thanked everyone for attending, and they were all invited back to the house for food and drink. Steve chatted to her and Tim and then made his excuses and left for home; he really didn't feel like making a social occasion out of it and still harbored memories of awkward si-

lences and dog-eared sandwiches at the funerals of long gone
aunts and uncles. As he made his way back to his car, he noticed a couple of men who seemed to be checking out all of the
mourners; they had "police" written all over them.

I reckon we haven't heard the end of this business yet.

Once the windows were wound down, the sun's heat drifted
out of the car, and Steve reflected on the scene. Jackie was obviously devastated; how much of this was due to shock and how
much to the loss of a lover was difficult to say. A closeness between Fiona and Tim, who had been very protective throughout
the service, was very obvious.

I wonder if anything is going on there? Maybe she's been
playing Ian at his own game. Well good for her.

Letting his thoughts drift away, he nosed the car out of the car
park and, to break the monotony, took a different route for home.
Somehow home didn't seem the right description any longer.
The place felt violated since the intruders and Jane's illness, and
no matter how much he'd dreamt of having this cottage, he knew
that nowhere would feel like home anymore unless Sheila was
there. In fact he felt that he'd learnt a profound lesson. It wasn't
bricks and mortar that were important; it was people.

Thinking about Jane gave him a pang of guilt, so he headed
for the hospital and after the usual routine was taken to see
her. She showed no sign of recognition, although someone had
done her hair and she looked less uncared for. He spent over
half an hour trying various ways that had been suggested to
him that might trigger some reaction, but in reality he might as
well have been talking to himself. It was frustrating yet tragic,
and he felt a deep sense of sadness and loss. Yes, loss; he really
felt that he had lost someone who'd been very close to him,
and there were no signs of her returning. As he was leaving,
a nurse asked him if he could wait a couple of minutes as the
psychiatrist would like to see him.

A few minutes later Dr. Avery appeared, beckoned him to
take a seat, and said that he was sorry to say that Jane had made
no progress in terms of recovering from her withdrawal state,

but that she had revealed a number of interesting details whilst under hypnosis, which they'd tried as a means of communicating. The information couldn't be used as evidence at any court hearing, but it did give some insight as to why she'd acted in the way that she had. In his opinion she was in no fit state to attend a court hearing, but his report would be available to the court in the very near future. Obviously he couldn't give any details but added that he thought it highly unlikely that Jane would be functional for a long time to come, if ever. He was sorry to be the carrier of such bad news, but felt that Steve ought to know what their thoughts were concerning her future and that he was welcome to continue visiting, but his visits were unlikely to have any therapeutic effect after the time that had elapsed.

After thanking the doctor for his candor Steve left the hospital feeling that effectively he'd attended two funerals in the one day. The drive home was busy and his concentration was on the traffic, but once in the village, he embraced the coziness of the pub and downed a large therapeutic scotch.

The following month had been extremely busy, and the mileage on his car had gone up in leaps and bounds, but so had the turnover of Foston. He was way ahead of his target, and if things carried on like this now that the business was solely his, he was facing a level of affluence only previously dreamt of.

Although he knew that it would eventually happen, he still got a surprise when the police telephoned to ask him to attend an interview with regard to Jane. Steve said that he was happy to oblige the following day as his diary was clear of appointments. It was only after putting the phone down that he realized that the word "happy" was not a particularly good choice.

The superintendent was pleasant and efficient and in the presence of a sergeant the background to his and Jane's relationship was thoroughly explored, checked, and re-checked many times. His whereabouts on several different dates were elicited, and thanks to his diary he was able to provide the information required. Some weeks later he discovered that all of his movements on these dates were double-checked with people who could corroborate his statements. He supposed that he shouldn't have been surprised, yet it all felt a bit unnerving. It was a bit like going through Customs with nothing to declare; you know you've nothing to hide but somehow still feel jittery. Still. Thank God he lived by a diary.

The questions had come thick and fast:

"What did he know about Jane's background, childhood and family?"

He had to admit to himself that he really knew very little detail about her past. '

"Was she very moody or violent? Was she violent during or after sex? Had she ever self-hurt? Did she have any eating disorders?"

There had been loads of other probing questions that were repeated ad nauseam. All he could say was that she had been perfectly normal and nothing out of the ordinary had ever occurred whilst she was with him. Okay, she had been obsessive about safety in the home, always checking and re-checking that doors and windows were locked and the kitchen had sprouted three fire extinguishers. But no, definitely no signs of violence at any time either during, before, or after sex.

Having been cautioned not to discuss their meeting with anyone, he was permitted to return home feeling totally wrung out and being convinced that he had been of no help whatsoever. There was also a sense of indignation that every last facet of his personal life had been put under a microscope for total strangers to pore over.

Once home he showered to wash away the feelings of distaste and, still in his dressing gown, wandered into the office, booted up his laptop, and for the first time that day his spirits lifted. Staring at him on the screen was a loving e-mail from Sheila. He quickly tapped out a reply and then sought solace in a large gin and tonic, which quickly hit the spot.

An early night beckoned as he was leaving the following morning for a business appointment in Scotland. Mercifully sleep came easily and blanked out the day's unpleasantness.

The Scottish meeting paved the way for further talks and was promising, but in the light of his recent successes he felt a little deflated not to come away with an order. He then mentally chastised himself because prior to the Tsang tie-up that would have been the norm.

He tossed up whether to drive home but came to the conclusion that a hotel room was a more attractive proposition than the long drive back that evening. The time on his own gave him the opportunity to digest the happenings of the previous day, and he managed to achieve some perspective; the guys were simply doing their job.

His mind was not yet ready for sleep, so he turned on the TV and watched a fascinating yet disturbing documentary on computerized crime. It was amazing how vulnerable companies and utilities were to expert hackers. The news followed and then some fatuous American comedy, and when he woke the following morning, the TV was still on.

19

Two days later and it was a morning of contradictions. The rain was heavy, but the sun was shining. Steve wanted to know how Jane, the woman who had been his lover, had become the zombie-like person whom he'd visited, yet dreaded what he might be confronted with. He felt guilty for the coward in him that half hoped that she would never recover, because then he wouldn't have to confront her with the Sheila situation, yet he knew that there was no turning back. He wanted to get to the court as quickly as possible, yet he wanted to linger at the cottage before leaving. Even when he arrived at the old court buildings in his county town of Chester, the sun gave a warm glow to the sandstone masonry, but the wind chilled him to the bone.

The court proceedings over the next few days filled in most of the missing gaps in the Jane saga. There had been no question of her making an appearance due to the lack of any change in her mental state. The psychiatric reports painted a tragic picture of mental decline but, nevertheless, offered a childlike logic that explained her actions.

Initially she had been regularly devastated at the loss of friends and familiar surroundings as the family moved around due to the many different army postings. This had created a lifetime of anxiety and loss, which had only been coped with by rituals such as her obsessions with safety, etc. A lot of her obsessive behavior had gone unnoticed as these were the very attributes that had initially made her an eager-to-learn pupil and then an ideal, conscientious employee. Obsession can often be mistaken for efficiency, and as a result businesses thrive due to such people. A number of her past actions slotted into place in his mind, and he recognized signs that had passed unnoticed before.

Apparently the fruitless efforts that she had made in early life to gain her father's approval and his final act of treachery by leaving her had set the pattern, and she had continued to try to please the men in her life in the hope that they wouldn't abandon her in the same way. Sadly this had not been the case. Like so many youngsters, her first serious relationship had only lasted a matter of weeks, but the effect of the break-up on her had been far more devastating than for most of us. Unfortunately this had been the first of a number of rebuffs that she had had to endure from the various unsuitable men whom she'd been attracted to. She'd been like a moth attracted to a candle.

In fairness to some of the men in her life, it had to be said that her intenseness had tested them to the breaking point, and they had been left with little option but to run backwards; this had formed a pattern of self-fulfilling rejection. To date the only person not to let her down had been Steve, yet he wasn't the one that she really wanted.

Interestingly, the breakup with Helen had not left any scars at all. She didn't feel rejected because by then she'd learnt that it was only men who did that to a woman.

The psychiatrist had explained that neuroses were built brick by brick, just like real buildings; no child was ever born neurotic; you had to be taught to be neurotic. The best teachers are parents and siblings because we learn by example. Numerous psychotherapeutic approaches had been tried to no effect, but eventually hypnosis had been the breakthrough that had enabled him to isolate the main "bricks" that had created her "building" and finally resulted in her confession.

Amazingly Jane had even coped with Bruce's initial withdrawal from her, due to his drug problem (it wasn't rejection of her; it wasn't him talking; it was his illness) and then his ultimate absconding. It was only when he finally admitted that he hadn't contacted her for fear of her leading his enemies to him that she cracked. And worst of all, not only had he left her, but he hadn't even trusted her. This had been the point when her neurosis converted into psychosis.

The black and white childlike logic had then cut in: the principle being "Remove the people who hurt me so that they can never hurt me again." Her decision was, therefore, amoral and the killing of Bruce was just a solution to her problem and was carried out with equanimity and no regret. The effect of these revelations upon those in court was surprising in the different behavior that it elicited. Some of the women sobbed quietly, one not so quietly. Others twisted handkerchiefs into incredible contortions, and even the odd man seemed to have something in his eye. However, the next bombshell was her admission to the killing of Ian, and this brought gasps from just about everyone. The report revealed that he had taken her out for dinner on one occasion when Steve had been abroad, his excuse being that she must be lonely with Steve away. After she'd had rather too much to drink, he'd taken her back to the cottage, he made a pass at her, and they'd landed up in bed. The following morning she'd felt very guilty and had gone to his flat to ask him not to tell Steve. Her persistent ringing of his doorbell had finally roused him from his bedroom to answer the door accompanied by the girl who'd been sharing his bed.

Just another notch on his gun!

Her new insight meant that she could prevent the bastard from ever doing that again to any woman, and she'd certainly achieved her task. Steve shuddered.

What if she'd found out about Sheila? I could have been six feet under by now.

In spite of the psychiatric explanations, he was also having a major problem in coming to terms with the fact that someone with whom he had been totally intimate over a prolonged period of time could suddenly become a cold-blooded killer. It was a revelation to him that people could change so drastically; he'd always thought that breakdowns just made you ill and unable to cope.

Unbeknownst to him, Jane had been taking sleeping tablets and medication for anxiety all of the time that they'd been together. She'd hidden this from him possibly because she thought that he, like previous boyfriends, would have shunned her if he'd thought she was in need of such drugs. The report suggested that she had probably hoarded medication in case she ever became suicidal but instead had used her hoard to eliminate her problems. It would appear that her doctor had given her a loaded gun, and like many gun owners, when pushed, she'd used it.

The medics felt that the accused had entered a psychotic state and was unlikely to recover in the short term, if ever, and that the killings had taken place as a result of her insanity. She'd shown no remorse at all due to her diminished responsibility; she simply saw her actions as a necessity for solving her problems. The recommendation to the court was that she should be held indefinitely in a secure unit for the criminally insane and should receive ongoing treatment. There was a lot more detail that emerged but in essence that was the outcome.

After two days of harrowing revelations of the mechanics of Jane's breakdown, Steve was left feeling drained, saddened but relieved that he too hadn't become one of the victims. It was a sobering thought that life and sanity could hang by a thread, and he also reflected that you only ever read about such things; they only happened to other people. How wrong could you be? What's more he'd often said, "You only really know someone properly once you've lived with them."

What a load of bollocks that had turned out to be.

The proceedings drew to a close, and the defense barrister made the point that if his client were deemed insane by the medics, her confession could not be relied upon and she should be treated rather than punished. It was a manful but somewhat forlorn effort at defense but nobody was really in doubt as to what had happened. The judge stated that he would consider all of the evidence presented and give his judgment in two working day's time. However, there seemed little doubt as to the outcome.

As he made his way to the car park, he caught up with Fiona and Tim who had both been at the hearing. For once Fiona wasn't a picture of calmness, and it looked as though the loss of Ian had finally caught up with her, but as they began to talk, it became obvious that she was very distressed but because of Jane's condition not Ian's demise. The graphic descriptions of Jane's breakdown had deeply affected her, and as a woman she had identified with a lot that had happened to Jane, particularly moving from pillar to post as a Forces child. She just felt eternally grateful that she'd been strong enough to survive what had been too much for Jane. Obviously she had grieved the loss of Ian but that had been years before his death, and she was totally pragmatic about Jane's role.

"It was bound to happen. If it hadn't been Jane, it would have been some cuckolded husband or betrayed mistress."

Tim, who was hovering a little awkwardly in the background, seemed very quiet but, judging by his nodding and body language, seemed to agree with most of Fiona's comments. He was very protective of her, and Steve felt reassured that he was there for Fiona. They both offered their sympathy to him and said that they felt washed out, so God only knows how he must be feeling. Did he want to come and stay with them? Steve thanked them for their concern but said that he would get home, because he was behind with some of his paperwork. In reality he just wanted to be alone to re-shuffle his thoughts. With all that had happened in such a short time, he was suffering from mental indigestion.

The empty cottage seemed to resent his presence. He didn't particularly like his own company at the best of times, but today his home was not a welcome refuge. The pub beckoned, and its atmosphere, the smell of food, and a pint of real ale soon restored his spirits, and although he didn't really marshal his thoughts, he returned to his bed slightly pissed and at least feeling human again. A full stomach, alcohol, and exhaustion eased him into oblivion and mercifully deep, deep sleep.

Tim had talked the evening away with Fiona and was finding sleep difficult as he lay surveying the ceiling of the guestroom. He'd loved spending the week with Fiona even though it was almost a form of torture for him—that agonizing mix of pain and pleasure. His mind wandered back to when he and Ian had been guests at a party thrown by a university friend of Ian's. They'd both been introduced to a vivacious young girl, Fiona, and Tim had been entranced immediately, but his inherent shyness had held him back, and whilst he was still trying to think what to say, Ian had moved in.

Typical Ian. And look how he'd squandered her love.

The army had been his one distraction, but he'd never gotten over Fiona; worst of all he'd never gotten over his shyness either. He desperately wanted to tell her of his love but was frightened, and the innate gentleman in him told him that this was not the appropriate time. He cursed the timing yet because of his bashfulness was almost grateful for the excuse not to do anything.

A tapping on the door startled him out of his reverie.

"Are you awake Tim? Can I come in?"

"Yes, of course."

He put the bedside light on, and Fiona walked towards him. She was wearing a pale blue satin housecoat (dressing gown to him), and as she reached him, she let it slip from her shoulders revealing that that was all she was wearing. Switching the lamp off, she slid into bed alongside him and put her finger to his lips to silence him. He needn't have worried about his inept fumblings for she guided and encouraged him, and finally he was where he knew he always should have been. Very early the following morning they both collapsed into an exhausted sleep entwined in each others' legs and arms but happy, oh so happy.

The next few days were blissful for Tim, and although he was concerned about what people might think, Fiona insisted that they should tell everyone as soon as possible that they were now an item, as she put it. They'd both wasted enough of their lives thanks to Ian, and all their friends knew what he'd been up to anyway. It was at this point that Tim made a firm decision to resign his commission. He'd been in the Forces a long time and would be financially secure, but most of all he didn't ever want to be away from Fiona again. Anyway, he'd only stayed in the regiment as long as he had because of the Ian and Fiona situation.

A week later he took her to a very special country restaurant and told her of his plans adding that he'd already been on the phone to HQ and set things in motion. HQ had agreed to release him early on condition that he remained a reservist, because his experience and knowledge of languages was too valuable for them to lose. Before she could make any comment, he took a jewellery box from his pocket, took out a diamond engagement ring, and asked her if she would wear it and eventually marry him. In typical Tim-style he then added that if she didn't like the ring, she could change it and that he realized she might need time to reach a decision and that, obviously, she could have as long as she wanted.

"Shut up you wonderful idiot man. Of course I'll marry you as soon as you want, and the ring is magnificent!"

"Phew, thank God for that! That was more frightening than Kabul on a bad night!"

Whilst on leave, Tim had arranged for his mail to be forwarded to Fiona's, and as he worked his way through the pile, he finally came to a letter from a firm of London solicitors advising him that they would like to meet with him, as he had been named as next of kin to Bruce Foster. The news came as a shock to him, not least because he couldn't quite see the old Bruce that he'd known using a solicitor.

Several days later, having arranged an appointment, he was making his way up a drab staircase in an old office block, sandwiched between a greengrocer and a Cypriot takeaway, in Stoke Newington. The reception area was surprisingly pleasant by contrast to the shabby exterior. Tim announced himself to the receptionist, and she said that Mr. Miles wouldn't keep him waiting for too long. In fact this turned out to be the case, and after a short wait, he was met by a middle-aged man who had that weary look of an overworked, disenchanted person to whom life had dealt a bad hand; let's face it, this wasn't exactly a prestigious office address. They shook hands, and Tim was ushered into a clean but soulless office that lacked any human touches or signs of family life, no photos, and no pictures.

"Thank you for responding to my letter."

"Not at all, I was intrigued."

"Firstly let me offer my condolences on your sad loss. Well, your nephew came to see me just before he left for India and said that he was starting a new chapter in his life, which he hinted had been somewhat chaotic previously."

"You could say that!"

"Anyway, very sensibly he decided to make a will even though he said that he had very little of any value to leave behind should he depart thence. I only wish that more young people would do the same; it makes everything so much simpler if anything like this happens."

Tim sat and listened as Miles explained some of the legal jargon associated with wills and the role of the solicitor, who was in this instance acting as executor. In short it boiled down to the fact that Tim would inherit everything, which really only amounted to a modest bank account, a life assurance policy, and a document box held in the safe deposit of his bank in Mumbai. Regrettably most of the bank account would be taken up by solicitor's fees, which left the policy and the box as the only real assets. Tim handed over his proof of identity and signed all the necessary papers, and Miles advised that he had arranged for the bank to release the safe deposit box and would be in touch in due course.

The fresh air was welcome after the stuffy office, and Tim walked briskly down the road with a mixture of emotions. He was sad at the loss of Bruce yet touched that he'd been named as next of kin. Sad at the loss of Jane's sanity yet angry at what had happened and at what had pushed her to such desperate actions. He found himself entering Clissold Park, which, unbeknownst to him, had been a walk of solace for Bruce on many occasions during his lonely sojourn in London. The solitude of the park was just what he needed yet totally unexpected in such a built-up area. In such a very short time life had been turned upside down for Tim; some changes had made him happier than he could ever have imagined, whereas others had been shocking and distressing even for someone who'd become hardened to the horrors faced by the SAS. These changes involved people known to him and loved by him. Gradually his brain pigeonholed the random emotions, and after an hour or so of sitting in contemplation or strolling, he felt sufficiently fortified to head back to the West End.

It was a totally new experience for shy, gauche Tim to go shopping for a woman. The jewellery was no problem, but the lingerie filled him with trepidation yet he wanted to spoil Fiona; from what he could gather, it wasn't something that had ever happened to her. Fortunately he'd sneaked a look at the size labels of her underwear in her dressing table drawer before leaving so was at least somewhat prepared before entering the Bond Street boutique. Mercifully the shop assistant minimized his embarrassment, complimented him on having the sizes at hand, and was extremely helpful. Half an hour later he left with a bag full of beautifully wrapped small parcels and a self-satisfied smile on his face.

Fiona met him from the train and that in itself was a treat as there had never been anyone that mattered at the end of his journeys previously. He filled her in on his meeting, and she too was surprised that Bruce had thought ahead enough to make a will; it was normally marriage and a family that pushed men into that sort of action.

Back at the house he settled into a comfortable armchair, slung his jacket on the coffee table, and plonked his parcels alongside him. Tidiness wasn't one of his virtues but, as Fiona came in from the kitchen, she was pleased to see that he'd made himself at home.

"Thought you'd like a glass of wine, dinner will be about an hour, is that okay?"

"That'll be great, thanks."

As they both sipped their drinks, he brought her up to date with all that he'd learnt in London and they both speculated on the contents of Bruce's mysterious deposit box.

The presents were a great success.

"I feel really spoilt."

"You deserve to be spoilt at last, and it gave me great pleasure to be able to do it. Oh! And there's something in my jacket pocket for you as well." It was lovely to see the little girl in this usually reserved woman as she retrieved the box from his pocket. Her face lit up as she opened it to reveal the gold bracelet that he'd bought at the beginning of his shopping spree.

"That is gorgeous!"

"Well, I'm just glad that you like it, but it can be changed if you're not sure and I won't be offended."

"I'm not letting go of this it's absolutely beautiful."

A week later and Tim returned to his regiment to work out his final stint before his return to civilian life. The commuting was a pain, but nothing was going to separate him from his bride to be. Fiona too was revelling in having a man that adored her, wanted to spend all his time with her, and whom she could trust implicitly. Their friends all felt that they were now getting the life that they both deserved and the happiness and fulfillment that had been missing from both of their lives previously. It was surprising how many of Fiona's friends now openly admitted that they'd only tolerated Ian because they were so fond of Fiona and that they were amazed that she'd never left him. All agreed that Tim was perfect for her, and he was quickly and easily absorbed into their circle.

At the end of the month a letter arrived from Bruce's solicitor giving the exact sum that the life policy had paid out, the final account, and the small residual balance from the bank account. Enclosed was a bulky envelope that had been in the bank safe deposit. Tim opened it and was astonished to find that it contained all of Bruce's copyrights and patents.

A quick phone call to Miles confirmed that the patents were transferable to the next of kin and that he would handle this for Tim if he so wished. Tim did so wish but suggested that Miles might care to use delaying tactics until Tim was finally discharged from the army as one of the patents could cause a conflict of interest whilst he was still employed.

"Mr. Foster, we solicitors never have a problem in delaying action, surely you know that."

Tim chuckled and thanked him for his help. He couldn't believe his luck; judging by the pending British Army order alone, the royalties from the encryptor copyright would be sufficient to top up his army pension to at least his present salary. Life with Fiona was going to be exciting and comfortable.

Six months later, free from the army and settled in a part time position with a crisis management consultancy, he was like a cat that had lapped the cream and felt more settled and content than he had ever been in his life. The icing on the cake was when he married Fiona at the local registry office with just the mandatory witnesses. For the first time in her life Fiona broke with convention, which had dominated her life. No big wedding this time; she was two months pregnant, and she didn't care who knew. Life had begun at last.

20

The judge's verdict raised no eyebrows and Jane was duly committed to a secure institution for the criminally insane, "insane" being a fabricated legal term that had no real foundation in psychiatric terminology. Suffice to say that, short of a miracle, she would spend most, if not all, of the rest of her days in a secure prison-cum-hospital. Steve felt a leaden sadness at the thought of someone so young, attractive, and intelligent who had been the victim of circumstance and had crumbled.

How many of us might have been only one incident away from doing the same? The thought frightened him. Strangely he felt all of his compassion channelled to her and none to Bruce or Ian; they'd been selfish catalysts in her downfall, and somehow weren't worthy of his sympathy.

One thing was for sure: after this he was going to make the most of every day of his life. The only certainty is the present, and happiness comes from being with the right people not from possessions like houses, cars, etc.

The following morning he was again driving to Manchester to pick up a flight to Kuala Lumpur but this time it wasn't business. It was far more important; it was to make sure that Sheila became the focus of the rest of his life. He wasn't going to let her slip from his grasp.

At the same time in Kuala Lumpur, Cecil Liu was sitting thoughtfully at his desk in the plush office that he had recently moved into. His re-honed entrepreneurial skills had quickly borne fruit, and he was now actually making more money than his not inconsiderable salary had been at Tsang Corp. It had been a busy day, but he needed to digest all that had happened over the last few months before making his way home. It felt good to be riding a success wave again, and he was eternally grateful that he had been given a second chance and that the past was written but the future beckoned.

The royalties on a variety of drugs had been regularly rolling in and swelling his bank account, but he missed the challenge of business. He'd been keeping a watch on a small company that primarily manufactured pharmaceuticals for other companies but did produce several lines of its own. Rumors were circulating that they had several very large orders in the offing but that they would need to expand in order to cope. The rumors also hinted that they were lacking in capital and, as a result, were between a rock and a hard place. The company was owned by its founder, the father, and his son, and the father wanted to retire but felt that the son would never cope on his own.

Cecil's initial meeting with the owners had been under the guise of introducing them to some of the companies who manufactured the drugs that provided his income. This ruse had given him the opportunity to study the workings of the factory at close quarters. The factory was situated on an area of scrubland that the family had bought for a pittance thirty years previously. The manufacturing plant occupied less than a quarter of the total area, and it was obvious that the old man had no idea how much land prices had rocketed over the last few years.

The production facility was streamlined and well run (this was the son's province), and there was plenty of additional land for expansion. It quickly became obvious that the son was progressive and far more capable than the father gave him credit for. He had actually wanted to obtain venture capital to expand but was horrified at the cost of doing so and was certain that he would be eased out after twelve months or so. The old man was firmly fixed in the past and was having real trouble grasping how the drug industry was developing. Cecil asked if he could take some photos of the factory to show his associates, and armed with these, he'd returned to his office and subsequently had long talks with his architect and business bank manager. Draft plans were drawn up and thorough company accounts investigation undertaken.

His bank manager had been extremely helpful and had come up with several suggestions that Cecil hadn't thought of for financing the deal. One big advantage was that they'd known one another during Cecil's Tsang days, and he was familiar with Cecil's shrewd business acumen. Also, he could see the great potential of the expanded company and congratulated Cecil on finding a business that was ripe for takeover.

At the next meeting Cecil dropped the bombshell: he'd been very impressed with their operation, could see the great potential, and was prepared to buy a majority shareholding in the company with the proviso (in writing) that the son, Lee, continued to run the organization. Cecil would put up the capital as a director's loan to fund the necessary expansion with an interest rate that was half of what any bank would have offered. Furthermore, he would bring business from his other connections as most of them were running short of production capacity.

After the initial deafening silence it was agreed that they should all meet again in a week's time as this would give the family time to consider the offer and make their decision. Judging by the body language, Cecil realized that Lee was not going to have an easy week with his father, but they wouldn't get as good an offer from any investment bank, and the old man looked tired.

Lee must have worked hard on his father and the deal was agreed in principle. The purchase had gone smoothly, and the first phase of expansion was well underway and actually ahead of schedule. Cecil had been spending a lot of time at the plant to get the feel of all aspects of the business, and whilst working in invoicing, he discovered that there was a small side to the business that he hadn't been aware of. They supplied morphine pump equipment for post-operative and terminal palliative care. Apparently Lee's father had seen a market for them whilst he was in India on a sales trip and had found a local company to manufacture to his specification. Ever since this range had produced a small slice of the company's overall profit and was easy to handle as they were made to order and dispatched directly from the manufacturer.

Inevitably he found a couple of minor problems but was pleased to discover that in general the business was well run, although some of the systems needed updating. The staff seemed relieved that the organization was moving forward; some had been concerned that if it didn't expand it would go to the wall and their jobs with it. As a result Cecil was viewed as a rescuer rather than a predator, and Lee positively blossomed now that he had a free rein. There was no doubt that his father had held him back, and he now arrived at work with a smile instead of ever-increasing worry lines.

Cecil's next step was to look at pending quotes for business, and here he needed Lee for guidance. The two largest jobs that had been quoted for were keenly priced, and Lee knew that the competition, all of whom were larger and had higher overheads, couldn't equal their prices without making a loss. Obviously Lee had done his homework, and Cecil couldn't fault his estimates.

"When are we due to follow up these quotes?"

"The closing date for both is next week."

"How long before we'd need to start production?"

"Approximately two months."

"Great, we will at least have the new phase for extra storage."

They left work that evening anticipating that next week would see their future workload multiply by at least one hundred percent. By the following Tuesday they were both forcibly reminded of the old adage: "Never count your chickens. . . ." Both of the major contracts that they had quoted for had been awarded to a competitor who had apparently under-quoted them by a substantial amount. Cecil and Lee were flabbergasted, but the customers, both European, wouldn't reveal the identity of the competition.

Lee started ringing around a number of associates and some of his moles, but nobody knew who had undercut them, and all of the usual competitors were equally incandescent and swore that they had not been accepted either. This was a serious set-back because Cecil had been relying on the increased turnover to finance his plans. He called in a few favors from Tsang days and eventually was given the name of the hijacker: "Pharmzest" who was based in Hong Kong. Further enquiries revealed this to be a holding company with manufacturing companies in China, The Philippines, and Indonesia.

None of Lee's contacts had ever heard of this company, and they were all amazed that a business with this production capability could suddenly appear out of the blue. So, it was these worrying developments that found Cecil late at his desk and pondering what he could do to help his company to survive. Hunger interrupted his thoughts, and he finally left the building and walked the short distance to a restaurant that he had recently discovered. The food was good reasonably priced Asian cuisine, and after giving his order, he sat at the bar savoring a cold beer. The thought of food must have focused his mind, and he took out his mobile phone and hit one of his speed dial numbers. There was a small delay in connection, and then Sheila's voice emerged clearly from his earpiece.

"Can I ask a favor?"

"Of course."

"Can we meet tomorrow? I could do with your help."

"No problem. What's wrong?"

"Nothing that can't be put right, but I think your friend at Foston could make a few enquiries that would be difficult for me to do without compromising my position. Anyway it's not fair to take up your time at this late hour, but can I meet you at your office at 10:00 a.m.? Incidentally, I do know the way!"

Sheila laughed and said that she'd be delighted to see him and she'd make sure that he got into the building this time. She put the phone down wondering what the hell that was all about and why Foston? Walking back into the kitchen, where Steve was preparing their evening meal as a treat for her, she quickly filled him in with the details of the call and suggested that he attend the meeting with her.

"Fine but that's for tomorrow; this evening I want you to sit down with the gin martini that you'll find waiting for you in the fridge, and your meal will be served for you in ten minutes or so—if that's alright with Madam?"

Sheila grinned, pinched his bottom as she passed, collected her drink, and made her way back to the sitting room as instructed. Steve was cooking Italian to remind her of that fateful Italian meal with her and Cecil and a bottle of Barolo was breathing to add the final touch.

They lingered over their meal, and he told her all that had happened recently, that he couldn't envisage life without her, and that he never wanted to be parted long term from her again. They both agreed and talked about him living in Kuala Lumpur as he could just as easily make business trips to Europe.

"What about your lovely cottage?"

"Somehow the place feels tainted and anyway it's empty without you."

"Well, don't sell it immediately, rent it out, and then you can make your decision at a later date."

At last he felt that he'd gotten his priorities right, and even if he had to be away at times in Europe, at least his base was in Kuala Lumpur with the woman he loved. When finally they fell into bed, he was asleep almost instantly. Sheila smiled at his face, which looked more relaxed than she could remember. Lovemaking would have to wait until the morning. Anyway come to think of it, she was tired too.

Breakfast was a hurried affair after a longer than normal stay in bed, but for once the traffic wasn't too bad, so Sheila made good time and they arrived almost on time. Once armed with a coffee, Steve gathered his thoughts:

"You know this is going to feel a little awkward; I haven't seen Cecil since all of his problems and I don't quite know how he'll react to me."

"Well, he was okay with me when I last saw him; it was almost as though nothing had changed, and it does seem as though he wants your help in some way."

Steve didn't feel totally reassured but decided that there was nothing that he could do but wait and see what happened. The phone rang and the receptionist informed Sheila that Mr. Liu had arrived.

Nothing changes, he always was early!

Cecil was shown in and was as immaculate and confident as Steve had remembered him. He shook Steve's hand warmly and without any sign of embarrassment said, "Well, as you know, I got myself into hot water due to my stupid actions, paid the price, and have bounced back. I've learnt my lesson and am never going down that road again. Let me say, however, that your appointment as European agent may have been made for the wrong reasons, but from what I hear, you have more than justified your position. Anyway, let me get straight to the point as I know that you are both busy people."

He went on to explain the details of his latest venture and how it was being compromised by this new upstart company based in Hong Kong.

"This could cost me a lot more than I can afford, and their prices just don't make sense. They are quoting below our cost price, and we are a small, efficient setup. I would like to learn more about their manufacturing plant, but they are bound to know of me. I realize it's a bit of an imposition, but I was wondering if you would be prepared to visit them on the premise of trying to persuade them to offer a complete package by including your range of equipment. Obviously I would pay all of your expenses and a retaining fee for your time."

"I don't have a problem with that. In fact I think I probably owe you for the great deal that you cut me when you were resident here."

Steve winked and shook Cecil's hand and realized that once again he was going to be Cecil's agent.

"I can travel on Monday so, if you e-mail all the details to Sheila, I will see what I can find out for you."

The conversation reverted to generalities, and then Sheila asked him if he could fill her in with the history of some of the clients whom she was about to deal with; his input turned out to be extremely helpful.

A Monday morning flight gave enough time during the
week for the two of them to explore all the possibilities of
their new life in Malaysia. Sheila insisted that, much as she
loved her apartment, they should look at new property as she
would like to start off with a place that they'd chosen together. So, any free time during the rest of the week was taken up
looking at real estate. They finally decided on a property that
was just being finished in a renovated colonial building about
half a mile from her present flat. It was bigger, had much
higher ceilings, was full of character, and was surrounded by
long-established gardens. The agent was confident that her
present home would sell very quickly, and before they really
knew what had happened, they'd put down a deposit on their
new home. Returning to the flat and somewhat in shock, they
demolished a large gin and tonic each. Steve texted the estate
agent friend who'd sold the cottage to him and asked him to
look for tenants and to advise what rental he might expect.
Their new life was definitely going into overdrive.

Monday morning arrived in record time, he boarded the
plane, and once settled in his seat, re-read the information that
Cecil had e-mailed over earlier in the week. There really wasn't
anything of any substance, so he'd just have to play it by ear
and see what he could glean at the meeting that he'd arranged
with the purchasing manager on Tuesday. Steve felt a frisson of
excitement; this trip was a bit different from the norm; he almost
felt like an espionage agent. Move over James Bond!

Settling back in his seat, he selected the in-flight film and had
to chuckle when he saw that it was one of the Bourne series.

The incredible skyline of Hong Kong slid under the wing
as the plane made its curving descent into the airport. On this
occasion he was only travelling with hand luggage, so he quickly made his way to the taxi rank, and although the traffic was
chaotic, it was not long before he was deposited at his hotel. A
quick phone call arranged a meeting with Pharmzest the following morning, and after a catnap he took the Star Ferry across to
Hong Kong Island and enjoyed a leisurely meal in Food Street.

Pharmzest's office was in a modern building in one of the side streets off Nathan Road, Kowloon. The waiting room was smart and functional but gave no indication of what business the company was involved in. After a few minutes the manager came out to greet him, and he was shown into an equally anonymous office. Steve outlined Foston's operations in Europe and stressed that he felt that they could be of mutual benefit to one another as the Foston range would give a complete package to Pharmzest and Foston would be able to offer contacts to Pharmzest. After seeing the Foston presentation, the manager seemed genuinely interested but pointed out that this office belonged to the holding company and that he would need to talk to the sales director at the production plant in southern China; he would ring Steve later in the afternoon if they wished to proceed further. Not wishing to leave empty handed, Steve asked for details of the pharmaceutical range that they manufactured and was informed that the main range covered sexual dysfunction, heart, leukemia, various cancer drugs, and others.

With the initial meeting over Steve went shopping: some shirts for him and a few presents for Sheila. The old days of cheap Hong Kong had now given way to designer Hong Kong, and he gulped at some of the prices. The property prices in the real estate offices made even London look cheap, and he was relieved that they were going to be living in Kuala Lumpur and not Hong Kong. As he retraced his steps to the hotel, his mobile rang and to his surprise it was Pharmzest offering to pick him up the following morning for a meeting at their production plant. Better than I could have hoped for!

With a good night's sleep behind him he was whisked back to the airport for a short flight into mainland China, and then accompanied by the Hong Kong manager, he was driven to the factory. The building was very modern and nondescript, and once through security, they were led into the reception area, which mercifully was air conditioned. It wasn't so much the heat that was getting to him but the humidity.

The plant manager, Mr. Chen, welcomed him and requested that he repeat his presentation, so that they could draw their own conclusions. The end result was the same, and they offered to let Steve have a brochure outlining the full range of their products. He in turn let them have his full catalogue, adding that he would like to see the production line in order that he could confidently recommend Pharmzest to his clients. There was a moment's hesitation, but then Chen picked up his phone, gabbled to the person on the other end, and moments later the production manager appeared with a set of protective clothing to enable Steve to enter the plant.

The production line was immaculately clean, running like clockwork, and most of the many women employed didn't even look up as he passed by. The manager proudly explained the workings of the factory, and Steve learnt that it had been open just under a year and was only running at one quarter capacity of the present building. However, the site had been chosen as it would enable quadruple expansion as sales increased. He enquired if it was a privately owned business and was told that indeed it was, but then the subject was changed making it impossible to pursue any further. He asked if he might take some samples back to show the quality of packaging, and it was agreed that a pack would be made up for him before he left.

With the grand tour completed they returned to the office, and Steve congratulated them on a superb manufacturing operation that greatly impressed him. He dreamt up a few more questions that would be expected of someone in his guise and was relieved that they also had relevant questions to ask about Foston. It would seem, therefore that his mission had been plausible and not raised any suspicions. Following tea he was given the traditional business present and a sample pack as promised.

At the end of a long day he sank a large whisky and phoned Cecil with an update and then fell into bed knowing that he had an early call the next morning for his flight to Kuala Lumpur. Drifting in that halfway state between sleep and consciousness, he wondered if the information that he'd gleaned would be of any use to Cecil and then finally submitted to exhaustion.

In fact, Cecil couldn't believe his luck when Steve handed over the sample pack. The production manager must have taken the pack from the wrong pile, because instead of just being sample packaging, the packs actually contained product. Cecil was delighted and profuse in his thanks and, as Steve left his office, rushed to the laboratory to have the products analyzed.

Cecil was not a patient man, and the ensuing week's wait for results had him pacing like an expectant father. It's often said that good things are worth waiting for, and this was no exception. Some of the product was spot on to the specification, but others had less than specified ingredients, but more dangerously some of the sexual dysfunction drugs had over twice the level of active ingredient specified and also contained unauthorized fillers. These were one of the ranges that Cecil's company had quoted for and lost to Pharmzest, the other being a drug used to control leukemia. The latter was arsenic-based and the sample contained a variety of contaminants.

Armed with his new-found information, he started to research sources of arsenic and found that China was a major supplier to large areas of the world but, because of buyers' stringent specifications, tended to manufacture to high levels of purity. He called in some old favors and eventually found that there was, in addition to standard quality arsenic, a small source of low grade arsenic being made illegally in Malaysia on his own doorstep. His informer was obviously frightened and wouldn't give specific details, but suggested that Cecil look close to a large lake near Kuala Lumpur and then rang off.

Cecil stared out of the window trying to think of where the plant could be. He knew the large lake that had been a flooded tin mine, but this was now beautifully landscaped and there was no industrial site there. No other place came to mind so in desperation he decided to drive over and explore thoroughly. As expected the lake and its surrounds were immaculate without a trace of any chemical manufacture. A shopping mall and residential apartment blocks had been built at the far end, and it was only when he drove around the back of these that he could see a secondary lake in the distance. This lake had some form of industrial plant alongside as well as several huge quarry-like pits.

On arrival his entrance was barred by security barriers and a high perimeter fence. A chat with the security guard was informative. The site was a combined state-of-the-art waste processing unit: rubbish was sorted with some going to landfill in the pits and the majority going into the huge incinerator. Cecil looked up at the huge smoke stack and was impressed that he couldn't see any emission; the guard said that this had been a condition imposed on the private operator. Sadly he was no nearer to solving the arsenic mystery.

It was a couple of weeks later after drawing a blank that Cecil was talking to David, the head chemist, at his own factory and explaining his dilemma regarding the plant location. The response stunned him because, as so often happens, the solution was simple. Apparently arsenic exposure causes cancer and early unsophisticated manufacturing methods caused many deaths amongst workers. If the plant they were looking for produced arsenic with contaminants then it was likely that the operators were using old-fashioned manufacturing techniques. The chemist's advice was to check with the Department of Health and look for clusters of high levels per capita of cancer. Any that were near a lake would be worth investigating.

Thanks to computerized records the data was on his laptop screen in minutes: Seven clusters and only one near a lake; the one he'd been looking at!

Back at the office he explained to David what he'd found in the records and what he'd seen at the site.

"I'd like to come and have a look at the site with you Mr. Liu.

"Sure, but why?"

"Well, arsenic is made by burning tin ore and passing the results through a calcine tower, and I'd be likely to recognize such a plant if I saw one whereas you probably wouldn't."

They set off for the lake the following day and looking from the car the verdict was that the incinerator could be capable of arsenic production, but to be certain it would be necessary to see inside the plant.

"If we don't stop these illegal producers, my job is on the line because we won't have a company. I'm the best person to know what's happening in there so, if you'll let me have the time off, I'll try to get a job laboring or whatever else is available, and see what I can find out."

"I won't forget you for this."

"You better not!"

Grinning, he wandered over to the security lodge and asked if there were any jobs available. The guard had no idea but gave him a phone number to ring. Once back at the office the head chemist managed to land himself an interview for a laboring job. Duly dressed down, he attended the so-called interview and was told to report on site at 6:00 a.m. the following Monday.

Monday was a long day for Cecil as he waited to hear what the plant contained. It was an even longer day for a chemist who wasn't used to heavy work. The phone call that evening made his wait worthwhile. The incinerator had been ingeniously designed as it was actually two incinerators with separate smokestacks and scrubbers contained in one outer shell to make it appear as one outlet. One incinerator was devouring ordinary waste whilst the other was digesting "waste" from the old tin mine spoil heap. The spoil would be of low grade and would, therefore, inevitably contain a variety of impurities but the feedstock cost nothing.

The incinerator plant was one laborer short the following day, and Cecil started to compile two reports, one with regard to the poor specification of Pharmzest product and the other to the Department of the Environment with regard to the actual operation of the incinerator plant.

A copy of his own specification for each drug tendered for was sent along with the Pharmzest analysis to the client, and he then sat back and awaited developments. In fact he was still waiting for a reply when the incinerator scandal hit the news. TV and newspapers carried the story and the underlying corruption that had turned a blind eye to what the plant was really doing. The fallout was massive, and somehow they had identified Cecil as the whistleblower, and the media were hailing him as a local hero.

He parked his car and was just turning the corner when he saw a gang of reporters around his apartment door ready to ambush him on arrival. Dodging back out of sight, he entered the building by the rear service entrance, let himself in, filled an overnight bag, and left the way that he'd arrived. A night in a city centre hotel will be preferable to facing that mob.

Next morning he was awake before his alarm call so he switched on the TV to catch up on what was happening in the world. The world news was the usual mix of doom and gloom coupled with the latest financial figures, but as he was about to get up, the local news showed pictures of his apartment block, more correctly what was left of the apartment block after the fire. The reporter made great play that the block contained the apartment of the recently hailed local hero who had uncovered the incinerator scandal. In fact, although forensic tests weren't yet complete, the fire was believed to have started in his flat. No corpse had been found, so it was assumed that he hadn't been home at the time. Two people within the building had been rescued and were being treated for smoke inhalation. Mercifully everyone else had been evacuated without injury. The building was gutted.

Minutes later and Cecil's mobile started ringing; the first were a number of calls from friends, all wanting to know if he was all right. The last was from David:

"My God, we've stirred up a hornets' nest haven't we? It looks like somebody wants you out of the way."

Cecil had to agree, but it was going to be difficult to keep out of the way of the enemy when you didn't know who your enemy was. One way or another he was going to have to find out who really owned the incinerator plant and take things from there. Once in the office he started digging for information on the computer. The company listed as plant owner was obviously a cover and was registered in Indonesia, but nothing else could be gleaned about the actual people behind the organization. He rang around a few influential friends and still drew a blank until he finally contacted the editor of the daily newspaper. He sympathized with Cecil's position and said that the rumors in the press world were that the owners were Chinese but operated out of Hong Kong.

The gloom of the underground car park with its faint smell of stale urine did little to lift his mood as he got into his car. However, as he burst forth into the bright sunlight of Kuala Lumpur he quickly returned to his normal self, and his organized mind started to process all of the jobs for the day. The traffic was its usual chaotic tangle, but finally as he reached the outskirts, he was able to put his foot down and was at long last making some progress when sod's law cut in and red traffic lights dictated otherwise. Quietly cursing to himself, Cecil braked and braked and braked. His foot had gone right to the floor with no effect, and he careened across the intersection, narrowly missing a lorry and accompanied by blaring horns. The car eventually came to stop by embedding itself in the wooden fence surrounding the garden of an old house and quiet descended. The police appeared from nowhere in no time at all, and a quick inspection showed that the brakes had been tampered with. They took him back to the police station, and after making a statement, he finished his journey to work by taxi. Once settled behind his desk with a glass of tea, he realized that he was badly shaken; the shock had only just set in.

It was some time later on in the day that Cecil realized just how powerful his enemies must be; the only way that they could have known which hotel he was staying at was if they had access to his mobile phone conversations, because he'd used his mobile to make the booking from his car whilst travelling to the hotel. Realizing that he was in deep trouble, he immediately thought to get out of the country and as far away as possible, but he knew that he couldn't leave when his business was in such a precarious state. He sat back in his chair trying to organize his thoughts when the phone rang.

"Hi Cecil, it's Sheila here, I've been worried about you since seeing the fire on TV. How are you?"

"Well, I've been better, some bastard sawed through my brake pipes, and I landed up in someone's garden. Mind you, that's better than the mortuary!"

"My God, that's terrible are you alright?"

"A bit shaken but otherwise okay thanks."

It must have been about an hour after this conversation when Sheila rang again to say that she'd told Steve what had been happening, and he'd mentioned that Tim seemed to have contacts all around the world from his SAS days; perhaps he might like to make a note of his phone number. Cecil thanked her and agreed that he had nothing to lose by having a chat with Tim. He had to face facts; he didn't know who was targeting him and had no means of tracing them himself. Shortly afterwards the police rang to say that they would be making their enquiries and were treating the matter very seriously, but Cecil knew that they had nothing to go on and that the case would soon be dropped.

Over the next few days he found himself constantly looking over his shoulder wherever he went and planned his movements so that he was always in public places, changing hotels daily. In fact his life had become almost nomadic, and he'd even resorted to using a different taxi firm for each journey. Tim agreed that Cecil was doing everything that he could to protect himself and, armed with the information that Cecil could give him, said that he would be delighted to have him as a client and see what he could do to trace the thugs who were after him.

The media publicity had been useful in one way, because it had given Cecil an excuse to contact the companies who had placed their orders with Pharmzest as opposed to his company. He informed them of the content of the samples of drugs that they had ordered, which he had had analyzed. Whilst they were obviously wary, they said that they would make spot checks on the first consignment to arrive and would withhold payment until the results were available. There was nothing else that he could do now but wait and see what happened, but at least he felt that he'd taken action to try to regain some form of control.

21

Fiona's pregnancy was going well, and she looked a picture of maternal health with her ever-increasing bump. Their friends were all thrilled to see how quickly she had adapted to impending motherhood. Tim was positively glowing with pride and almost wanted to pinch himself each day as he found it difficult to believe how happy he was.

Cecil's predicament had alarmed him, and he'd quickly set in motion enquiries throughout the Far East and was now awaiting replies somewhat impatiently. In fact one line of enquiry was through Bruce's old company in India. One of his contacts in Taiwan, who had agreed to delve around for him, had tipped him off that arsenic was also used in the manufacture of semiconductors. Tim had made enquiries in India to see if they had been offered any cheaper than normal product from China, and sure enough they had and the manufacturer was Taiwanese. He'd dispatched an e-mail with the identity of the company and a request to see if his contact could find out the identity of the supplier of the raw material. Although it seemed like an age to Tim, in reality the e-mails started arriving in a relatively short time. Various probings with regard to the owners of the Malaysian incinerator plant pointed through a trail of dummy companies to a holding company in Hong Kong operating under the name Pharmzest. The Taiwanese semiconductor company turned out to be totally respectable, but their arsenic supplier was a mineral company who was also traceable back to Pharmzest. It was at this point that Tim realized that, much as he didn't want to leave Fiona alone, he would have to travel to Hong Kong to dig further; there was only so much that could be done without personal involvement.

He eventually arrived home after a long day and felt somewhat guilty when he announced that he would have to leave in two days for Hong Kong. Fiona's reply completely threw him: "Great I'll come with you; I've always loved Hong Kong, and I can do some shopping for myself and our baby."

"But you're pregnant!"

"Precisely, I'm pregnant not ill! So that's settled."

This was one hell of a girl that he'd married, he reckoned, and so, two days later they flew east together.

Using the hotel as a base, Tim called in some old army intelligence favors and very soon the workings of Pharmzest were being dissected bit by bit with trails leading to the mainland, Indonesia, Malaysia, and Europe. The convoluted trail kept leading back to one Shanghai-based individual known by the single name: Tam. Tam came from a previously respectable wealthy merchant family, but his activities now encompassed illegal drugs, prostitution, and just about everything unsavory, as well as legitimate business. Although he was purportedly only in his thirties, his wealth was phenomenal, his caution was legendary, and he spoke half a dozen languages apart from Chinese. Both Chinese and Hong Kong police were totally frustrated as they were certain of his activities, but neither had ever been able to prove his involvement, and as a result he led a charmed life and added even more millions to his existing billions of dollars.

Tim and Fiona enjoyed an extra day on the island and then stopped off on their return at Kuala Lumpur. Cecil was impressed with the progress that Tim had made in such a short time and was fascinated at the string of cover companies that all appeared to be owned by Tam. The appearance of Pharmzest on the list was no great surprise, but he was brought up with a jolt when he saw the name Anglo Oriental Trading. So Tam had been the shadowy figure backing Pang's activities that had screwed up my life!

With Tim and Fiona on the flight back to the UK Cecil had time to gather his thoughts and quickly realized that he'd made a very powerful enemy, and that Tam's activities were so widespread that he really had no effective hiding place. He decided to take advice from Tsang's legal director whom he'd kept in contact with and who, unlike most of his colleagues, had not been judgmental. He made a phone-call, and they agreed to meet for dinner that evening; this gave him the rest of the day to make notes of all the vital information that he'd gleaned.

After the main course, the dessert arrived accompanied by a sinfully nectar-like pudding wine, and the conversation turned to Tam and the implications of all that had happened. Cecil marveled at the lawyer's incisive mind that seemed to absorb information effortlessly whilst rejecting anything extraneous. As a result he quickly had the whole situation encapsulated, and his synopsis actually clarified the whole picture for Cecil.

The barrister's conclusion was that Cecil would never be able to outrun Tam and that the latter had a vested interest in Cecil's death. Cecil shuddered. The best approach would be to attack rather than defend.

"How the hell am I going to attack him?"

"You're not, the police are!"

He went on to explain that Cecil was now in possession of most of Tam's activities complete with addresses, etc. The police had been desperate for this sort of lead for years, but their sources had not been able to cut corners in the way that Tim's had. This gave him a very potent weapon and the police would be able to use it against this unscrupulous "Mr. Big."

The more Cecil thought about it, the more sense it made, and he decided to act on his friend's suggestion the following day. With the subject of Tam mentally filed under "pending" they went into the lounge to enjoy a large brandy and coffee to top off their dinner.

Next morning he put a call through to a tired sounding Tim and told him of the previous evening's conversation. Tim agreed with the lawyer's assessment and suggested that they contact the

Hong Kong chief of police who wanted Tam and would liaise with the Shanghai police who were equally eager to nail him. Apparently, since the return of Hong Kong to China, the liaison between the countries had increased dramatically, and this would work in Cecil's favor. Tim felt it would be better if he made the contact as he was known to the people concerned, and Cecil was relieved as he would have felt out of his depth dealing directly with the police. They agreed to talk again at the end of the week unless anything urgent cropped up in the meantime.

Cecil picked up his unread newspaper and flicked through the headlines. His eyes settled on a small item: "Drug importer killed." The report went on to describe how Tony Pang had been run down by a hit and run car a few hundred yards from the prison gates following his release. After interviewing witnesses, police were treating the incident as murder, and the theory was that it was related to one of the drug gangs.

Cecil shuddered; the enemy certainly had long-reaching tentacles, and he also felt a twinge of sorrow, because although Pang had created problems for him, he had to admit that he had actually liked the guy. He could no longer delude himself; if this was what they could do to anyone who could be a threat to them, he was frightened, really frightened! Fortunately his phone rang, and Sheila's voice sounded calming. He quickly slid into telling her how helpful Tim had been and thanked her for suggesting the idea. They chatted for a while, and he felt much better by the time he put the phone down, although in the back of his mind he was very aware of his vulnerability.

Several days later he took a call at work from an officer of the Hong Kong police. They were just checking and confirming various facts with Cecil and said that they would call again as soon as they had anything to report.

Well, at least someone is doing something!

Steve's curiosity was getting the better of him, so after several aborted attempts, he finally rang Tim to ask what news he had regarding their joint espionage mission. In truth he'd got a real kick out of his snooping. Tim confirmed that there was ongoing action in Hong Kong, and he also mentioned Pang's murder, adding that Tam and his cronies were obviously running scared and were eliminating any incriminating contacts. He thought he should have some more meaty news by the weekend and would keep him in the picture. "Reckon we make a good team, you and me. Let's hope we can nail the bastard before he does any more harm."

Steve couldn't argue with that, and he felt rather privileged to be allowed a little access to Tim's cloak and dagger world. Also, the more he got to know the man the more he liked him, and with impending fatherhood, there was a definite softening and less of a military bearing. However, in the meantime it was going to be difficult to concentrate on work, and the weekend seemed light years away.

After all the excitement of the last two days, Saturday loomed up unexpectedly, and Steve was taken by surprise when Tim's call came through. Both Hong Kong and Shanghai authorities were overjoyed at the insight into Tam's activities that Tim and Steve had unearthed but were frightened that if they initially instituted criminal proceedings against Tam, his lawyers might get him off on some minor technicality. They had, therefore, instructed forensic accountants to check out all of the cover companies to see if they could nail him on tax evasion. This would give them watertight charges and buy time whilst they prepared further criminal charges. Steve could appreciate the logic in this approach, and he recalled that that was how the US authorities had finally trapped Al Capone.

Tim would contact him again as soon as he heard of any more developments, but TV news beat him to it the following evening when, snuggled up to Sheila on her comfortable sofa, he was shaken to hear a report that a group of companies owned by Tam had been suspended from trading due to tax irregularities. Tam had been "helping the authorities with their investigations."

"Christ! Sheila we've really stirred things up, and they're moving at warp speed!"

Moments later the phone rang. Cecil wondered if they'd heard the news and what did they think would happen next, etc. Steve brought him up to speed, and they then both agreed that things were moving very much faster than either had envisaged.

22

The Shanghai office, which was the impressive nerve center for Tam's worldwide operations, was a mass of computer equipment and complicated phone systems that enabled him to maintain communication with all of his far reaching branches. Today he was anything but the stereotypical inscrutable Asian, more like a raging bull. He was incandescent and his finance director was on the receiving end of a tirade whilst the company lawyer was being harangued on the speaker telephone at the same time.

"I pay you more in a month than most men earn in a year just to cover our tracks and keep our affairs hidden from prying eyes. Okay some of our operations are, shall we say, dubious, but they are always under the auspices of companies registered in countries that are not too fussy about such things. So how in fuck's name do you land me in a situation where half of the authorities in the Far East are snooping around my companies and preventing us from trading?"

The hapless finance man tried to explain that he had covered every possible attempt at investigation through normal accounting channels, but someone must have had illegal access to some of their company records.

"Not my problem. Tell that to your next employer, you're fired!"

The lawyer came off somewhat better as he explained that he could deal with any claims of criminal activity against the company but tax and finance were not his remit. Apart from a sore ear, as a result of the phone being slammed down on him, he came away unscathed and still in employment.

Tam had always worked on the principle of only appointing people who were under an obligation to him. Today would be payback time, and he spent the rest of the day calling in favors. However, by the end of the day nobody was able to throw any light on who had divulged information, and the best assistance offered was that they would be as obstructive as possible to any investigations. He also secured assurances from all of his sources that they would warn him if there were any signs of impending disaster. For a man who was always in control, this was a very poor compromise, and he was not enjoying the alien feelings of insecurity. Any funds in excess of those required for the everyday running of the business were discreetly moved to safer venues abroad, and that completed the damage limitation for the day. However, like all good businessmen, he had contingency plans in place should everything go belly up. There was a private jet permanently on standby at the airport, and his personal fortune had long since been dotted around the world so that he could leave at a few minutes' notice, and thanks to the internet continue to function from a base outside of China.

Tam was the latest in a long line of merchants, and they'd frequently had to become adaptable to changes in circumstances, but that didn't mean that he relished the thought of upheaval, and he would resist to the very last. Marriage had always represented an unacceptable tie to him, but he had enjoyed a series of glamorous girlfriends each of which had been unceremoniously dumped as soon as she started looking for commitment. Easier to travel lightweight!

Topaz, the latest eye candy, had been enjoying the Shanghai club scene with him and was the daughter of a retired army General. She'd been introduced to him by her cousin, who was the company secretary for Tam's holding company. She was very intelligent, very ambitious, and very athletic in bed: Tam had introduced her to the joys of cocaine-enhanced sex, and she'd managed to exhaust even his appetite for the bizarre. Tam liked his sex wild and with domination, and she was at her most excited when administering discipline. In short, they were an ideal sexual partnership: him somewhat of a masochist and her somewhat of a sadist. Her main interests were sex and money so the relationship had lasted longer than her predecessors, because she seemed content with what was on offer rather than demanding more.

Topaz was an unusual beauty as her eyes were almond shaped, and her breasts larger than the average Chinese girl's, although neither had been surgically enhanced. She oozed confidence and turned heads wherever she went, which appealed to Tam's oversized ego, as he derived great pleasure from seeing the envy in the eyes of other men as he entered a room with her on his arm.

It was now early evening, and he had plugged as many loopholes as possible, so the rest was in the lap of the gods. Time to relax, so he called Topaz on his mobile and arranged to meet her at the apartment he had recently bought for her. He gunned the Porsche and as the engine note built to a crescendo, so did his sexual arousal. By the time he pressed the intercom to her penthouse, he could feel the adrenaline of anticipation and the hardness of his erection fighting for liberation from his designer jeans.

She opened the door wearing a leather basque and thigh boots and handed him a small silver tray with two lines and a straw. They both sniffed deeply and eyeing one another hungrily hurried to the bedroom where they did some serious damage to a bottle of Krug before choosing from the extensive array of sex toys and bondage gear. In no time at all the worries of the day had been banished from his mind as he slid into sexual ecstasy.

They eventually succumbed to sleep for a short spell, but the cocaine was winning over fatigue, and they were both buzzing on awakening, so decided to head for a favorite casino. The cab decanted them at the main entrance, and the doorman welcomed them warmly; he knew that Tam always tipped generously and wanted to make sure that he was remembered when they left. Re-fuelled with champagne, they made straight for the roulette table, and after a short spell of losing they hit a winning streak.

He supplied the money, and she the numbers. The teamwork resulted in one of the largest wins of the night once again proving the old adage: "Money makes money."

With a large wad in his pocket, after cashing in his chips, Tam steered his stunning accomplice to a waiting taxi, and they left for a nearby trendy disco where they danced away the final traces of the stimulant from their bloodstreams.

At 3:00 a.m. the traffic was normally quiet in the city, so it was particularly unlucky that a speeding taxi, driven by a driver who had put in sixteen hours on duty, should plough into their cab as they were returning to her apartment. The impact was on Tam's side, and whilst she and the driver were shaken but unscathed, he was unconscious and obviously seriously injured. An ambulance arrived on the scene very quickly in response to her mobile call, and she accompanied him to the nearest hospital. The accident and emergency department was busy but efficient, and to her great relief Tam regained consciousness during the examination. He had sustained a blow to the head and even without an x-ray it was obvious that he had a broken right arm and lacerations.

After what seemed an age, he was put to bed in a side ward, and the doctor summed up his injuries as concussion, a fractured right arm, several broken ribs, cuts, bruises, and various soft tissue injuries. He was to stay in hospital overnight for observation and the reduction and setting of his arm would be carried out the following day. However, once all of his injuries were known, his consultant advised that he should stay in hospital for at least a week. The caged wild animal would probably have died from boredom, but for the regular visits from Topaz who regaled him with all the "rehabilitation" ideas that she'd dreamt up for him on his return. He, on the other hand, felt totally out of control with regard to his latest problems and was desperate to escape and be in the driver's seat again. Continual checking of his mobile phone for warnings of impending doom resulted in nothing but an eerie silence.

During her enforced spell of celibacy, Topaz had time to catch up with her father who had recently been very inquisitive about her boyfriend. She wasn't really surprised at her father's concerns as she was fully aware that Tam had the reputation of being a playboy as well as a ruthless businessman. She decided not to tell her father of Tam's accident, as he had already expressed worries about Tam's high speed driving in the Porsche; it just wasn't worth the hassle of explaining that they'd actually been in a taxi. They enjoyed some quality time together and he took her to one of her favorite restaurants; he enjoyed spoiling his little girl with good food and good wine.

Cousin Tony, the company secretary, had been very grateful to the General, his uncle, for covering up his brother's illegal private enterprise whilst in the army. He was about to be investigated and could have been charged with corruption if the General hadn't intervened and hushed things up. Like Tam, he worked on the principle that it was always helpful to have people under an obligation to you; you never knew when it could be useful.

Recent Chinese Authority enquiries, resulting from Tim's probing, had been relayed to the General via his old grapevine. It was now time to call in a favor, and who was in a better position to reveal Tam's activities than the company secretary? Also, this was personal; he was extremely unhappy with his daughter's choice of boyfriend, whose reputation was well known to him, and he knew that she wouldn't listen to any advice that he offered. Instinctively he knew that Tam was bad news and anything that he could do that would remove the creep from her life was okay by him.

In spite of the apparent quietness that Tam was experiencing, in reality there was feverish activity taking place simultaneously in forensic accountant's offices, police headquarters, IRS departments, and Customs and Excise offices in four different countries. Encrypted e-mails were flashing around the world, and everyone concerned shared the buzz and excitement of cornering a prey that had eluded them for far too long. There was a quiet confidence that success was finally in sight, but everything hung on the Chinese tax authorities being able to bring a watertight case against this slippery eel of a businessman. The day before Tam's release from hospital the final pieces of the jigsaw slotted into place and the police left their Shanghai headquarters for the hospital.

The everyday mundane routine of the hospital administrator was thrown into chaos when his secretary announced that a posse of senior police officers was demanding access to Tam's ward in order to arrest him for alleged tax evasion, fraud, and various other pending charges.

Once he'd recovered from his initial shock, he explained that he couldn't help them, because the patient had discharged himself that morning. The tip-off from one of his minions had been timely and already the Gulfstream Executive jet was thrusting its way into the sky en route to the Congo. Tam had invested heavily in countries across the north of Africa, and the Congo was convenient because it would not cooperate with extradition orders, and the tax laws were easy to bend.

23

Tim, Cecil, and Steve shared the news on a conference call, and although they were disappointed that their quarry had escaped, they were consoled by the fact that a large part of the Tam Empire would be smashed, and there was always the hope that he would eventually slip up and be caught. Tim had been in regular communication with the various government spook departments, and it was amazing how wide-reaching Tam's activities had been. Fortunately he'd made a number of enemies along the way, and they had been only too pleased to assist in his downfall even though some of them were little better than he was.

The general consensus was that the majority of the known Tam activities would be closed down along with a considerable number of suppliers. The drug trade in Europe would be seriously dented and so would a lot of the Eastern European people-trafficking that fed the sex trade. The more that they looked into what the businesses involved, the more evident the domino effect became. Fake medical drugs, internet scams, vice, fixed gambling, stolen cars, and smuggling were but a few of the ever-increasing list of ramifications of their investigations.

All of the authorities involved were extremely appreciative of Tim and Steve's efforts, which had produced such great results when their own combined efforts had been so unproductive because they'd been hamstrung by their own rules and regulations. There was, however, a Taiwanese fine chemicals company that regularly appeared in the accounts but wasn't listed as a subsidiary company. The company supplied various outlets across Africa and the investigators were certain that it was somehow involved but weren't sure how. Would Cecil be prepared to visit this company as a potential customer? His knowledge of the business, Taiwan, and the fact that he spoke Chinese would be invaluable.

Two days later Cecil was in the air heading for Taipei and looking forward to his clandestine mission and staying with his father for a few days as a base for his undercover operation. The old man's mood had immediately lifted when he heard that his son was on his way, and Cecil realized that although he never complained, he must be lonely since his mother's death several years ago. Perhaps he could persuade him to come and live in Kuala Lumpur?

At the same time that Cecil was thinking about his father, back in the UK Tim was abandoning his usual aplomb and showing the first signs of panic as he drove Fiona to the hospital whilst she coped with increasingly strong contractions. Fiona, on the other hand, was calm and was also managing to reassure Tim. She was faintly amused to see this normally self-contained SAS man totally out of his comfort zone but loved him for this unexpected new-found vulnerability.

Tim attempted the impossible by trying to drive sedately yet fast at the same time and breathed a sigh of relief as they eventually reached the hospital maternity unit. The midwife who greeted them seemed unbelievably calm, and he wondered if she really appreciated the seriousness of the situation. Fiona climbed into a wheelchair, and they made painfully slow progress to the labor suite where, after what seemed like an eternity to him, a doctor finally examined her. Apparently all was fine, and it would be some time yet before the baby was born.

This is going to be a long night.

In fact Fiona and the baby proved the doctor to be wrong, because within an hour Tim was holding his newborn son and, against all odds, this battle hardened soldier had tears rolling down his face. Childbirth had been an incredibly emotional experience for him, and he felt overwhelming love and admiration for this remarkable brave woman, his wife.

Fiona was very tired but otherwise fine and was utterly delighted with her longed for baby. She drifted off into a contented and well-earned sleep whilst Tim crept out of the room and proudly phoned everyone to inform them of the arrival of Benjamin, their son. Cecil received the good news by e-mail on his mobile as he arrived at Taipei and was able to send his congratulations by return. Even he had to admit that modern technology was amazing. A baby had been born less than half an hour ago on the other side of the world, yet he knew about it already. In his father's youth it would have taken weeks for a letter to travel by boat to announce the new arrival.

Taipei city is set out in a symmetrical plan, and in less than an hour his taxi turned into the familiar alleyway of his home. A brief knock on the door brought his father from the living room, and the old man's face was a picture of joy as he greeted him. Cecil noticed how stooped his father had become as he led him through to the cramped kitchen where he had prepared his favorite meal that his mother always used to make for him. It dawned on Cecil after the last year's ups and downs that these were the values that really mattered, and he vowed to spend more time with his father and to move him in with him if he would agree and thus make life easier and less lonely for him. He also made a mental note to arrange a bone density test as well. The spinal curvature had happened very quickly, and he wondered if his dad's diet had been going downhill recently now that he had nobody else to cater for.

Cecil's food tastes had become very sophisticated during his travels, and he'd forgotten how fantastic the simple food of home tasted. They lingered over their meal and then caught up with all of the local news until the old man finally fell asleep in the armchair, which for some years had been his prized possession. Cecil couldn't help smiling when he noticed that the chair was still encased in its protective plastic cover. He left him for an hour or so and then gently woke him, and they both headed for the comfort of bed.

The next few days were a strange melding of unfamiliar family life and work. Cecil took his father out to eat at several local restaurants and learnt to swallow his embarrassment as his father bragged about his son to everyone that they met. He hadn't realized that his father was so proud of him and shuddered at the thought of how close he'd come to shattering his father's illusions.

Posing as a potential buyer, Cecil had made an appointment with the sales manager at the Pharmzest factory to discuss the possible supply of bulking agents for some of his own pharmaceutical products. The factory was modern, surrounded by manicured gardens, close to the airport complex and producing highly competitive, quality product. The range that the factory had claimed to produce was genuine so, in view of this, Cecil requested a tour of the production facility to check on hygiene, quality control, and batch tracking. That would present no problems if he cared to return the following day. He didn't consider the delay to be suspicious as he would have done exactly the same at his facility to ensure that there were no indications of customers' identities. No point in giving away customers.

The return visit revealed a very efficient and well run production unit and, as he had guessed, no trace of any customer's identity. They produced a wide range of chemicals including stabilizers, bulking agents, surfactants, and nitrates, all of which seemed innocuous to him. His time in the plant was limited, and he couldn't see anything that caused concern, and in fairness he was allowed access to all departments. In fact the price of the product was so competitive that he actually placed a genuine order for delivery to his own factory.

That night he lay in bed unable to sleep, his mind replaying what he'd seen. There must be something that he'd missed but what? He ran through all the chemicals that he'd seen and the various types of plant equipment but still drew a blank.

If only David was here; he'd understand the chemistry. It's no good. I'm not going to sleep; there's nothing for it but to get out of bed, boot up the laptop, and e-mail everything to David for his opinion: chemicals, plant description, and countries supplied.

There was nothing else that he could do, so he shut down the computer and finally fell asleep, although on waking the following morning he wouldn't have known it. A stiff neck and fuzzy brain didn't really reflect a good night's rest, but things improved a little after his father produced cold herbal tea and a breakfast of fresh papaya. Cecil realized that he must have inherited his early rising habit from his father, and once his head cleared, he decided to explore his father's reaction to the possibility of moving to Malaysia. To his utter astonishment the suggestion was met with enthusiasm. "There's nothing to keep me here now, and if you can put up with me, it makes more sense for us to be close together; I'm not getting any younger you know."

Cecil breathed a sigh of relief; he'd expected to have a battle on his hands, but on the contrary, it was agreed that they would travel together the following day. An agent was appointed to pack up anything important (not that there was a lot!) and forward it to Kuala Lumpur and also to arrange the sale of the property.

Cecil checked his e-mails and eagerly opened the one from David which read:

DIOXINS—HIGHLY TOXIC DEFOLIATING AGENTS (AS USED IN VIETNAM) WHICH CAN BE USED TO WIPE OUT YOUR ENEMY'S CROPS AND COVER OR, IF USED AS POISONS, TO WIPE OUT YOUR ENEMY!—ALSO, USED IN MANUFACTURE OF EXPLOSIVES. -DAVID

So that's what they were supplying to that group of African countries; he'd better pass on David's speculations to Tim and Steve who could then fill in the various investigating agencies. Closing down the laptop, he felt a glow of satisfaction that his trip had been successful on both fronts.

That evening he took his father out for a final Taiwanese meal but assured him that he would be able to eat equally good Chinese food in Kuala Lumpur. Later on their return he helped to pack clothes and a few essentials ready for the following day's journey. He reassured his father that he could arrange for some of his favorite pieces of furniture, like the famous rocking chair, to be sent to Kuala Lumpur. The old man beamed and surprisingly was not the least regretful at leaving. Cecil felt a pang of guilt for not realizing that his father must have been desperately lonely. The flight home was a civilized mid-morning departure time, so there was no great panic at leaving. It was only when they entered the departure lounge that his father confided that this was the first time that he'd ever flown. It hadn't dawned on Cecil, who had become totally accustomed to air travel, that his father had only ever travelled within Taiwan and then only by train, bus, or taxi.

In fact, the experience proved to be a great success with his father who, apart from eating his meal, spent the whole time glued to the window even when there wasn't anything to see. The journey from Kuala Lumpur airport to the apartment was also a source of great entertainment, and Cecil felt that it was almost like having an excited child alongside him. However, he was gratified to see his father so cheerful and obviously without the least sadness at leaving his roots.

Back in the UK the doctor introduced himself to Fiona and informed her that she would shortly be going down to minor ops. theatre for a bit of "tidying up." She wouldn't be in theatre for long and the injection that he was giving her would be sufficient to keep her asleep whilst he sorted her out. He asked her to count to ten, and she only made it to four before darkness descended.

Tim had been busy at his office when he received the e-mail from Cecil and was cursing his luck that he'd left his laptop at home and with it the addresses of the various people that he needed to contact. There was no option but to slip home but that meant passing the hospital, so dad might as well drop in and see Benjamin. As he approached, the door of Fiona's room opened and an unconscious Fiona was being wheeled out on a trolley with Benjamin in a crib at her feet.

"Is anything wrong?"

"No, just taking her down to theatre for some tidying up."

Tim smiled acknowledgement, turned away and then something didn't seem right.

Doctors don't normally push patients around on trolleys and when do babies get taken to theatre with mothers.

Spinning around, he leapt on the "doctor" from behind and put excruciating pressure on the man's neck. "I think you better tell me what the hell you think you're up to, and who you're working for if you want to survive the next ten seconds!"

Just as he was about to permanently depart, the spluttering explanation was that he'd been hired to kidnap mother and baby and deliver them, in the private ambulance that he'd arrived in, to a nearby airfield. She'd only been given a sedative and would recover very soon. The fake doctor had no knowledge of the identity of his hirer and had been paid cash in advance at a pre-arranged drop-off point; the outstanding balance would be paid in the same way. Tim toyed with the idea of calling the police but concluded that it would take too long and that they would be handicapped by regulations.

He reapplied his neck hold, rendered the impostor unconscious, dragged him into a laundry store, stripped him of his bogus uniform and donned it himself, pocketing the ambulance keys. He made a quick mobile call to some Hereford-based chums, who now ran a mercenary security organization, to arrange a meeting at the airfield and then he pushed Fiona and babe back into their ward and rang the emergency bell before leaving.

The ambulance was parked right outside the fire exit, and Tim sped off for his airfield rendezvous whilst trying to fasten his safety belt. Fishing in his pockets, he managed to locate his mobile and called the hospital to make sure that Fiona had been found and was okay. They enquired who he was, and once he'd identified himself, they reluctantly said that there had been a slight problem but that she and the baby were fine; perhaps he would care to come in for a talk? Feeling great relief, the little boy in him came to the surface, and he couldn't resist putting the lights and siren on. Twenty minutes later he killed both to prevent announcing his arrival and was struck by the coincidence that Shobdon was where Ian had departed from and could have been where Fiona would have left as well.

The car park was right next to the clubhouse so he parked up and made his way to the enquiries desk. "I'm just delivering a patient for transfer, any idea who is supposed to pick her up?"

The guy behind the desk looked blank but said he'd check to see if anyone knew anything about it. After phoning around he eventually learnt from the control tower that an air ambulance plane from London was scheduled to land in ten minutes time. Tim thanked him and, as soon as he was back in the ambulance, phoned his friends who were dotted around the airfield and brought them up to speed. Right on schedule a twin-engine turboprop could be seen on final approach, and as all the observers around the airfield watched, it continued to make a perfect landing. The aircraft sped along the runway then slowed rapidly and the nose dipped as it came to a halt. The pilot made a hundred and eighty degree turn, back-tracked the runway, and was shaken rigid to see a Land Rover approaching from the opposite end; what he couldn't see was another one closing in from behind him sandwiching the plane to prevent any escape. Nor was he aware that both vehicles were full of armed personnel.

The plane turned off onto the grass taxiway, the pilot shut down both engines, and the propellers windmilled to a standstill. By this time the aircraft was surrounded by soldiers brandishing automatic weapons, and both pilots and the air traffic controller were in a state of shock. Tim took control and escorted the two pilots to a nearby hangar where questioning would commence. Meanwhile some of the remaining soldiers temporarily disabled the aircraft, to ensure that it couldn't return to its base, and ordered the air traffic controller to divert all incoming aircraft until further notice.

Both pilots turned out to be genuine employees of an air ambulance charter company and were just carrying out instructions to pick up a patient from a waiting ambulance. However, some quick phone call enquiries struck gold. The air charter company was a solely owned subsidiary of Tam's holding company, and the instructions for the flight had been e-mailed from Tam in the Congo. Alleluia! A direct criminal link to Tam at last!

The air traffic controller was informed that he could recommence aircraft movements. Two of the military technicians restored the aircraft to its operational state, and the pilots were given permission to fly back to London, after signing sworn statements with regard to their instructions and flight plan. They both looked relieved and were obviously very upset that they'd been used as pawns in the proposed ransom kidnapping. The Land Rovers were driven away from each end of the runway, and the sleek plane lined up, took off, and climbed out glinting in the sun as it headed southeast.

Tim thanked his mates who all agreed that they'd enjoyed a bit of activity, and he then retraced his steps to the hospital and his new family. Fiona was a bit shaken, Benjamin was still asleep and totally unaware, and the hospital administrator was cringingly apologetic. Tim let him off the hook but strongly suggested a review of security and then concentrated on cuddling and comforting Fiona.

By the end of the day she was back to her normal self but was aghast at the power that Tam had been able to wield from such a great distance away. Tim pointed out, consolingly, that this was the nail in the coffin for the man who had put them all at risk. Fiona was just so grateful that her husband had such useful friends that he could call on even though he'd left the army.

24

As Sheila put her office phone down, she tried to digest all that Cecil had just told her. Life with Steve certainly could never be described as dull; in fact her feet had hardly touched the ground since they'd met. Unfortunately her time for reflection was short lived as an e-mail memo from Robert Young informed her of an unscheduled meeting that had been called by Alec Jackson, who had apparently flown in from the States the previous evening. Half an hour later, she was sitting with Robert and several other key personnel waiting for Alec to put in an appearance. Typically, the CEO burst through the door, hurried to his seat at the head of the table, dumped his briefcase under the table, and waded straight in:

"I've been reviewing all of the different aspects of our business and have finally focused on our Electronics Division. In my opinion we are spread far too thinly. We have some aerospace involvement, but the majority of our work is reliant upon the medical field. There's nothing wrong with this, but we should be more involved in military and security contracts than we are.

"Let's look at security first: every government, bank, health service, police force, and IRS is terrified of their records being breached and what are we doing about it? Sweet F.A.! Well that's going to change.

"If we move on to the military scene, it becomes obvious that we are doing nothing whatever to tap into the vast amount of armed forces logistics contracts. We only look at the glamour business of guidance systems, but they only represent a fraction of the bread and butter work that is available to us.

"I have already had talks with our production people, and we could cope with additional work quite easily, and when the load becomes onerous, we will expand our manufacturing plants. However, rather than waste time getting up to speed, I am proposing to make a number of acquisitions of companies already involved in these areas and will then want to rationalize technical, production, and sales teams to optimize our effectiveness."

He then sat down as abruptly as he had started and almost as an afterthought added: "Any questions?"

There was a stunned shuffling of papers and a somewhat uncomfortable pause until Sheila broke the spell and asked if the other companies' sales managers would be under her authority or autonomous within their own company.

"You're a bright girl Sheila; I've given that considerable thought and decided to make you overall divisional sales director and the individual sales managers will report directly to you. You, in turn, will report directly to me. I will advise you of the various acquisitions as soon as they are complete."

There were a few minor enquiries from other staff members all of which were dealt with very quickly and then the "whirlwind" departed and the others returned to their various offices. Robert turned to Sheila with a wry smile; "He doesn't let the grass grow under his feet does he?"

She had to agree. Alec was a guy who got things done, and as she mulled over what he'd said, she couldn't argue with his logic that a wider spread of work would certainly make sense.

A week later and an e-mail from Alec informed her of the first takeover. The company concerned was a medium-sized outfit based in Texas that specialized in military and shipping logistics. She read through the attached report on the company and saw that it had achieved phenomenal growth for about five years but had plateaued in the last two. Alec's summary explained the tail-off in growth as being due to under-capitalization, and Tsang would be able to inject the necessary funding to take it into the next phase of growth.

It was to be another three weeks before details of the next merger came through, and this one was a company specializing in all forms of electronic security. Company expansion had been steady and they already had some enviable clients including the British Army. The company AI Electronics was based in India and the owners were keen to recoup the capital that they'd sunk into its start-up. The name rang a bell with Sheila, but she wasn't certain as to why. It was only when she mentioned it to Steve that evening that things slotted into place. They both had to admit that it was an outlandish coincidence that Tsang should end up owning Bruce's old company. An e-mail put Tim in the picture, as he was travelling to London to meet with the security services, and he was delighted; doubtless Tsang would increase sales and that in turn would increase his royalty dividends.

His meeting at the Security Services building overlooking the River Thames proved to be very interesting. The harvesting of incriminating evidence against Tam from all the authorities involved was complete. But how to get him out of the Congo? The consensus was that going through official channels would be unlikely to produce a result and, even if successful, could take years. If they did get him out and bring him to the UK, some flashy lawyer would plead for his human rights, and he'd probably end up escaping the net.

The afternoon's brainstorming evolved a plan of campaign that they all felt was likely to succeed. Some palms would be greased in the Congo to ensure that people were missing from their posts at appropriate times, and Belgian Special Forces, who still had good contacts in the Congo, accompanied by UK SAS, would spring the quarry out of Africa. He would then be spirited off to Shanghai where the Chinese security services were chomping at the bit to interview him. The various authorities along the way would oil the wheels of the operation wherever possible.

A date was set for the following week, after all arrangements had been made, to secure the services of a Hercules aircraft to transport the Special Forces into Africa and subsequently pick them up with their prisoner. The plane was ideal for short takeoff and landing duties yet could also accommodate all of the soldiers and equipment involved. Arrangements were made for the aircraft to land and re-fuel in southern Turkey on its return. The journey onwards to Shanghai would be in a military version of a business jet, and Tam would be accompanied by five army escorts.

In the ensuing few days, visas were processed and all the other necessary paperwork was produced for those involved, and Tim, as a reservist, was temporarily co-opted into the army again so that he could be part of the capturing party. This gesture was beyond his expectations, and he was thrilled that the powers that be had agreed to let him go. He phoned Fiona to tell her that he'd be staying in London until he left for Africa. She understood that he had to go but urged him to be very, very careful as his family loved and needed him very, very much. Tim melted; he'd never had anyone to say that to him when leaving on previous missions, and it gave him a warm feeling inside.

In no time at all he found himself back on familiar ground as he collected his kit at Brize Norton. The rest of the group arrived shortly afterwards, and after attending their briefing, they made their way to the waiting Hercules and climbed aboard. With the engines at full throttle the whole body of the aircraft vibrated and buzzed as it strained against its brakes like a huge tethered animal. Finally the pilot gave it its head, and in no time they were climbing away from the airbase at what seemed an impossible angle.

Meanwhile, in Africa Tam had settled in remarkably quickly. Initially he'd been devastated at having to leave China and was even more pissed off at having a lot of his operation closed down. Within two weeks, however, he'd realized that the bulk of his money was still intact and whatever he'd created previously he could do again. Virtually every official in this country was open to a bribe, so re-building his empire should be very straightforward, and he wasted no time in making himself and his wealth known to anyone who might be useful to him.

His first move had been to source and fly in Eastern European women. The socializing paid off, so the visas for the girls presented no problem. Government officials in the city always drank in one of the hotel bars after work and left with a minimum of two girls before eventually returning home to their wives and families. Tam had spotted a niche market; they invariably left with black girls, but the real prize was a white girl. He'd initially met with some resistance from local pimps but reassured them that he would not use black girls and would not, therefore, tread on their territory. What the dimwits didn't realize was that before long the demand would be entirely for white girls and that their girls would be sitting twiddling their thumbs.

So far so good. The next move would be to set up a legitimate business to act as a cover for his other dubious activities. After looking through the local business magazine, he settled on an air freight transport company that was listed as being for sale. A meeting with the French owner revealed that he was going back to Europe due to health problems and that he'd become jaded at the need to constantly deal with corruption. The offer of a cash sale secured a discounted purchase price, and Tam found himself the owner of several vans and, more importantly, easy access to the airport cargo facilities.

He'd also rented a very flash apartment on the outskirts of the city, and having lived there for a short time, he was convinced that it was the ideal position. Again an offer of cash secured the purchase of the property, and he now became a property owner once more. The adrenaline rush of starting a new business cut in, and he sent a taxi for one of his white girls to help him celebrate and to ride the adrenaline wave. His visitor was a beautiful Latvian girl with classic high cheekbones and jet-black hair. In spite of the heat and humidity, she was wearing high-heeled boots.

She accepted a vodka and tonic but refused a line, so Tam also poured himself a drink but followed it with a snort. By the time they reached the bedroom, he was high as a kite and the sex was over very quickly, but her dominatrix role continued until she was exhausted as well as him. She left with the best money she'd ever earned, and he made a firm decision to "rescue" this girl and keep her for himself; in fact he would move her in.

The Hercules had been flying just above tree-top level to avoid radar detection and finally made an impossibly steep approach to a disused runway that had been located previously by a high flying reconnaissance plane. Reverse thrust slammed in, and they came to a shuddering stop in an unimaginably short distance. The raiding team bundled out down the ramp and silently made their way towards flashing side lights of a vehicle at the edge of the airstrip. The driver greeted them in broken English; he was a Belgian "sleeper" and was thrilled to be activated. Earlier he'd liberated one of Tam's vans from the airport complex at Brazzaville and the irony was not wasted on the other men. Locating Tam's home had been easy as the Chinese millionaire's flashing of cash had received its fair share of local publicity and rumor.

It was exactly 2:00 a.m. that all hell let loose. The stun grenade that had been lobbed through the open ventilator had exploded with a deafening crash; there was a blinding flash and the room filled with smoke. Tam struggled to wake and to organize his brain into some semblance of comprehension of what was happening but, before anything registered, strong arms grabbed him from behind, his arms were pinioned, and a hood pulled over his head. He could hear other people in the room, but nobody spoke; then he was dragged out and roughly frog-marched to a waiting stolen van, strangely enough, one of his own.

Coughing violently from the fumes, he landed heavily on the van floor, and immediately several people sat on top of him, and without a word spoken they careened off towards the airstrip. En route his hands were handcuffed behind his back and his shoes were removed and searched for any weapon; none was found. For the first time in his life Tam experienced real fear; fear for his own safety but also that deep-seated fear of a control freak who finds themselves totally out of control.

The vehicle skidded to a halt, and Tam was blindly dragged to his feet and, with what was obviously a gun, prodded between his shoulder blades and propelled up the ramp into the bowels of the Hercules. He felt himself being strapped in and for the first time a voice said, "Don't kid yourself that this is for your safety; it's just that if there's an emergency, we don't want you rolling around and injuring us!"

The reply in Mandarin roughly translated to "Sod off you bastard."

But what Tam wasn't prepared for was an equally quick reply in immaculate Mandarin: "If I hear one more word out of you, believe me, I'll enjoy doing to you what your minions have done to so many of your victims."

Tim wished that he could have seen the astonishment on Tam's face for the little sod must realize that he couldn't even hide behind his language any longer.

The take-off noise, vibration, and incredible climb angle all built up Tam's anxiety, and his adrenaline level was even greater than his usual cocaine assisted norm. As the pilot leveled off at a low level altitude, Tim removed the hood from his prisoner's head.

"So that's what the lowest form of life looks like."

"Who are you?"

"Someone you're going to remember for the rest of your life and wish that you'd never crossed."

"Where are you taking me?"

"Back home to your roots where your government wants to talk to you and is prepared to offer you free board and lodging."

Tim went forward to join his team and congratulate them on a well-oiled operation, leaving Tam in silence to build up his anxiety and feelings of isolation. Although it wasn't the most direct routing, the plane set heading over the sea to clear the country's radar network, and they were finally able to climb to a realistic altitude, and the flight became much smoother as a result.

To everyone's relief the rest of the trip was uneventful. The tired pilot was grateful that the approach to Incerlik had the luxury of full instrument assistance, landing lights, and a ten thousand foot runway unlike the Congolese airstrip. He greased the plane onto the runway, and once disembarked, the team and their prisoner were escorted to accommodation for rest and sleep before the next stage of the journey to Shanghai. Obviously Tam, unlike the team, had the exclusivity of a military police cell to relax in.

Tim woke having slept the sleep of exhaustion with the realization that he was glad this wasn't his everyday life any longer and wondering how his lovely wife and baby were. He mustered the rest of his crew, and after a hearty breakfast courtesy of their hosts, they escorted a handcuffed, disconsolate Tam to the small jet waiting on the tarmac. With preflight checks complete they were given immediate clearance for takeoff, and within a few minutes, the sleek sand colored aircraft scythed its way eastwards climbing to forty-two thousand feet where there was a minimum of traffic. This time the group was able to catnap in comfort and relative silence, and they relished the unaccustomed luxury.

The flight was smooth at that altitude, and after an hour or so, Tam had dozed off. This gave Tim the opportunity to closely look him over. Surprisingly the guy wasn't particularly imposing: short, slightly overweight with a round puffy face, definitely no screen idol. On the other hand, the clothes were expensive as were the loafers and the Omega watch. It just showed the power of money and of having a hold on people. He too closed his eyes and drifted off again.

Foston's sales figures were up by eighty percent on the previous six months, and Steve was delighted; what's more, without having a partner to pay or consider, he was able to award himself a pay raise. The estate agent in the UK had e-mailed him to advise that they'd received an offer of the asking price for the cottage, and he'd told them to accept it and make all the necessary arrangements for the sale. It seemed strange that he felt no sorrow at the prospect of losing his onetime "pride and joy." A few moments contemplation later his thoughts cleared, and he concluded that the cottage was a past chapter of his life. He now knew that his future focused around Kuala Lumpur and Sheila; priorities should be people not places or possessions.

Work-wise Steve was inundated, and after talking it over with Sheila, he agreed that they needed additional staff to cope with growth. The decision was taken to employ a full-time manager in the UK, and interviewing would take place on his return to the UK. The job description would cover the handling of all of the daily routine office work and liaising with Tim whenever he was working for Foston. Thanks to computers the applicant would be able to work from home and there would be no need for the additional overhead of an office. Steve felt a sense of relief as this would enable him to concentrate solely on sales.

Sheila too was overloaded with work thanks to the newly acquired companies and, with Robert's agreement, had taken on a PA by the name of Mavis. The lady was highly efficient, dumpy, didn't wear makeup, and had no dress sense whatever. Steve's comment, after first meeting her, was that she wasn't a patch on Cecil's old PA. Sheila laughingly said that it was to prevent him from being tempted.

They treated themselves to dinner at a trendy restaurant to celebrate the easing of work pressure, and it was during the meal that a text message arrived from Tim:

CARGO SUCCESSFULLY PICKED UP AND DELIVERED.

"It really is amazing the way that guy gets things done."

"Yes, but Fiona must have been worried out of her mind. I know I would have been if it had been you."

They raised a glass to Tim, Fiona, and baby Benjamin and relished the moment wondering what the outcome would be.

In Shanghai Tam had been unceremoniously dragged from the plane, shoved into China's version of a Land Rover and taken to an interrogation unit. The building was featureless with very few windows, and it was with a sinking feeling that he entered the huge double doors. The admission officer examined a photograph in his folder, looked at Tam, then nodded, and he was abruptly taken to a cell. The door slammed behind him, and he surveyed his new penthouse: one bare lightbulb, one wooden bed with straw mattress, a bucket, and not even a chair. Not really the sort of accommodation that he had been accustomed to

Suddenly loud music started playing from a concealed loud-speaker and occasionally the light went off. Thirty-six hours later without food, water, or a wink of sleep the door opened, and he was taken to an interrogation room along the corridor. The two soldiers escorting him thrust him through the door, and a smartly uniformed officer slammed him into a chair and started firing questions at him:

"Have you ever taken drugs?"

"No."

"Have you ever dealt in drugs?"

"No."

"Were you involved in vice?"

"No!"

A side door opened and in walked an elderly man in civilian clothes but with a military bearing. Savoring the moment that he'd longed for, he looked straight at the indignant prisoner and retorted: "That's not what my daughter has testified!"

Tam had no idea who this ranting old man was or what he was talking about. The door opened again, and there stood Topaz, her eyes flashing with anger. She turned to face him head on, and he could see the hatred and scorn in her face as she pointed at him and said, "Yes, that's him!"

She turned her back on him and left with her father. Too late he understood the truth of the adage: "Hell hath no fury like a woman scorned."

His interrogators returned to the job in hand. More and more questions and each answer accompanied by a beating.

After what seemed like an age, he was dragged back to his cell and then unceremoniously dumped on the floor. The door slammed shut behind him again. His brain ached as much as his body, and he longed for sleep, but now realized that it was definitely not on the immediate agenda.

He must have drifted into some form of sleep when he was once again taken to the interrogation room. Deep down, he knew that he was sunk without trace but managed to keep denying everything until, after a further twenty-four hours of food and sleep deprivation, his resistance was shot and he admitted everything. Provisionally he was charged with drug trafficking, living off immoral earnings, and internet fraud; these were charges that they could immediately substantiate, others would follow. A court hearing date was set and e-mails beamed their way around the world triggering off even more searches into the distant corners of Tam's murky empire.

Topaz's father still had some friends within military intelligence, and they had no compunction, on behalf of their old friend, in dealing out the thrashing of a lifetime to Tam when he returned to his cell. It was hard to tell whether loss of consciousness or sleep came first, but when he finally awoke and managed to open his one working eye, he wished that he hadn't. He checked his limbs to see if they worked. Arms and legs seemed intact, but most of his fingers were unusable and the pain from his right shoulder didn't augur well for his collarbone. Unconsciousness finally embraced him with more mercy than he deserved. However, on waking he was now left to contemplate his fate until the day of the hearing.

The days dragged interminably, the food was appalling, and the stench in his cell was overwhelming as the guards regularly "forgot" to empty his latrine bucket.

25

Steve had come to the conclusion that Sheila was his idea of perfection: a woman who always looked wonderful, was a great listener, highly intelligent, independent, and a fantastic lover. What more could a man want. They'd recently had a great time making their mark on the new apartment, and for the first time in his life, Steve had actually enjoyed shopping. Occasionally in his quiet moments his mind drifted back to Jane, and he felt a tinge of guilt at finding it increasingly difficult to conjure up a picture of her face in his mind's eye.

I suppose life moves on.

After a longer than expected delay since Tim's text, Steve was relieved to hear Tim's voice on the phone. "Sorry I haven't been in touch, but I didn't trust the Chinese phone line to be secure and I didn't want anything to screw up what we'd already achieved. I'm on my way back and calling from our military base at Incerlik; I'm happy with the security standard of the line here, because we put it in. Tam's in custody and initially has been charged with drug trafficking, living off immoral earnings, and internet fraud, but believe me there's a lot more to follow. He'll be an old man if he ever sees the light of day again.

"The pick up went without a hitch, no injuries, and my chaps were brilliant. I'm just thrilled that I've had the opportunity to clip this bastard's wings; this had become personal in a big way. Hopefully by the time we've finished, he'll be stopped from creating any more misery. I'll be back in the UK tomorrow and will ring you if there's any more news."

Steve rang Cecil and brought him up to date, and they both agreed that Tim had done a fantastic job, and that it looked as though all of their efforts were going to pay off. Cecil went on to say that it was an ill wind, because he'd just taken delivery of his order from the Taiwanese chemical company, and it was ahead of schedule, of excellent quality, and he'd definitely use them again.

Sheila's reaction to the news was one of relief, and she hoped that the whole business would be cleared up quickly, so that she and her man could concentrate totally on their work and on their life together. Somehow their feet didn't seem to have touched the ground recently. In spite of all the hassle, it was hard for her to take in how easily Steve had blended into her life, and it could only get better with more time.

Back in Herefordshire, the door opened and a voice boomed out, "Return of the wanderer!"

Fiona rushed into the hallway and flung herself at her man and held him so tightly that he had trouble breathing. She started to sob convulsively blurting out, "I was so terrified that we'd lost you. Don't you ever, ever leave us like that again!"

Deep down though, she knew that if called upon, he'd go again. She had seen how alive he'd been recently and had to accept that the soldier in him was a deeply rooted essential part of his life. He held her close until eventually she cried herself out, and it dawned on him that he'd never seen Fiona cry like this before; she must have been very frightened. As calmness descended, he made his way to the nursery and gloated over his sleeping son and heir who had that angelic look that sleeping babies invariably have, but obviously his was the most special.

Cecil's business, like Foston's, was expanding fast. The elimination of the bogus competitor had resulted in all of the original contracts being re-awarded to him, and new referral business was also coming in on a daily basis. The buzz of commerce had been missing from his life for far too long, and he relished getting back into the swim and the challenge of building a large concern from nothing.

Living with his father could easily have been problematic, but in fact it had turned out remarkably well. It was just like having a quiet housekeeper; meals were ready when he returned from work, the apartment was clean and tidy, and the only downside was the afternoon phone calls demanding to know his exact time of arrival home to ensure that the meal wasn't spoilt. He wasn't accustomed to having to answer to anyone, but he'd quickly realized that this was a very small price to pay for having a father who had shed at least ten years. Gone was the frail old man image, and in its place was a younger looking, more mentally alert, and seven kilo heavier companion. There was also good news from the consultant who'd confirmed that there were no bone density problems, just inadequate calorie intake.

Most entrepreneurs have compulsive personalities, and if they hadn't been workaholics, they would probably have been alcoholics or gamblers. Cecil was now fully aware of his compulsions, but realized that he must never gamble again; business was his only safe outlet. In his journey of self-discovery he had also finally admitted to himself that he'd led an asexual life of denial rather than admit that, given free rein, his preference was for men and not women. He had no idea how his father would take this news, but he wasn't prepared to start their time together dishonestly.

That evening with dinner out of the way and fortified by a good bottle of wine, he broached the subject with trepidation. To his astonishment his new-style parent informed him that he'd always suspected as much due to the absence of girlfriends and that the only surprise was that it had taken so long to surface. So far as he was concerned the only thing that mattered was that Cecil was happy. The reaction from all of his friends turned out to be exactly the same; most had commented that although he wasn't camp, his obsession with detail, fine clothes, and the absence of any woman in his life had led them to naturally assume that he was gay. Phew! What a relief! He could at last be himself.

The following morning he crept around as quietly as possible so as not to disturb his father. He had to leave very early to prepare for a meeting with a supplier. He made himself a cup of tea before leaving and, just as he was leaving, he spotted a note on the breakfast bar:

Cecil,

This is your life and your home that you've been kind enough to share with me. I am more grateful than you will ever know. I could not have a better or more caring son, and if there are any people that you feel sufficiently strongly about to want to bring home to stay, I would be very hurt if you didn't.

Love

Dad

Not surprisingly he walked to his car with a lump in his throat but with joy in his heart. There was perhaps a morsel of regret that he hadn't previously credited his father with such understanding and compassion.

It just shows it's never too late to learn.

26

Unlike those of Europe and America, the Chinese legal system operates phenomenally quickly, which is probably more humane for both the wrongdoer and the wronged. No years of wrangling as in the West. In truth the ideal system probably lies somewhere in the middle of the two extremes.

Tam's case turned out to be an exception to the rule as several months had dragged by before the hearing date was finalized. The delay had been due to worldwide investigations into his activities and had resulted in yet another crop of charges. So, by the time he entered the courtroom, his injuries had healed, although the deformities in his fingers would be a lifetime reminder of his interrogation.

The proceedings bore little resemblance to a European court, and as the list of charges was read out, nobody was left under any illusion that the prisoner would walk free. Tam was in prison fatigues, stripped of fine clothes, jewellery, and dignity and was no longer an imposing figure. The evidence against him was indefensible and his "legal representative" made only a feeble effort to offer pleas of mitigation. The prosecution was quickly allowed to cross-examine and in no time had tied him up in words and shredded any defense that he tried to offer on his own behalf.

The judge speedily summed up all of the charges and asked Tam how he pleaded. "Not guilty" was the reply, which produced uproar in the courtroom. The judge demanded silence and made his views very clear before finding him guilty. Sentencing was withheld for two weeks pending final investigations; in the meantime he would remain in custody. No luxury of a jury here, although in all honesty the outcome would probably have been the same. Tam was led away in handcuffs, a disconsolate figure, but all those involved could only focus on the misery that he had generated around the world and not on the misery that he now justifiably faced.

The news filtered through from Shanghai to Tim who in turn relayed it to his friends. Everyone, both friends and the various authorities, breathed a sigh of relief that they had finally clipped Tam's wings and taken him out of action. In the ensuing two weeks, prior to sentencing, Brazzaville had made token diplomatic complaints to the British and American governments, but in truth they had no idea who had spirited the undesirable alien from their shores. What's more, they didn't really care; it was just that their pride had been ruffled. So, no one was surprised that after the initial rumblings nothing further was heard from the Congolese authorities.

Tim had been waiting patiently for the Chinese to let him have details of Tam's sentencing, but the silence had been deafening. In fact it was Steve who spotted a small item in the Telegraph World News section, which was little more than an announcement concerning the execution of Tam, a corrupt trader, who had brought disgrace upon The People's Republic.

There was no further elaboration but in fact Tam had been executed by firing squad without all of the final investigations being completed. In reality the government had heard enough to warrant imposing the death sentence, and you can only kill a man once. Cecil, Tim, and Steve were incredulous at how quickly justice had been dealt out, but with their knowledge of his activities none of them could muster any regret.

An American firm of forensic accountants had been engaged during the investigation, and they were now given the task of closing down Tam's various businesses and salvaging what money that they could. Drugs were seized and destroyed, but partly as a result of a suggestion from Cecil, the various government IRS departments agreed that the cash and proceeds from the sale of assets should go into a trust for the rehabilitation of drug addicts.

Cecil had pointed out that most of Tam's wealth had come from illegal drug dealing and that it would be obscene if the IRS were seen to profit from such activities. Surely, the people to benefit should be those who had been ensnared by Tam and whose lives had been wrecked. The argument was persuasive; the IRS knew he had them by the short and curlies, and as a result the trust had been set up with a very healthy bank deposit.

With Tam out of the way all three settled back into their own business routines. Back in the UK Steve's estate agent and lawyer had completed the sale of the cottage. His mortgage was paid off, and the equity gave his bank balance a healthy blood transfusion.

Sheila and Steve arrived home from a hard day at Tsang, and while she started to prepare their meal, he opened a bottle of wine and switched on the TV. The newsreader rambled on about economic talks in America and then started a report of an explosion that had totally destroyed a nightclub in Kuala Lumpur. Scores of people had been killed and many more had been injured. Steve was reminded of the Bali bombing scenes that he'd seen on TV several years previously. The report stated that no group had yet claimed responsibility, but it was thought to be the work of some Middle Eastern radical organization.

News reports so frequently show atrocities that one becomes desensitized, and at this point Steve had virtually mentally switched off when he heard the reporter mention that the building had been owned by the well-known Malaysian conglomerate, Tsang Corp. Both he and Sheila were rooted to the spot as the reporter explained that the nightclub's owners had leased the ground floor and that it was not certain if the attackers had targeted the club to wreak havoc with Malaysian tourism or whether it was a direct attack against Tsang Corp.

Sheila knew that the company had a large property portfolio but wasn't aware of individual buildings involved; it wasn't her remit. However, within minutes her mobile rang, and Robert requested that she return to the office, because they needed to plan a response to the press. The meal was abandoned, and they both drove back to work in silence.

Robert was already there when they arrived, and he beckoned them to follow him to his office. Sheila had never seen him look so grave, and as he shut the door, his opening comment was "I think we may be in very deep shit."

The company public relations officer joined them, after a few minutes, and gave them a short briefing. Apparently the Security Service, Police, and Fire Service had all liaised and the combined opinion was that Tsang was the target rather than the Malaysian government. Their reasoning was that there were many more high profile targets within the city if the attackers really wanted to damage tourism.

The logic was undeniable, but initially none of those present could offer a reason as to why Tsang should be targeted. However, after an hour of brainstorming, the pieces of the jigsaw started to fit:

Sheila worked for Tsang, and she had a relationship with Steve who was also associated with Tsang.

Tim worked for Steve on occasions and, therefore, indirectly for Tsang.

Cecil had worked for Tsang.

Tsang Corp. had a number of sensitive contracts for American companies involved with defense.

The worrying aspect of these links was that whoever was behind the bombing knew a great deal about all concerned, their private lives, and their various roles in Tsang Corp.

The meeting concluded that their press release should play down any link to Tsang; there was no point in feeding publicity to the enemy's propaganda machine. It was agreed that all of the people involved should be informed immediately but cautioned not to talk individually to the media. All statements should be made by the company PR department. Everyone exchanged mobile phone numbers, so that they could share any developments at the drop of a hat, and with that the meeting dispersed.

Fiona was clearing the breakfast dishes when she took the call for Tim; she knew what the look on his face meant. Fifteen minutes later a helicopter landed in their paddock, and looking rueful, Tim was whisked off to London. She realized that it must be something very important, as there was no way that he'd have willingly left her and Benjamin again so soon.

The helicopter landed on a pontoon moored on the Thames, and a waiting launch completed the journey to Vauxhall Bridge. It seemed no time since he'd last walked through the entrance of Britain's Thameside security headquarters. He wasn't an admirer of modern architecture but made an exception where this building was concerned; it was functional but actually looked attractive.

The briefing was an eye-opener, disturbing, and totally unexpected. Britain's security listening station (GCHQ) at Cheltenham had monitored a number of messages that linked several radical organizations from Yemen, Saudi Arabia, and Pakistan, all of whom had been involved with the Kuala Lumpur bombing. As was so often the case, it was doubtful if one overall organizing body could be identified so the usual somewhat nebulous term "Al Qaeda" had been used as a label.

Some of the disparate groups were known to British Intelligence; others were not and were now being investigated in their various countries of operation. Apparently Tsang Corp. had been specifically mentioned in a number of intercepted messages and likewise the individuals' names with the one exception of Cecil Liu.

Once again Major Foster was asked if he would head up the investigating team and also be prepared to travel to the Middle East, because of his contacts in that area and his fluency in Arabic. There wasn't a moment's hesitation in agreeing; they were all at risk, Fiona and Benjamin included, if this business wasn't sorted out. He called Fiona to let her know that he was going to have to stay in London to head up an operation, but that she was not to worry as he was not doing anything risky. She sighed and simply replied that she reckoned she'd have to get used to this but that he was to be very careful.

The first breakthrough came from an unexpected source: Shanghai. Much to everyone's incredulity the Chinese had completed all of their enquiries, albeit after Tam's execution, and had found that a number of his companies had Arab partners. The countries where these companies operated required a native to be a fifty-one percent shareholder. The shutting down of a number of the businesses was inevitably hurting the Arab partners financially. Although the identity of the shareholders was made available, it didn't mean anything as they were, almost without exception, local lawyers acting as nominees.

Tim was provided with false papers and passport and the cover of being a golf course irrigation consultant. It was felt that he would have credibility and would have access to most of the Arab countries with this story, as they were all competing to offer the best championship courses. The next day's flight to Oman departed on time, and as Tim left the aircraft at Muscat, the hair dryer–like heat hit him in the face. A military staff car screeched to a halt on the tarmac, and he was quickly side-stepped through the VIP arrivals hall and, with a minimum of formality, decanted onto the pavement outside the arrivals hall. This time a more luxurious staff car was waiting, and he was greeted by Jonathan Miller, a Major, with whom he'd shared a number of hairy assignments in the past. Jonathan had been filled in with the rough details of the mission on a secure phone line. It was made clear to Tim that the evening was already spoken for and was going to be a mixture of a fair amount of reminiscence, a reasonable proportion of catching up, and a hell of a lot of alcohol. There was no arguing, so he decided to go with the flow.

As the evening progressed and before they became too pissed, it became clear that Jonathan had been doing his homework. A number of the radical group leaders' locations had been identified, and although there were several countries involved, it was apparent that the main activities were in Yemen and Saudi. Up to date photographs had been obtained where possible with the obvious qualification that individuals would change their appearance if they suspected that they were being tailed. Most of the photos were of respectable looking business types. There was also an accompanying profile with each photograph covering all known details on the person concerned and in most cases the background tied up with the image. Also, there was a separate file of satellite photos of the terrorists' homes.

"Jonathan, I can't thank you enough; this will definitely give me a head start."

"Good. So now let's get down to the serious business of enjoying ourselves. It's been a long time!"

Before setting off the following morning, nursing a king-size hangover, Tim had a meeting with the senior intelligence officer and asked him what he knew of the people involved. The information was sketchy, but there was one group that kept cropping up that called itself: "The Assassins of Satan."

Little was known about them, except that a number of the intercepted messages originated from Riyadh. There were no actual addresses but a number of coordinates. Tim decided that this was as good a place to start as anywhere and hitched a lift on a military transport plane heading for Saudi.

Encoded messages had preceded his arrival, and yet again he was fast-tracked through the airport and taken to a consular building that fronted British espionage activity. A protracted meeting with a "Cultural Attaché" was less than helpful in shedding more light on the "Assassins of Satan" but did give a firm address for the location that had produced the most intercepted messages. It was agreed to locate a covert listening vehicle with directional microphones as close to the building as possible. Tim hoped that modern technology would make this viable, as he was not willing to risk tipping off the group by trying to install bugs within the building.

As it happened, the reception was acceptable, and they were able to record all conversations emanating from the house. Inevitably the vast majority were of no value whatever, but various snippets started to build a picture of the outreaches of the group.

After one particularly long, hot day Tim was luxuriating in a soothing bath at his hotel whilst listening to the BBC World News. The US president had made veiled threats yet again about

Iran and, not surprisingly, had upset a variety of Arab countries. There'd been a number of predictable responses, some measured and others more aggressive.

The phone rang jolting Tim out of his warm reverie. A staff member from the Consular Office read an e-mail transcript to him:

"America seeks world domination and exploits the world's oil and mineral supplies. America has nuclear capability yet resents any other country having the same defenses. The West is a puppet of America and hides behind its skirts. America and the West are the personification of Satan and we, the Assassins of Satan, will bring about its downfall."

This was the message received by the BBC and was the first time that the organization had identified itself; he felt sure that they were angling to be contacted. Experience told him that radical groups like this could only survive with the nurture of publicity, and he was certain that they would contact either a newspaper or radio station within the next forty-eight hours. Through his security contacts he had a message sent out to all media outlets to contact a secure number if they were approached. He'd informed London and it was now a waiting game.

Contrary to his expectations nothing happened for three days and then not as expected. The listening post van, disguised as a telephone installation vehicle and parked near the terrorist building, reported that a number of people were congregating and it looked as though there was about to be a major meeting. Fortunately Tim's hotel was not far away, so he hurried to join the guys with the earphones and was just in time to see three of the people in his portfolio of suspects arrive. He just had time to grab a paper cup of surprisingly good coffee before the meeting started.

The conversation was in Arabic which was no surprise, but what was a surprise was that the voice was that of a young female. None of the photos in Tim's file were of a woman, so this one had slipped through the net. However, the officer in the observation van had seen her enter the building and was able to identify her as Lisa Khan and, as an aside, "A bit of alright!" Apparently Lisa was an academic political activist of

Pakistani origin whose views had got her noticed by the security services, but who to date had not caused any major problems. She had written articles with an anti-American slant for Amnesty International and various other organizations and had regularly appeared on TV. As the meeting got under way, they were relieved that the directional mikes were working well and reception was sharp and clear.

From the onset it was apparent that Lisa was in charge, and her first comments surprisingly referred to Tam:

"Most of you had at least heard of Tam even if you hadn't met him. Well although he was potentially very useful to us, because of his worldwide contacts, he became somewhat of a liability due to his inability to keep his trousers zipped. He is now of no use to us at all as his business empire has been shut down, and he's managed to get himself executed into the bargain."

There was a stunned gasp from those in the room before she added, "This was our first major setback."

Then she turned her attention to one of her group around the table, Ali Aziz, a known troublemaker originally from Yemen, and tore into him for his stupidity in bombing the Kuala Lumpur nightclub.

"Don't you idiot men ever listen to anything that I say? You ask me to lead you in your mission and then totally ignore what I say!

"You've done things your way for year after year and look where it's got you—NOWHERE! You are still living in the dark ages. Don't you realize that you will never have as many weapons as the US and the West? Okay, you will be a constant thorn in their flesh, but you will never bring them down. If you do things my way, we will bring the West to its knees, and that's what you want isn't it? So let's get things clear; if anyone does their own thing again, I am out of this and you are on your own. Is that clear?"

There was a general murmuring of consent mixed with overtones of discomfort. Those listening in the van were amazed that these hard-headed terrorists were prepared to take such a dressing down from and be led by a woman. The Middle East is not renowned for giving women positions of power let alone being dictated to by them.

From the surveillance team's point of view the good news was that they had now discovered the identity of the Kuala Lumpur bomber.

Lisa continued, "You all know my views, and history is on my side. Just look at what happened with the IRA and Britain. Violence against Britain only hardened attitudes of both government and the public against the IRA; exactly the opposite of what they were trying to achieve. What finally brought the government into talks with the IRA was when they were hit in their pocket. The 'troubles' were bringing the Northern and Southern Ireland tourist economies to their knees and inward investment was totally drying up. The cost of pouring money into Northern Ireland was becoming prohibitive and the government was forced to talk to and offer respect to the IRA.

"So let's recap so that none of you are operating in ignorance: The Middle East has in the past given the world mathematics, geometry, navigation, and astronomy, yet America and its puppets look down their noses at us. Once they discovered oil here they courted us for their own ends, but believe me they will dump us when oil and gas are exhausted.

"My aim is to use all of our resources to support the electronics, pharmaceutical, automotive, and other industries in the Far East in competition with the USA. This will bring their own manufacturers to their knees due to their higher labor costs, and at the same time we will aim to dry up the availability of oil from the Middle East. That way we will strangle their economy; we will strangle Satan. Only then will they listen to us and treat us with the respect that we deserve.

"I need your assurance that nobody will act individually. If we are to succeed, it will be as a group-led mission not by the efforts of an ill-advised individual hero.

"Tomorrow I will send you an encoded e-mail outlining your individual tasks. Although you will see that we each have our specific roles to play, you must realize that our strength is dependent on our working as a team. We will meet here again a week from today to formulate our next moves, and for you to discuss any queries that you may have concerning your tasks."

The rest of the meeting was spent outlining which companies would be financially assisted to set up in competition to America, although, much to the disappointment of the listening crew, the source of money for investment was not revealed.

Several hours later Tim was chairing a Security Services meeting to review the results of the day's eavesdropping. There was general agreement that Miss Khan was a powerful, charismatic, and dangerous new element in Middle Eastern politics, and whilst everyone agreed that the move away from violence was to be welcomed, they could also see the devastating effectiveness of Lisa's approach if she was capable of bringing it off. The whole balance of world power would change and the US would cease to be the superpower. There were several wry comments that this might be an improvement, and one wag volunteered that Bush and Blair would have eventually achieved something worthwhile after all.

Tim requested all information available on Lisa Khan, because she was obviously the brains of the outfit. They agreed to keep listening in to and recording any conversations from the group and also discreetly contacted the ISP that Lisa was using, and a bug was attached to the phone line of Lisa's building. It was agreed that no contact would be made with the now known bomber, Aziz, as they didn't want to scare off the whole group; they'd keep him on ice and pick him up when they were ready.

In the meantime messages were flashing around the world with a view to trying to profile the new first lady of terrorism; but was it terrorism if no violence was involved?

The pooled information from all of the agencies involved became available towards the end of the week and, for the first time, gave them some idea of whom they were up against.

Lisa had been born in Karachi to a mother from an affluent land-owning family and a consultant physician father. The family had moved to London during her early teens, and after leaving school, she had attended the London School of Economics where she gained a first class degree. After university she'd worked for a couple of NGO's and had then become involved with a pair of London-based Pakistani radicals who appeared to have been responsible for raising her awareness of the "Satanic" role of the West.

Lisa had attended a conference on "Solutions to Third World Poverty" in Geneva two years previously, had met Tam who was the keynote speaker on the subject of "Investment in Underprivileged Countries" (obviously feathering his own nest). It must have been at this time that they'd decided to liaise, because their association could be of mutual benefit. He would have had an eye to the profits that could be made, and she would have seen his money as the solution to directing trade away from the West. For the last eighteen months she'd been living with her boyfriend, Sharif, at the address where the meetings were being held. Sharif was the son of a wealthy fruit exporter and had been brought up in Damascus but had left Syria for Saudi to finish his education. He had subsequently eked out a living as a freelance journalist for various Arab publications, although with the family wealth it seemed unlikely that he was solely dependent on this source of income. His articles were well written, could not be considered radical, but nevertheless, they displayed a subtle anti-western flavor. It was hard to see where he fitted into the picture. Other than that there was nothing significant in his profile except for regular meetings with a number of exceedingly wealthy Saudi businessmen, all of whom were business contacts of his father.

His first love was computers, and by all accounts he was some sort of computer prodigy, if there is such a thing. As a student he'd hacked into the university computer and altered the CVs of all of his lecturers and gave some of them very lurid pasts. He'd nearly got sent down at the time and only escaped through the combined effects of promising never to do it again, some string pulling by his father, and a large donation to university funds. Inevitably he'd become a student hero, and the incident had entered into college student mythology. It appeared that nowadays, when not working, he spent most of his time and money on computers, which one of the guys pointed out didn't leave too much time for Lisa.

Aziz was a totally different kettle of fish, an ill-educated Yemeni hothead who'd been in regular trouble with the police for violence at various demonstrations. He'd attended a known training camp in Pakistan and was considered to be unstable and extremely dangerous. It was not known how Lisa had come in contact with him, but it would appear that she was already re-gretting his involvement.

Tim thanked everyone for their input and closed the meet-ing by suggesting that they re-convene the following week af-ter Lisa's next meeting. Obviously, if there were any major developments beforehand, everyone would be kept informed. As the door of his temporary office closed, he sat back in his chair and took stock.

The pieces are starting to slot into space, and most impor-tantly, we've identified the weakest link in their organization.

27

Steve was woken early by an irate phone call from a Kuwaiti hospital administrator. He had supplied a network of Tsang state-of-the-art intensive care equipment, and the machines had functioned faultlessly until yesterday. Today, however, there had been a total catastrophic failure, which would have been fatal for a number of patients but for the vigilance and skill of the anesthetist on duty.

Shocked into wakefulness as the details seeped into his struggling brain, Steve said that he would get technicians there as soon as was humanly possible. In the meantime he would arrange for the technical manager to contact them to see if he could offer any instant advice. He rang off and immediately contacted the technical department to forewarn them, but they had already been called from Kuwait. Not just Kuwait but Ankara, Dubai, and a number of American hospitals all of whom were experiencing the same problems. He could sense panic spreading virus-like throughout the department, and it was obvious that they had no clue what the cause was; this was well-tried equipment that had never malfunctioned previously.

Bad news travels fast, and it was less than an hour later when the press rang the company after receiving a tip-off. The public relations officer did his best to fend them off, but this was a big emotive story, and the hounds had scented blood. He was certain that it wouldn't be long before they were camping out in the car park complete with support vans, TV cameras, and satellite dishes.

At Tsang headquarters an emergency meeting was convened with Robert, Sheila, and the poor harassed technical manager in an attempt to plan some form of coping strategy:

Offer maximum technical support to all customers involved.

Other customers using the equipment had not been affected so far so where did the problem lie?

Try to isolate and find the common denominator.

Inform all users to be alert to a potential problem.

Seek feedback from all users.

They could think of nothing else that they could do, until they received feedback, other than to cross their fingers, hardly a scientific solution. Robin impressed on them the importance of keeping their mobiles switched on, in case any further developments arose. Communication was vital if they were to ride out the situation.

Once back in her office Sheila rang Cecil to see if, in his past incarnation at Tsang, he'd experienced any problems with this particular product range. Cecil was flabbergasted; there'd been no problems whatsoever, not even with the prototypes. He asked where the complaints had come from, and his incisive mind quickly isolated the common denominator. All of the customers are American or are American-funded hospitals.

Thanking him profusely, she immediately rang Robert and told him what Cecil had said.

"Of course, why didn't we see that? Let me patch in the Tech. Department."

They took onboard the information, and it seemed to catalyze their thoughts as they then pointed out that no single machines had been involved, only groups of machines run as networks to an overall master computer. The problem, therefore, must be within the controlling computers and not the slave machines.

As soon as Steve heard the Tech. Dept. findings, he rang Tim and his immediate reaction was that someone must be hacking into the control computers and altering the command programs. Steve could see the logic of this but pointed out that if this was the case, it meant that there must be a mole inside Tsang who was feeding the identity of the US-funded customers.

"Not if they've hacked into Tsang's mainframe!" was Tim's reply.

Steve realized that, if this was true, the ramifications would be massive and devastating, but so far all that they had to go on was surmise.

The investigators weren't the only people who'd been busy. Lisa had secretly appointed a minder for Aziz in the hope that he could be controlled, and coded e-mails had been sent to various parts of the world to begin the first stages of her scheme. It had taken her a long time to put together a competent team, but a chain was only as strong as its weakest link, and Aziz definitely worried her. Aziz was unaware of his new shadow but still smarted at the treatment that he'd received from the woman Lisa.

It would never be permitted in my country, and I'll make damned sure she pays for her insolence. She might be clever, but what a waste of time when everybody knows that if you hit the enemy hard and violently, it frightens them into submission.

Aziz was not entirely alone in his feelings; the rest of the group recognized that he was an idiot, a hothead, but they too felt uncomfortable with the way this woman lorded it over them, although they were open-minded enough to recognize the sense in what she was preaching. So, it was with mixed feelings that they all turned up for the end of week meeting.

Sharif had tactfully warned Lisa not to be too imperious, so she opened the meeting in a low-key manner, effectively patting them on the head before kneeing them in the balls:

"Welcome gentlemen and congratulations on what you've achieved this week.

"Firstly, you may have seen a couple of items in the press and on TV concerning hospital equipment failures around the world. Well, we are responsible for that, and it's just the tip of the iceberg; the problems are much more severe than was reported, and they are playing things down due to government pressure. Thanks to our IT genius we are in control of a lot of

US hospital intensive care units. Already you can see that we have the capability to hurt and embarrass our enemies. The public will lose confidence in both the politicians and the hospital authorities and will wonder what will happen next. Morale will be decimated.

This, however, is just the beginning. What they don't realize yet is that we are also in a position to take control of US air traffic control and the mainframes of a number of their major banks."

There was a stunned silence in the room as the ramifications sank in, followed by a ripple of applause. In the listening van a gasp of amazement escaped from everyone.

Aziz sullenly piped up, "What makes you think that we've got enough people to handle something on this scale?"

"We don't, and we don't need many, because we aren't going to handle it that way. Once we've proved to them our ability to carry out our threats, we will charge the other potential victims for protection; they will have to pay up or face ruin. The large sums involved will form our seed fund for investment in companies that will compete against the Americans and beat them at their own game. The beauty of the plan is that it will be US money that wrecks the US economy.

This is the last time that we will meet in this building, as now that we are active, we may soon come under surveillance. We will be moving to a new base today, and you will receive encoded details in the next few days."

There were no further critical comments as each member digested the genius of the plan. Any misgivings about Lisa evaporated except where Aziz was concerned.

Her smart ass ideas don't alter the fact that she's a bitch and must be taught a lesson.

Tim and his fellow eavesdroppers were awestruck but had to admire the elegance of the plan. They watched the various members of the group disperse and head off to their respective hideouts and then returned to their temporary command post to hatch a plan with a view to trying to thwart the efforts of the Assassins of Satan. After hurried discussions it was decided that both US and British Security should be informed immediately, and Tim was adamant that only British Special Forces should be involved in Syria, as they were already on the ground and were less confrontational than the Yanks.

The ensuing secure conference call was unanimous in reckoning that Sharif must be the "IT Genius" referred to and that he should be taken out immediately. This action would have several effects:

He would be rendered inactive.

He would give them the details of his hacking and reprogramming, so that the potential victims could be protected. (The two diplomats present shuddered at the confidence that Tim had in his ability to get Sharif to reveal these details.)

Lisa would be deprived of her soul-mate.

The Assassins of Satan would realize that they were not invincible.

After various arguments regarding joint and unilateral responsibilities the conference call closed, and each country set the wheels in motion for their counter attack. Tim's first concern was to trace Sharif, so he contacted GCHQ Cheltenham for their assistance in intercepting any calls and for breaking any codes involved; he stressed the urgency involved in stopping Sharif's activities.

The wait was exasperating but relatively short in real terms. The vast network available to GCHQ revealed that Sharif was booked on a flight to Qatar the next day where he could doubtless be a great nuisance to the Americans who have a major base in the state from where they run their Iraqi operation. The booking was only for Sharif, so Lisa must be holing up somewhere else.

A couple of hours later and they had the new address for Lisa: a house on the other side of Riyadh. This information had been a gift from Aziz, the loose cannon, who having received the coded details promptly rang one of the other members and gave the address over the open telephone line.

Tim hand-picked an old SAS friend now working for a Saudi company in Riyadh, and they agreed that Sharif should be taken out before entering the airport. There were too many watching eyes inside the terminal building, and the political situation was still very delicate in Saudi. A quick check of Lisa's new address was fruitful because Sharif was seen entering the building; his route to the airport the following morning was, therefore, now a given.

That evening Tim had a long chat on the phone with Fiona but decided to omit anything that might worry or upset her. There seemed no point in unnecessarily causing anxiety when there wasn't anything that she could do.

It was an early start the following morning as the flight to Qatar left at 9:00 a.m. Sharif's taxi arrived at 6:30 a.m. and was following a military Land Rover when about two miles from the airport the vehicle in front slowed to a stop. The taxi driver looked in his mirror and saw a similar four-wheel drive pull up directly behind him effectively sandwiching them. In a flash both Land Rover occupants were at each side of the taxi brandishing automatic weapons and ordering Sharif out of the taxi in fluent Arabic. The taxi driver looked terrified but was quickly pacified with triple the fare and warned that, if anyone asked, he hadn't seen anything.

Sharif was hurriedly bundled into the back of one of the Land Rovers, handcuffed, and both vehicles disappeared in a cloud of dust leaving a very confused taxi driver gazing disbelievingly at the wad of notes in his hand.

Once back at the base Sharif was quickly "persuaded" to reveal all of the information that was needed to protect the vulnerable companies and services. It wasn't too difficult as he had no professional training in resisting interrogation. Like most sensible people he had a great fear of pain and, in his case, a desperate need to keep his fingers in working order. In fairness, as a computer geek, it seemed that Sharif had been primarily motivated by the challenge of hacking into supposedly unassailable secure major computers, whereas Lisa had seen the potential of his skills and had used him for her own idealistic ends. The relevant programs, passwords, and computers involved were flashed around the world, and it was almost possible to hear the huge corporate sigh of relief—so far so good.

As the news filtered through to Tsang, Steve visibly brightened; he'd had visions of all that he'd worked for becoming worthless if there had been an inherent design fault in the product. Sabotage had not initially entered his head, and he now realized how vulnerable computers rendered us. However, Steve's relief was nothing by comparison to that of the technical manager who visibly beamed as he set about the task of de-bugging and protecting the mainframe computer.

News circulates very quickly in Saudi, and although no exact details were available concerning the identity of the man who'd been lifted, the Saudi police authorities were already demanding information from the CIA and the US Consulate. Nobody likes things happening in their patch when they are not in the picture. The chief of police was discreetly advised that no details could be given, but that there had been a joint venture undertaken with their own and British Security Services. The response as he put the phone down: "No bastard ever keeps us in the loop!"

The controller announced his decision to pick up Lisa and the rest of the group, all of whom by now had been identified and targeted. The first move was on Lisa's new hideout, and once again Tim and his right hand man were assigned to "bring home the bacon." Tim smiled inwardly at the unfortunate turn of phrase.

Not wishing to announce their arrival, the Land Rover arrived sedately (not normally Tim's style of driving), he parked around the back of Lisa's house, and Tim's accomplice heaved himself over the high wall into the rear garden whilst Tim walked around the building to the front door; rank has to have its perks. At a given radio command, with guns at the ready, they burst into the house and met in the central hallway. No sign of anyone and an eerie silence. Cautiously they moved from room to room checking every possible hiding place until finally arriving upstairs at Lisa's bedroom; they found her.

She was lying across the bed, her gold colored silk pajamas in disarray and her throat cut. She was dead, very dead. The likely weapon lay on the floor: a typical razor-sharp tribal dagger.

It would appear that Aziz has finally taught her the promised lesson.

"Shit, I know she was a dangerous pain in the arse but that shouldn't happen to anyone, let alone someone as gorgeous as that!"

Tim couldn't argue with his mate's summing up; even in death this woman was beautiful. They were careful to leave everything as it was and retreated cautiously from her room but made a thorough search of the smallest bedroom, which was being used as an office. CDs and memory sticks were collected and a brand new external hard drive still in its packaging was opened and used to copy the hard drive of the laptop.

On their way back to base Tim radioed the consulate, brought them up to speed, and requested them to notify the police, so that they could investigate the murder scene and remove Lisa's body.

The ensuing de-briefing was somewhat somber. They had intended to remove Lisa as an operative, but nobody had envisaged the need to eliminate her permanently. It was agreed that Sharif should be told of her death, and Tim agreed that he would take on the unpalatable job.

Sharif was visibly shattered at the news of Lisa's death. "I knew she was playing with fire; even tried to warn her to back off from bullying some of the hotheads."

Although the lad was involved, Tim couldn't help feeling for him; he obviously cared deeply for her and was grief-stricken, but it was debatable whether she had ever felt the same for him. To Tim it seemed more likely that Sharif was just a useful tool in Lisa's overall plans and the "romance" was a necessary ruse to keep him on side.

In the meantime news was filtering through that members of Lisa's group were being picked up one by one. Most were very talkative when questioned, and as a result a number of previously unidentified members were rounded up. However, one person was still at large: Aziz.

On the bright side, Tim was receiving reports that were coming in thick and fast that the computer systems had been compromised, but all had now been repaired and were functional again, and the IT boffins had put in place new firewalls and various other new security features to prevent further problems.

Stable door and bolting horses? Anyway, how much confidence can we have in security arranged by technicians who left us vulnerable previously?

Two days later and whatever complacency that he might have harbored took a shattering blow. Subsequent discussions with Sharif had been unproductive until he was seriously "questioned." The results of this interrogation showed that the terrorists had plans that would prove more crippling than anything that had been dreamt of to date. Advanced electronic jamming equipment had been developed that aimed to neutralize US navigation and communication satellites.

Without the satellites, both military and commercial aircraft would have to rely on old- fashioned navigational aids, which were vastly less accurate, and various defense departments would lose their snooping abilities. In short the US and its allies would, in modern terms, be left blind and unable to target any enemy accurately. The more Tim thought about it the more terrifying the prospect became. It was only now that he realized how much his army life had been dependent on satellite communication.

Late night discussions with Steve had made Sheila painfully aware of how vulnerable their medical range was to computer crime. Advanced technology brought with it ever more sophisticated crooks, and it would only be a matter of time before they faced the same challenges again. So it was in a somewhat anxious frame of mind that she boarded the flight to Mumbai, not relishing spending time away from her man.

The following morning after a bumpy flight, which had offered little chance of sleep, she was met by a mercifully air conditioned car sent by AI Electronics and whisked away from the chaos of the airport to the peaceful company headquarters.

The managing director was an impressively good-looking man in his early fifties with impeccable diction and manners, yet there was genuine warmth in his welcome. He led her into the boardroom and introduced her to a corporate team of both senior management and technical experts. After the ritual tea and introductions the stage was handed over to her.

"What I am about to reveal must be treated in total confidence, but I feel that it is essential information for you to assess the seriousness of our problems and, hopefully, to enable you to come up with a solution."

Professional as ever, Sheila tried not to let her anxiety show as she outlined the happenings of the last couple of weeks. She was impressed at how quickly the technical wizards showed their recognition of the magnitude of the problem; it was like watching lights come on in a building at dusk.

She went on to describe the types of equipment that had been affected and then to cover other ranges of product that she felt might be vulnerable. Also, she explained what steps had been taken to try to prevent further cyber-tinkering but added that she felt that this was only a temporary sticking plaster. There was general nodding of agreement around the room, and it was suggested that she be given a guided tour of the factory whilst the relevant experts pooled their knowledge and hopefully came up with some solutions after lunch.

One production plant was like any other to Sheila, but she realized that this was just a way of getting her out of the way whilst they got down to brainstorming. However, she was impressed with the incredible cleanliness; the place felt more like an operating theatre than a production plant. Various heads of departments were wheeled out and introduced, and each attempted to explain what was going on in their area of specialty. She couldn't fail to be impressed with the sense of pride that they all exhibited in their work and in the company.

Lunch was a delight; unlike so many work canteens, the food was a selection of northern Indian dishes, which were spicy and creamy but not too hot. In fact the food must have been good because in spite of Sheila being desperate to hear if they'd come up with any solution to her problems, she was still able to appreciate it.

The meeting reconvened at 2:00 p.m., and the technical director had not only pooled the input from several departments but had prepared a full presentation outlining their proposals.

God, these people don't let the grass grow under their feet; I reckon we've acquired a damned good asset in this company.

The director commenced with typical Indian politeness: "I don't wish to minimize the steps that your company has taken to protect itself from internet crime but feel that we may be able to make further improvements."

By the end of his presentation it had become obvious to Sheila that he had been very diplomatic as the measures taken to date were shown to be woefully inadequate. Having demonstrated the existing shortcomings, he had gone on to show that, by utilizing some new hardware of their manufacture and some extremely complex and revolutionary software produced by one of their subsidiaries, they could become impervious to attack.

"Gentlemen, I am most impressed and can't thank you enough for explaining things in a way that even I, as a non-expert, can understand. I now fully realize how vulnerable we were and still are and will be recommending my board to adopt your proposals immediately."

"Thank you for your kind comments and please do take a copy of our presentation with you to show to your colleagues."

Leaving for the airport, Sheila felt a great sense of relief that the problem had been thoroughly examined and equally thoroughly resolved and that they would never be confronted with the frightening scenario of losing control of their own equipment ever again. She also made a mental note to run any new products past their Indian associates in future to assess any potential vulnerability. The flight back to Kuala Lumpur was uneventful and, after food, wine, and the soporific effect of watching a film, she actually managed to sleep, not something she often achieved on planes.

Two days later the Tsang Board adopted AI's proposals, and an e-mail order was placed for the necessary hardware and software along with arrangements for commissioning technicians to install the equipment in Kuala Lumpur. Everyone breathed a sigh of relief, and Alec in typical style congratulated himself on arranging the purchase of their new-found saviours and promptly sacked the IT manager.

28

On several occasions Steve had tried to speak to Tim but had only succeeded in reaching his voicemail, so when the phone rang, he was relieved to hear Tim's voice at last. Initially Tim seemed somewhat preoccupied, but as Steve outlined what AI had managed to achieve for Tsang in terms of computer protection, Tim's attention was immediately engaged and he exclaimed, "Thank heavens! They may be able to solve some mammoth problems that I'm confronted with. Can't say more than that on an open phone, but I'll contact them immediately."

Having put the phone back on its base, Steve was left wondering what had got the usually unflappable Tim so rattled; it had to be something very big. Two days later Tim was at Heathrow Airport to meet a team of experts from AI. Together they flew onwards to the US for the meeting that had been arranged at the Pentagon.

None of them had ever seen the vast building other than on newsreel footage, and the scale of the place left them thunderstruck. One technician commented that it had the same menacing aura of a Stealth bomber, and the others had to agree.

The security was unsurprisingly impressive, but eventually, having jumped through all of the hoops, they were shown into a conference room, which was dominated by a vast oval table, and instructed to immediately fill in confidentiality forms.

The room quickly filled with top brass and a General, who took the chair. He welcomed them; choosing not to reveal that there was any real threat to navigational satellites, he posed a "hypothetical" problem and they were asked to come up with a solution should such a vulnerability ever occur.

AI's technical director was the first to speak: "I'm sorry but without knowledge of the coding and existing protection of the equipment, we can't possibly work out any counter measures."

The General chairing the meeting looked a little flustered and pointed out that this was classified information and couldn't possibly be released.

Tim's admiration for the excruciatingly polite Indian director went sky high when he heard the reply, "Then I'm sorry Gentlemen but you are beyond the help of anyone. We cannot overcome your vulnerability if you cannot disclose your operating system. This is like human relationships; one cannot know pleasure without revealing one's vulnerability to pain.

I fear that we have been wasting one another's time, and as we are all busy people, we should stop doing so and part company."

The language, although slightly archaic, hit home, and after some huddled whispering it was agreed that details of the operating systems would be made available if the team would be kind enough to stay and study them. It was at this point that AI's experts realized that the Pentagon must be in deep shit. There was no way they would reveal this sort of information otherwise, confidentiality agreements or not.

It took just over a week of intense work to come up with the answers, and although a number of the somewhat isolationist Pentagon staff had been skeptical of the Indian technicians, when they were confronted by the analysis of their problems and the team's proposed solutions, they had to admit that they were being taught a salutary lesson and that they no longer had all the answers.

The Pentagon techs' egos took a further hammering when one of the other Generals present demanded to know why their own staff hadn't foreseen the vulnerability or come up with any solutions. There was an embarrassing silence.

AI signed a defense contract and the Official Secrets Act forms before leaving and agreed to commence work immediately on their return to Mumbai. They left the following day, and Tim made his own way back to London, Fiona, and Benjamin.

In fact when he arrived home, he was met not only by the family, but by Steve who had just arrived to visit some of their clients. Steve had previously rung Fiona to speak to Tim, and she'd explained that he was returning that day from the States, and so he'd accepted her invitation to stay with them.

Freshened up, and with Benjamin in bed, they caught up with all of Tim's news over one of Fiona's superb men's food dinners and a good bottle of wine. Steve had been badly affected by the problems that Tsang had been experiencing but was horrified when he realized what the implications could have been worldwide. Tim also mused on the coincidence that it was Bruce's old company in India that had surfaced to become the saviour of the West.

After dinner both Sheila and Cecil were brought up to speed by e-mail and they were equally flabbergasted when they read the details on waking and realized the potential consequences of what might have happened.

The next few days proved very profitable for Steve and Tim as they visited both old and new clients and returned with a sheaf of new orders for Tsang products. After interviewing several applicants for the post of Foston's UK manager, Steve and Tim finally settled on Jean. Jean had been a hospital procurement officer and was ideally suited to the job, and her appointment would shed a load from both Steve and Tim. Most importantly, they both felt that they could put their trust in her.

Foston was fast becoming a highly profitable business and a major asset to its Malaysian associates; more to the point, Steve no longer had an overdraft, and he knew that his future was secure. For the first time in his life he felt that he had actually become successful in his own right, and he experienced a pang of regret that neither of his parents was still alive to witness it.

With business completed in the UK the weekend found him back in Kuala Lumpur and in the arms of Sheila who had been waiting at the airport. The journey to the city passed quickly as they exchanged news, and Steve felt the warm sense of contentment of being with the person that matters most to you.

Her car was deposited in its undercover parking space, and as soon as they were in the apartment, she was startled to see him apparently stumble. However, he quickly righted himself and, perching on one knee, handed her a small leather box whilst asking her to marry him. The opened box revealed a beautiful sapphire and diamond engagement ring.

"Of course I'll marry you my love, but where did you get this; it's gorgeous!"

"The only flight that I could get had a stopover at Dubai, so it seemed like an ideal opportunity. Do you like it?"

"Like it? I adore it."

The rest of the weekend was a blur of bed, dining out, and telling all of their friends the good news. The wedding date was set for two months hence, which didn't give her long to prepare, but she didn't care just as long as she was going to be with her Steve. Neither of them could believe how happy they were.

Monday brought a special delivery of their first wedding present. Cecil in his usual efficient style had beaten everyone else, and they were now the proud owners of a fabulous large painting of the view across the lake from the hotel that Cecil had moved Steve to on his first trip to Kuala Lumpur. The enclosed note read:

A beautiful view for two beautiful friends to remind you of where it all started.

Love & Happiness to you both,

Cecil

Jean proved to be so efficient that Steve felt confident enough to spend the next two months in Kuala Lumpur, and Sheila breathed a sigh of relief that she wouldn't be left to organize everything herself. Inevitably the time rocketed by and, with all of the preparations hopefully in place, they were heading for the airport to meet Tim and Fiona and various other guests of Steve's from the UK. The rest of the week disappeared in a haze of champagne; just about everyone who delivered a wedding present also came armed with a bottle of bubbly.

The one thing that could be relied upon was the weather, and Saturday morning was its usual sunny self as everyone headed to the church. Steve was fidgeting nervously alongside Tim, the best man, and there was a general buzz of conversation from the pews. The organ changed from background sound to boom out the arrival of the bride, and the conversation dissolved as everyone turned around to try to get a glimpse of her. Sheila looked even more stunning than usual, the white of her dress contrasting with the bronze of her skin, as she walked down the aisle on Cecil's arm.

Cecil released her arm as they reached the chancel steps. Steve turned to greet her and immediately filled up when he saw how beautiful she looked. I have to be the luckiest man alive!

With their vows completed and, thankfully, no objections, they signed the register and, with the organ thundering, emerged into brilliant sunlight for what seemed to be endless photos. The reception was at the Colony Club; the surroundings were beautiful and the food and service superb. Eventually, tired but happy beyond belief, they said their farewells to all of their friends and flew off to Langkawi Island for a well-earned honeymoon. The rest of the guests were staying on for a week to explore Kuala Lumpur and Cecil volunteered himself as their tour guide.

29

Police in Saudi, Oman, and Yemen had been busy building cases against the remnants of Lisa's group, who had been rounded up with the help of information gleaned from Sharif. Some were hardcore terrorist material, but the majority were easily-led youngsters with misguided aspirations. However, all were going to be dealt with equally and were likely to spend a considerable time behind bars.

Tim felt slight tinges of regret that the least dangerous were going to be tarred with the same brush as the worst but could see no other solution and, somewhat uncomfortably, had to let the proceedings take their course.

Interrogation had produced some interesting details with regard to the distribution of funds to various Far Eastern countries. Some of Europe's most respected banks were about to experience acute embarrassment and would doubtless be reviewing their procedures and enquiries with regard to the source of funds and their ultimate destination. Profitability and volume of business had definitely overridden regulation and morality.

Amongst the governments, police forces, and Customs and Excise authorities there was general feeling that a massive blow had been dealt to a wide range of underworld activities around the world and that the planet would be a better place for the removal of those involved.

Talks between the West and the Arab States were quietly evolving, and whilst nobody was under any illusion that there would be a speedy breakthrough, there was an encouraging sense that things were moving in the right direction. Interestingly, a number of major US companies were now sending key personnel on intensive Arabic language courses, hopefully a sign of respect and an admission that you don't win wars by not talking to your enemy.

Thanks to AI Electronics the Pentagon considered itself more secure than for many years and was confident that it could react quickly to any future threats that might arise. Both navigation and communication satellites were now ring-fenced, and hospital and bank computers were all protected. The Pentagon had taken the unheard of, but very sensible, measure of employing some of the country's best criminal hackers to try to break into their computers but AI's systems had proved impregnable. At last there was a restoration of confidence which had been progressively slipping since 9/11 although Intelligence Services were more vigilant than ever.

GCHQ, Cheltenham had picked up some worrying loose talk concerning a possible bomb attack on an American base in Qatar and had tipped off the US Army. So, following up on the intelligence, a small group of US Special Forces had silently moved into position around a building on the perimeter of Doha Airport. The building was a preparation plant that produced food for airlines, schools, hospitals, and the armed forces. There was no sign of activity outside the factory, but the night shift could be seen working inside the building. The surveillance team hunkered down to wait for some activity. It was just as the rose tinge of dawn fringed the horizon and the velvet black sky that a roller door clattered open and a refrigerated van slowly emerged. As the van turned onto the main road, a typical battered workman's bus settled in behind it as a result of radio messages from the lookouts. What those in the van were unaware of was that, instead of the usual construction workers, the bus was full of armed marksmen.

It soon became obvious that, as per the tip-off, the van was definitely making its way to the military base. The senior officer on the bus radioed his CO suggesting that they should run the van off the road before it could do any harm.

"For Christ's sake don't! It's probably a bomb on wheels. Loud hail them and order them to pull over. If they don't comply, stay well back and shoot out the tires."

The loud hailer was even louder than they could have believed, but either the driver was stone deaf or he was hell-bent on achieving his goal. The bus dropped back from its quarry, the side door slid back, and a marksman leaned out precariously. Staccato automatic fire drowned the sound of the diesel engine, and the speeding van veered off the road, leapt into the air, and crashed down on its side. The dawn sky became mid-day bright as the explosives-loaded van detonated. Screeching to a halt, the bus spewed out its passengers, but it was some time before they could get anywhere near the blazing vehicle. The driver would be a cinder, but the passenger had been thrown out as the vehicle flipped over before exploding. He was draped over a rock, his face a grim rictus, his neck broken like a twig.

The operation had gone like clockwork. No injuries, except the enemy, and the van disposed of before even approaching, let alone entering, the gates of the base, and there had been no American casualties.

The first reaction to the episode was that this was somewhat of a setback in what had generally been positive progress. However, the incident eventually turned out to have an upside; the van passenger's body had been identified as Aziz. Ironically the proponent of violence had died by his own loose talk and violence. Lisa's prediction had come to fruition.

Tim had been regularly receiving updates from his contacts around the Middle East, and he breathed a sigh of relief when he heard the news. He'd always felt that Aziz was the most dangerous and unpredictable of the whole rabble. He had a vivid picture in his mind's eye of Lisa on her deathbed, and although she was far from being guiltless, he somehow felt that justice had been done on her behalf. Once you had intelligence on people like Lisa, you could second think what their next move would be but not with characters like Aziz.

Several days later Tim heard that the US security services had investigated Sharif's computer activities and had come to the conclusion that the guy was bordering on genius. They had, therefore, granted him freedom from prosecution provided he worked for them to develop programmes that would enable them to snoop on potential enemies. He had been only too pleased to cooperate, and again Tim was pleased as he felt that the man had been entrapped by Lisa and used.

Pharmzest had become a thorn in the flesh of the Taiwan government as their enquiries had unearthed the fact that the company had been solely owned by Tam. Their first instinct had been to close it down, but that would have created hardship to a number of companies who were reliant on its legitimate products. Nationalization was another approach but one that they didn't wish to go along with. The final decision was to seek a buyer, and in view of his recent assistance Cecil was given first offer. His reaction was one of surprise, and he asked for a day or two to consider all of the ramifications.

After careful consideration his decision was that, although the company's order book would justify the necessary merchant bank loan for purchase, he would be over-stretched with his present company's existing commitments. He was disappointed because the manufacturing facility was superb and the forward ordering book was enviable. On the other hand, he was pleased that his old gambling instinct was under control.

The response was totally unexpected; if he would merge the company with his, he would be offered tax breaks that would make the deal impossible to refuse. In short if he would remove their source of embarrassment, they would be very, very grateful. Cecil's luck had certainly returned big style. That evening he took his father and friends out for a celebratory banquet at one of Kuala Lumpur's best Chinese restaurants; by coincidence the restaurant was called Liu's.

30

A fortnight later, a sun-kissed relaxed couple returned from their tropical idyll to their Kuala Lumpur apartment and were met by a mountain of mail and a full answerphone. Steve played back umpteen unimportant messages but was intrigued by one from Tim requesting that he and Cecil make themselves available for a meeting in London with himself and the British government as soon as possible. A subsequent phone call to Tim failed to reveal any further information about the meeting as Tim refused to discuss things on the phone.

After only a week with his wife in their new home, Steve met Cecil, and they boarded a flight to London, appreciating the luxury of the first class seats that had been booked for them courtesy of the UK government. The flight was thankfully uneventful, and they arrived relatively fresh at Heathrow where they were met by Tim, who ushered them to a waiting car. After battling through the usual chaotic traffic, they eventually arrived at one of Mayfair's best hotels. Tim suggested that they book into their allotted rooms and all meet in the bar in half an hour's time.

The bar was luxurious with fabulously soft feather cushioned sofas, subtle lighting, and rich wooden paneling. Cecil and Steve sank into one of the decadently comfortable seats and were both taken aback to find that a barman had silently materialized alongside them to take their order. Their drinks had just arrived when Tim entered the room accompanied by a rather stiff looking character whom he introduced as "Colonel Phelps."

"Please, call me Brian. Firstly, welcome to London. Obviously this is not the place to discuss tomorrow's meeting, but I just wanted the opportunity to spend some time socializing with the three of you beforehand, and it also gives me the opportunity to wine and dine you as a small token of our gratitude for your recent assistance in curbing our Middle Eastern 'friends.'"

The miniature speech was delivered in an overly formal clipped and somewhat old-fashioned manner, which hinted of his military background and the circles in which he now operated. He then caught the barman's eye and ordered his and Tim's drinks and added that all the drinks for his party were to be charged to his account.

The evening progressed, and as the wine flowed, his demeanor mellowed, and he became almost human. Either that or their perception altered in direct proportion to their intake of both food and wine, each of which were memorable. As they said their farewells to Tim and Brian, they were told that a car would pick them up the following day at 9:00 a.m. Tired, replete, and still none the wiser as to the reasons for tomorrow's meeting, they returned to their respective rooms.

Steve woke to blazing sunshine streaming through his bedroom window and realized that he'd forgotten to close the curtains last night. I must have been tired.

He breakfasted with Cecil who was equally eaten up with curiosity about the pending meeting. They backtracked over some of the recent events and had to admit that life had taken some amazing twists and turns during the last year. However, by the time they made their way to the hotel entrance, they were still in the dark as to what the meeting had been convened for.

With clockwork precision their car arrived at the hotel entrance, and as they sat back in the Jaguar's luxurious leather-smelling comfort, the driver eased his way into Park Lane's constant traffic. Soon they were crossing Vauxhall Bridge, and the sun was sparkling off the Thames as it sluggishly meandered its way through the city. The many communications aerials glinted on the roof of the MI5 building ahead of them and looked like futuristic sculptures. The car pulled into a security entrance, and the driver handed them temporary passes to gain entry to the building but advised that they would receive full security checks once inside. Cecil looked somewhat puzzled at the cloak and dagger conversation until Steve explained that this was the home of Britain's "Spooks." Cecil must have been taken aback, because he actually raised an eyebrow.

ID checks and frisking completed, they were shown into a waiting room and, a few minutes later, the familiar face of Tim appeared around the door: "What in God's name are they doing letting two undesirables like you in here?"

They both grinned and followed him along the corridor where they were ushered into a large conference room. A group of people were already sitting around the central table and deep in conversation. All stood up as they entered, and the by now familiar voice of Brian intoned, "Ladies and Gentlemen may I welcome and introduce you to Mr. Liu and Mr. Dalton. These are the two gentlemen along with Major Foster, whom you all know, who saved our bacon recently."

Once they were all re-seated, Colonel Phelps introduced them to the various personnel who ranged from the US Ambassador and the Minister for Defense, to a variety of communications experts. He went on to outline the roles that his "Unholy Trinity" (as he called Cecil, Steve, and Tim) had performed and, judging by the expressions on the faces of some around the table, the seriousness of recent events was news even to them.

"Firstly we would like to, once again, express our gratitude to you for the outstanding work that you did on our behalf, and secondly we would like to ask yet another favor. Would you be prepared to be retained by Her Majesty's Security Services to act on our behalf if necessary in the future? You see you have a unique combination of talents and businesses that involve travel around the world without arousing suspicion and a proven track record. Also, the military knowledge, electronics expertise, and language fluency makes for an irresistible package. As you will see from the contractual folders that are in front of you, the financial arrangements will be attractive, but you would have to make yourselves available at the drop of a hat. We realize that you will need to discuss our proposals, so I am suggesting that we have a fifteen minute break, and we will leave you alone to digest our offer."

Quiet descended as they read through the contents of their folders, and Steve was the first to break the silence: "The Unholy Trinity has a certain ring to it, and I must admit that I've never felt as alive as I have in the last twelve months. I'm certainly up for it and the financial terms seem more than generous."

The others nodded in agreement. Cecil, who had always been an essentially moral man, felt that this was his chance to repay society for his fall from grace, and it was obvious that Tim would be delighted to still have a tenuous military connection. Fifteen minutes later, the rest of the group filed back into the room, and there was spontaneous applause when they heard that The Unholy Trinity was on board. Just as everyone was preparing to leave, Steve was shocked to hear himself say, "Yes, it would appear that we are all happy in principle to help wherever and whenever we can, but if the Ambassador will forgive me saying so, there seems to be a recurring problem. The West sees the Middle East as a vital supply of oil for its ever-increasing needs and The Middle East sees the West as a greedy customer that will discard them like an old shoe if it comes up with alternative energy supplies.

There is inadequate dialogue, and in all honesty the largest proportion of Western diplomats and politicians involved are so insensitive that they haven't even taken the trouble to learn Arabic let alone understand the ancient culture of the Arab nations.

Gentlemen, how would you feel, as an Arab, in those circumstances? Surely by now you must recognize that the West is hated in these countries, but have we ever asked the Arabs what we can do to overcome their grievances with a view to harmonizing our societies?—No!

If we don't start working along these lines, we will have continual problems, and as recent events have shown, there is no guarantee that we will always come out on top. What's more, the drain on our economies of constantly trying to out-wit what we call terrorists is crippling, and it is a war that can't be won."

Steve sat down flushed with embarrassment and a number of those present squirmed awkwardly at Steve's passionate out-burst. Amazingly he found an ally in the US Ambassador who said, "Young man that was said with great passion and makes a hell of a lot more sense than most of the bullshit that I've been listening to back in the States. I will, with your permission, relay your comments as soon as I get back to the Embassy."

There was a mixture of surprise and relief around the table, and the rest of the afternoon was spent signing The Official Se-crets Act, ironing out details like insurance and life assurance as civilian schemes would be invalid whilst in Security Service employ. The financial package was generous, but what none had expected was a large tax-free gift each, from the US government in recognition of their recent assistance. All in all it had been a pretty good day.

Steve was still in a state of shock for being so outspoken but also experienced a sense of satisfaction that, perhaps, his inabil-ity to keep his mouth shut might just pave the way towards some form of reconciliation.

When they finally left the building Tim turned to Steve: "You're a dark horse; I didn't see you as a diplomat cum politi-cian, and I reckoned your little sermon would go down like a lead duck. Just goes to show what little I know, because in real-ity it seems like you might have got further in a few minutes than the rest of them have done over the last few years! Well done Steve."

In fact Tim's surmise proved to be accurate. Within a month of the meeting a "Summit" had been convened between the ma-jor Arab States and the West to seek a way forward, and there was an obvious willingness to seek compromise on both sides. The US was also paying serious attention to the Israel/ Palestine situation and was being far less one-sided in its approach.

Steve settled back to his busy schedule and was somewhat surprised at how quickly he had melded into Malaysian life. With part of his recent windfall, courtesy of the US government, he'd bought a half share in a second hand four seat Cessna 172, something he'd never dreamt would be possible. The aeroplane wasn't young but it was in excellent condition and was exceptionally well equipped with the very latest navigational instruments. Steve was enjoying flying from the local airfield, on the outskirts of Kuala Lumpur, and the hours in his log book were totting up quickly now that he was liberated from British weather. One of his first flights was a romantic one when he flew Sheila over the hotel with the huge lake where they'd first realized their mutual attraction.

Sheila had furnished their new home beautifully whilst at the same time apparently effortlessly overseeing Tsang's ever-increasing group of associate companies. They'd both given up homes that they loved without any qualms so that they could start afresh together: Steve realized that, for the first time in his life, he felt totally happy and contented.

Cecil busied himself making money and building his new rapidly expanding empire. However, this time, just like his two friends, he had returned home to his partner; yes, Cecil now had a live-in partner. Father had been true to his word and had totally accepted Simon, the new man in Cecil's life. In fact Simon had become a firm favorite of the old man and could do no wrong. Before arriving in Kuala Lumpur he'd worked for a merchant bank in Singapore. The product of an American father and Chinese mother, Simon was highly intelligent and worked as finance director for a large automobile manufacturer. He was not overtly gay, which fitted in with Cecil's own understated personality.

Tim was revelling in fatherhood and was fully occupied with his consultancy work and his Foston activities, but in his quieter moments he had to admit to himself that he missed the camaraderie of the army, not surprising when it had been his only family for so many years.

Although they were all enjoying life, unbeknownst to each other, all three men had been missing the thrill of the recent past and secretly hoped it wouldn't be too long before the Unholy Trinity would be unleashed into action again. Not a sentiment that they could confide to their partners though.

In fact, although it seemed to be a lot longer, in reality it was only several months later when a call from Tim rallied The Unholy Trinity to action again. This time the Security Service advised that the starting point of their mission was Burma. In spite of every effort by the West, opium production was running out of control and crime around the world was multiplying on the back of it. There was a desperate need to find out why.

SYNOPSIS

Steve Dalton, a young electronics graduate and keen private pilot, starts his own medical equipment business in partnership with a wealthy friend from university days. His life in a sleepy Cheshire village has offered no preparation for what is to come. Business takes him to Malaysia, and although he pulls off a superb deal to become the agent for a major medical equipment corporation, he soon finds his life under threat and becomes embroiled in a web of crime and murder reaching from China to The Middle East and Africa.

Illicit drugs, bogus medicines, and vice are all involved in the crime syndicates that Steve encounters. A chance alliance with Cecil Liu, a shrewd and dapper Chinese businessman but compulsive gambler, and Tim Foster, an ex SAS officer, creates a uniquely qualified trio who take on the awesome task of protecting the West from Middle Eastern terrorists whose aim is to wreck the American economy and make America pay for its own downfall.

The Saudi-based plotters are led by Lisa Khan, a highly intelligent woman, and thanks to the near genius skills of their computer expert, they are able to render American navigation satellites, Security Services, bank, and hospital computers entirely at their mercy. For the first time in modern times America the superpower is totally vulnerable.

Life accelerates to a hectic pace, and Steve finds himself on the run from assassins who mistake him for their real target.

Never in their wildest dreams did the trio expect to find themselves in such unlikely places as the Pentagon and MI5 yet this is where their new life takes them.

Steve, Cecil, and Tim now known to the Western security forces as The Unholy Trinity find that their shared dangers and truly life-changing experiences cause each of them to completely re-evaluate what really matters in life and to make serious changes in their personal relationships. The many twists in their lives encompass romance, personal challenges, and the fulfillment of a number of secret dreams.

ABOUT THE AUTHOR

Anthony Dickenson is married to his artist wife, Gail, and they live in the countryside on the borders of Cheshire and Shropshire in the northwest of England. Between them they have three children, six grandchildren, and Lily, their Jack Russell dog. Anthony has been an acupuncturist and osteopath, based in Chester, for thirty-five years and has lectured extensively in Europe, the Far East, and Australia. He is a qualified private pilot, a keen pianist, and his interests include music, travel, and crosswords.

Over the years he has written many articles for professional and commercial magazines. The Strangling of Satan is his first novel.

Printed in the United Kingdom by
Lightning Source UK Ltd., Milton Keynes
140225UK00001B/7/P